# Half Plus Seven

T0164287

Dan Tyte was born and raised in Cardiff, Wales. He studied English Literature at the University of Liverpool before becoming a PR man, pushing everything from professional sports to pop music. He has written newspaper columns, for men's magazines, for literature magazines and was a music journalist but got out before the beer went flat. He's contributed to Amazon No#1 Best-Selling PR books. This is his debut novel.

www.dantyte.com
@dantyte

# Half Plus Seven

## Seven

### Dan Tyte

PARTHIAN

Parthian
The Old Surgery
Napier Street
Cardigan
SA43 1ED

www.parthianbooks.com

First published in 2014
© Dan Tyte 2014
All Rights Reserved

ISBN 978-1-909844-41-4

Editor: Susie Wild
Cover design by Jack Hudson www.jack-hudson.com
Photography by Kirsten McTernan www.kirstenmcternan.co.uk
Typeset by Elaine Sharples
Printed and bound by Edwards Brothers Malloy, Ann Arbor, Michigan

Published with the financial support of the Welsh Books Council

British Library Cataloguing in Publication Data

A cataloguing record for this book is available from the British Library.

For Rebecca

# Chapter 1

When I woke up at the strange house in bed with the 39-year-old psychic, I didn't yet know how Sister Gina would change my life. Sister Gina was a psychic too. But we'll get to her later. I'd drunk a bunch of booze the night before and ended up in the arms of another. This kind of happens a lot. More than it should for a man of my experience. But to be greeted at first light by the ageing face of a fading earth mother 10 years my senior, well that's kind of a new low. Or high. Half full. Half empty. Half crazy. Half happy. Let's just call it a benchmark. It's a new BENCHMARK. Let's rewind to how… Christ I can't even remember her name… at least once you'd think I'd be able to remember their name. Let's call her The Mystic. This is how she found her way to my side. It was a Friday night and I'd been at a bar in the town.

It'd been the usual sketch. I'd had a pint which turned into three at lunchtime and had zoned in and out of consciousness at my desk for the rest of the afternoon. My boss had asked me to file a report on the Henderson campaign by 3 p.m. but I'd crawled out of it by blaming the more culpable fuckwits I had the pleasure of spending five days a week with. Come 4 p.m. my body was craving another drink. I'd looked around the office and could only see Pete. The last PR man standing. I grabbed his attention with a snarl and before either of us knew it we were stood at the nearest bar discussing the merits of the latest batch of strawberry beer.

'Well it might not put hairs on your chest, but it's not half bad you know.'

'Quiet, Pete. Get me another one.'

And repeat.

Pete came and went and other voices passed through my brain over the ensuing hours. The Hi Honey I'm Home hours. The Hi Honey Oh Fuck You Don't Exist So I'm Going To Go And Get Plastered Hours. No checking little Dave's long division, no asking Alice about ballet class. Just drinking. And thinking. And thinking about drinking.

Before I knew it, I was asking the outline of a smallish man in a double-breasted jacket and a well-worn badge of honour what his purpose was, where he'd been and if his mother loved him. He looked at me like I was strange or the town drunk. Turns out I was neither, either or both depending on what day it was or who you asked. Before the clock struck ridiculous, the cognitive side of my brain battled with the booze to convince my body that a breather might be a good idea.

Left followed right followed left followed right followed left to the door of the bar.

The cold air hit me. My brain oxygenated. My senses sharpened. My hands reached into my pocket for a cigarette. I had remarkably soft hands. You'd have thought I swam in lakes of Fairy Liquid before breakfast every morning. My father's hands were man's hands. Bricklayer's hands. Coarse, cut, knowing. My wear and tear was in the brain box. Mental. Metaphysical. A clusterfuck of failed relationships, shot down dreams, hypochondriac breakdowns, parental indifference and bullshit jobs had seen to that. And it wasn't getting any rosier.

The maze of city streets was dotted with people like Pacmen; shoppers, sinners, losers, winners. I already knew which I was.

'Need a light?'

'Erm… yes.'

'Well, do you want one?'

'Erm… yes.'

An experienced hand reached out of the vacuum to light my smoke. A tattoo of an eye snaked past. The movement was hypnotic. Stay sharp.

'I can sense your aura. You're troubled. Why are you so troubled?'

'I can sense your aura too. It says you're a loony cat-hoarding tree hugger.'

She shook. Or perhaps I wobbled.

'Why are you so angry?'

I took a deep breath. In through the nose. The air hit. The brain whirred. Out through the mouth.

'I'm sorry. I really am. My dog died last week. Mauled by cats. Poor Timmy. It's just you looked like a cat person is all. And it all came flooding back. The screech… the fur… the whimper. Let's hope all good dogs do go to heaven.'

'Oh.'

'Let me buy you a drink.'

'Um…'

I took a long drag on my cigarette and grabbed the eye-etched hand. Back into the sea of depression. Back indoors. But not alone.

'I've made you a cup of chai.'

A questioning noise spluttered out of my mouth. I generally couldn't talk until I'd sunk two cups of tea in the morning and found it even harder to enunciate when being offered a cup of God-knows-what by God-knows-who.

'What the fuck is that…? And where the fuck am I…? And who the fuck are you…?'

Flashback.

Falling up the messy stairs of a house to a bolted door. Darkness. Candles. Strong smelling candles. Cheap nasty liquor. Bullshit talk about who we used to be 2 months ago, 200 years

5

ago. Changing the subject. Lecturing, aggressively, dismissively. Fumbling. Spilt drinks. Pulled hair. An ageing body fading from the light. The eye-etched hand blinking, sagging, giving. Sweat.

Nothingness.

'Well if you don't want it I'll just give it to the plants. Probably too much goodness in there for you anyway.'

'Do you have normal tea?'

'What is "normal"? You're certainly not "normal".'

'Well your voodoo has got something right.'

'You shouldn't mock the spirits you know.'

The room was dank and decaying but decorated with garish symbols of mysticism. Much like its inhabitant. Purple velvet birth charts pinned to damp-risen Artexed walls. Discoloured portraits of Indian spirit guides. A latent smell of cat's piss.

'You were mean last night. And this morning. I can sense you're not a well person. But there's something about you that I like. And the sex… it was like you'd been possessed by some higher power. You were almost in a trance.'

I sat up and rested my back on the headboard. This was not how I dreamed my Saturday mornings would be. I had to get the hell out of here. Where was the door? My blurry eyes scanned the room. The garish decor did not mix well with my hangover. There it was, bookended by joss sticks.

'Thanks, really, thanks. I think it's time I left and went back to the real world. You must have a tea leaf reading or a seance to get to.'

Her smudged-grey eyes looked at me. Not with anger or disappointment. With pity. I got out of the bed, grabbed my jeans from the trinket-strewn floor, pushed out of the door and almost tripped down the stairs trying to put my shoes on.

By the time I'd stumbled my way through the streets back home, it had dawned on me that I hadn't eaten for about 24 hours. Not a morsel. Not unless you counted drink, fags, chai and some bits of a hippy that I'd be best off forgetting about.

My body needed something. Craved something good. Something healthy. Something regenerative. Something to purge it of its sins. The house was empty. The cupboards weren't far off. The sum total wouldn't have looked out of place at a Harvest Festival in an inner-city comprehensive: a few own brand tins, half a pack of basmati rice and Chow Mein flavour Super Noodles. At Mother Hubbard's the cheap Chinese nutritional nothingness was an oasis in the desert. A shitty puddle of one but an oasis all the same.

But it wasn't just hunger that was eating me. Just as a carpenter laughs in the face of splinters or a lifeguard to getting his flip-flops wet, a drinker should become immune to hangovers. Migraines, dizzy spells, nausea; nothing more than an occupational hazard. A mild distraction that lasted all of two drinks until the next day's. But not for me. They fucking killed me and were getting worse with age.

It started with the headaches. A dull thump that constantly lived in my head like a mental stutter. But like a gimp with a limp, constant pain could be lived with, worked around, understood, dealt with. The dry mouth was a bitch. It wasn't pleasant to spend the day with a kisser that tasted like the population of Bombay had discarded their cigarette butts in it the night before. But it was bearable. You could brush your teeth. Use mouthwash. Chew gum. Or smoke more.

Wild weekends always brought me closer to God. This isn't the Road to Damascus. A Catholic education had ripped up that map. Rather the night before made the morning after a collection of what felt like final heartbeats. And it was these palpitations that slayed me. They were the unknown, the joker in the pack, the fly in the ointment. Headaches weren't going to kill me. A dry mouth wasn't going to kill me. But my heart stopping? That'd sure as the sun setting be my untimely end.

But even worse than the tremors? The sense of guilt at last night's crimes. Where had I been? Just what had I done? Nagging doubts are a fucker when you spent a fair proportion of your life in a state of non-remembrance. I caught my reflection in the stainless steel oven's splashback. The bluntness of the mirror blurred my features but I knew them by now. My face was symmetrical enough, barring a small scar above my left eyebrow, earned by answering my dad back in between brushing my teeth as an 8-year-old, his push in my back causing me to headbutt the chrome tap, the spat-out toothpaste turning pink with blood. Green eyes sat on dark bags above cheekbones they used to say you could hang your coat off. You'd just better not weigh down the pockets these days. A five o'clock shadow set all day over a square jaw, a dimple in my chin being cute or corny depending on your tastes. Once blonde hair was pushed off my forehead, still going strong at twenty-nine, its colouring doing me a favour in keeping grey at bay. I knew I still looked good. Goodish. I knew I had looked better. I knew another 5 years of this lifestyle and I could forget it.

Dear Mr McDare,

Thank you for taking the time to visit us recently.

At the MediHealth Wellness Centre we identify health risks that may affect you in the future, so you can do something about it now. Following your consultation with our healthcare experts, we would offer the following advice:

- Giving up smoking altogether
- Cutting back on number of units of alcohol drunk each week to 5 units
- Exercising for at least 30 minutes a day
- Visiting your GP and explaining your concerns regarding your ear and your genitals

As the country's pioneers of preventative health, our health-check is intended to keep you in the best of health. Following the recommendations contained within this letter can help you achieve this and live a healthy and happy life.

Sincerely,

Dr L. Taylor

# Chapter 2

I worked in a medium-sized office, which is to say there were about fifty other lemonheads doing the same shit I did to varying degrees of authority, success and interest. The shit was writing bullshit for bullshitters to sell bullshit. Or PR to you. Public Relations. Relations with the Public. It's fair to say that if you wanted a job which showed you the world only cared about money, and the odd pat on the slimy back – which in its wicked way led to, you guessed it, money – then this was it. I duped people for a living. Which, as you're beginning to discover, was quite a sad one. Heck, a lot of the time I even duped myself. Which is what made the moments of realisation that smacked you bang on the bridge of the nose at ten to four on a Tuesday afternoon all the more poignant. Chocolate bar brands sponsoring never-seen-their-dick fatsos to eat balanced diets, reality TV stars trying to reposition themselves as relevant, selling the 'social benefits' of a multi-million pound housing estate and its subsequent new fume-spewing road to dumb-fuck mothers with Ventolin-sucking kids. If your shit needed shining, then my chamois was at your service. And damn the consequences. They just didn't make for a nice story. Every PR man since Goebbels knew it.

Having spent the bulk of my working life selling in stories on behalf of everyone from greedy blue-chips to not greedy enough wafer-thin F-listers, it was inevitable my imagination would sometimes daydream headlines where I was the protagonist. 'Bill in Thai drugs bust: I'm innocent', 'Railroad death of drunk spin doctor', shit like that. The hacks at *The McDare Mercury* were canny copywriters on the topics of doom, gloom and disaster. The poor readers needed a good war to cheer them up. I put these thoughts not down to narcissism but a normal by-product of the job. When you picked up the news rock to see the squirming ants underneath, you realised anyone – repeat ANYONE – with a good enough jawline/tits (delete as applicable), the right wind and the wrong PR behind them could become 'famous' almost overnight. So why not me, if only in my own head?

It was a Monday. A day which I un-stereotypically liked. Full of hope, aspiration and purpose. This is the week your shit life changes. You straighten up. You make a difference to yourself. To society. All of these hopes evaporated like steam off piss in the desert by 11 a.m. when you realised you weren't going to make a difference, to yourself or society, and the only purpose you had was to get the story out of the door and follow closely behind it.

It was 11 a. m. Time for a cup of tea. Like most things in my life, tea drinking was taken to excess. Even an innocent pleasure such as this could be turned into a crutch when seen through the eyes of a dedicated addict. I think it was the ritual of it which drew me in. Ritual loomed heavy for lapsed Catholics. Boil the kettle, warm the pot, scatter the leaves, pour the water, let it steep, splash the milk, strain the leaves, pour the tea, stir. Hit. After three or four cups, your body reached a caffeine plateau and subsequent cups made you strung out and scratchy. Bad for you. Bad bad bad. Everything was bad for you these days.

Pete was in the kitchen. The office kitchen looked like it had been moved pine door by pine door from a mid-1990s show home. Yes, this was the height of homeware for the Mondeo man and his Asda Price wife hoping to social climb onto some soul-destroying development called something like Sovereign Chase or Cunts' Horizon. And now it lived in our grey little office, looking as out of place as a sunbather at a wake. But it had tea and biscuits and often this was all that mattered.

Pete had his back to me but it was evident he was resplendent in the office wear of the damned. A cheap shapeless suit hung from his podgy late-30s frame, looking as comfortable as a Jihad Warrior hanging from a crucifix. Plasticy slip-on loafers finished the look. From behind, his hair seemed like a good solid cut. One you could set your watch to. But as he turned around to greet me it was clear that an identity crisis occurred in the mirror every morning at around 8.30 a.m. as he worked wet look gel from the root up, not quite sure whether to play it edgy or safe and ending up with a compromise which ticked neither box and that a grandmother would find hard to ruffle without losing the family silver in.

'Ah, hello there, young man. How was the rest of your weekend then?'

Pete was stood next to the boiling kettle. His hearing was selective at best, irrevocably damaged at worst.

'I drank, wandered town, met some people, went to an all night drugs party, was sick on myself, was sick on a girl, got up, got lost, had a fight with a man taking his kids to football practice…'

Pete was straining to hear me over the water.

'Sorry, buddy, I didn't quite catch all of that. Sounded like a nice weekend though. You seemed to be talking to a rather lovely lady when I snuck out of the side door of the pub. You know three is my limit on a Friday. Foolish to ruin the next day, especially when the garden centre's got a sale on.'

The kettle had boiled and Pete poured the water into his cup. It said 'My Other Mug is The Holy Grail' in an italicised font on the side. It never failed to make him titter. Some of his drink spilled onto the mock marble counter.

'Oh Christ. Oh no, I blasphemed then. Now I'm not religious but I do have my own little beliefs. Every time I take the Lord's name in vain, I feel like I'm one step further away from heaven and one step closer to eternal damnation.'

I got out of the kitchen as quick as I could. Fuck the tea.


The annoyance thresholds of those who spent the majority of their waking lives marking time close to each other could be broken by the most nominal of noises. Sometimes it was the chime of a text message tone or the way they laughed sharply, just once, when reading a forwarded email about misspelt road signs from someone in accounts. These little things punctuated the nine to five not as a common comma but as a rarely seen semi-colon; eyebrow-raising, abnormal, unwanted; chipping away day-by-day until the listener snapped.

'Will you just shut the fuck up with that sneeze of yours? It's driving me slowly INSANE.'

With me, it was a cough. An irregular but virulent cough. It came, it produced, it went, it bothered. Usually-sympathetic colleagues turned and shot scornful stares. People talked in the kitchen. Emails were sent. I had to be told. Concentration was being broken. Trains of thought derailed. Germs being spread. It was Carol who came to talk to me.

'Have you got two minutes? There's something sensitive I'd like to talk to you about.'

Intrigued, I spun around on my chair and gave all 5 foot 2 inches of her my complete attention.

'Let's go to the breakout room. I've made you a tea. Just how you like it.'

I said nothing, but stood up and acceded. Carol smiled a mumsy smile and turned to walk to the room at the end of the open-plan floor. She had the look of a woman who had once been pretty, deep in her distant past. Never sexy or fuckable, just 'pretty'. Like when she was fourteen, but was far too conscientious to do anything about it, staying in doing her biology homework listening to Donny Osmond when her less pretty friends had stuffed socks into their older sisters' bras and gone uptown to suck some bouncer's cock in return for free entry to a theme pub.

'You need to see someone about it. Everyone is worried about you. Really. A cough can be a sign of much deeper problems. Are you eating well? Are you looking after yourself?'

'Yes I'm eating well, Carol, thanks. I even had one of my five-a-day this morning. Amen to Minute Maid.'

'Your health shouldn't be a joke, Bill. It's important. One of the chaps in my quiz team had a similar tickle you know. Sometimes we'd mishear important questions because of it. Turns out he had cancer. Dead now. We kept the name, "The Fab Four", though. In memory.'

'Thanks for brightening up my Monday and scaring me half to death, Carol.'

'Just get it seen to, Bill. It's important you're well. We rely on you here.'

It was Carol's concern that pushed me towards the Medi-Health Centre. Well, that and the fact that I'd spat blood in the urinal earlier, but mostly Carol. The blood had been appearing sporadically in the mucus I'd hack into the bog every time I'd take a piss. Which with the amount of tea I drank, was higher than average. It's not right for young lungs to be coughing up blood but when you'd been caning Marlboro Reds since a first sly drag behind the scout hut on your twelfth birthday, I tended to see my breathers as aged in dog years. Well worn-in. Loved, if you will. There was bound to be a bit of wear and tear every now and again, right? That's what I kept telling myself anyway. And why I'd put off seeing anyone about it for so long. Who wants to go to a small room to have some kid you would have bullied at school give you really bad news? Not I. I hated going to the doctors. All those sick people spreading germs over each other. Sneezing kids. Whooping pensioners. Shell-suited teenage mums. Shit magazines. So when Carol talked me around, there was no way I was crossing the threshold of an NHS establishment. Each visit came with free MRSA.

Every once in a while I'd splash out on a purchase. Generally it was upgrading to a double, but very occasionally it'd involve some hint of altruism. Like the time I bought my mum a Toby Carvery. Or the time I signed up to be a Cancer Research donor after being hounded by some white, dreadlocked mistake on my fag break and didn't cancel my direct debit as soon as I got back to my desk. A down payment for the future I reckoned.

This time it was a £299 comprehensive health check. I figured it was a small price to pay to stop me from thoughts of my demise. That the chest pains were just a hangover. Not the end of days. My days that is. A little MOT for little old me. I'd only spend it on fags anyway. Peace of mind. Fuck, I'd pay twice for peace of mind. The doctor would have to be Einstein crossed with Emmanuelle to give me that though. This was a good decision. If I keep telling myself I might actually believe it. Good good good.

The Medi-Health Centre was located about seven miles across town from my office. I'd booked the pool car under the auspices of going out to meet a hot new lead and blocked out a few hours next to my name on the whiteboard which acted as a bubble-written surveillance tool on our movements.

'You're taking the car?' asked my pod neighbour Jill. Jill spent her weekends training to be a yoga teacher despite being the least calm person I'd ever met.

'Yeah.'

'But shouldn't you be taking this "hot new lead" out for a three course with wine?'

'No. He doesn't drink so we're meeting at a Starbucks.'

'Fucking hell, Bill, when in Rome is it? You? Not having a drink? Ha.'

Jill emitted a piercing shrill, which managed to infer surprise and degradation all at once.

'See you later, Jill. Hold all calls, yeah?'

'Whatever.'


The pool car would have been better off being driven into a pool, being as it was the culmination of the collective shitty nick-nacks of the retards I had the displeasure of working with. You really did never know what you were going to find. On this occasion, which while unique was symptomatic of every time I got behind the wheel, my tan brogues stuck to a cluster of diet bar wrappers (Carol's) while a *Best of Sting* CD sat at a right angle on the ledge above the glove compartment (Pete's). I daren't open the glove compartment. This was often for the best.

As I drove across town, thoughts danced as clumsily as teenagers pilled up on their first half in my head. I was about to enter a situation which presented the very real possibility of bad news, a situation that I usually avoided at all costs in preference of the laissez-faire of social comatose, either through work, love, life or drink. What if this doctor told me, no doubt in an 'I'm-a-£300-an-hour-concerned-friend' kind of way, that 'I'm sorry Mr McDare, but you're fucked'. I couldn't really complain, could I? I've been caning it like there's no tomorrow ever since I could remember because it didn't really seem like there was much else to do. But what if there was no tomorrow? Would anyone care? Would I care? Sure, people would be surprised (not shocked), supportive and look at me with the same pitying, superior eyes normally reserved for the skinny, fly-ridden Africans on the give-us-your-money adverts. But secretly, deep down, they'd be hoping the same as me – that this sorry excuse for an existence could be over so they could get back to their soap operas, their goofy kids, their new kitchen appliances and the new restaurant in town, without having to give a thought to someone who maybe, just maybe, didn't want the life they thought they were meant to be living.

# Chapter 3

The waiting room at the Medi-Health Centre was everything the NHS one was not. It was a different kind of sickening. With a slight whiff of potpourri rising through the usual air of sterility, peach ceramics and carpeted walls, it gave the impression of an early 1990s leisure centre run under the firm but fair stewardship of a second-favourite aunt. Pan-pipe interpretations of hits of the 1960s hung in the air. It was the kind of muzak I'd imagine was played in the great glass elevator that greeted you when you'd snuffed it, the chimes of 'Hey Jude' leaving you unsure whether the lift was going up to heaven or down to hell.

'Mr McDare. Your Medi-Health Wellness Check is ready to commence. Would you like to follow me?' said an effeminate in dark chinos and a green Medi-Health embroidered polo shirt, whose name badge said 'Leo' but you could bet your last smoke went by 'Cleo' at some ketamine cave every Friday.

'Sure.'

So follow him I did, down a corridor decorated with pictures of active, happy-looking fuckers, into the heart of the muzak. We stopped outside a door marked 'Consultation Room' and the queen knocked twice, smiled and almost curtseyed before sliding back from whence we'd come.

'Do come in,' said a voice, husky as hell. Immediately all thoughts of slow, painful death evaporated – I entered the room to be faced with a lithe, late-30s, brunette knockout. She looked like the kind of girl who in a parallel universe I'd have been happy to take home to meet my mother. Non-conventionally attractive, no doubt intelligent, with a spoonful of sinfulness piled to the top for my own good measure. I imagine we'd laugh in all the right places at her dinner table talk of the patient who came in that day with a model aeroplane stuck to his hand, and as conversation turned to the relative merits of Swiss and Austrian ski resorts, her size seven heels would tease the inside of my trouser-leg under the table, promising another hot, sweaty night of animalistic feasting in the master bedroom of our paid-for-in-cash suburban town house.

'I'm Dr Linda Taylor but you can call me Linda. Dr Linda.' Fuck, she was feisty too.

'What we're going to do this morning...' She paused as she rechecked her computer screen for my name. '...Mr McDare.'

'Bill, please.'

'...Bill, is run a series of painless procedures to paint a holistic picture of your health and well-being. Think of it as an MOT for the body. And if our motor cars are deserving of an annual check-up, we here at the Medi-Health Centre are of the mind that the body – the most important machine of all – is certainly worth a once-over too.'

'Certainly Linda... Dr Linda.'

'Right then, Bill, in order for you to get the most out of your assessment, it's important that we have an open and honest dialogue so I can consider all the information in my overall recommendations. Are we agreed to being open and honest with each other?'

'Yes, Dr Linda,' I said, thinking how I'd like to see her open and honest.

'To begin I'd like you to give me a brief overview of how you see your current state of health and why you've come in to see us at the Medi-Health Centre today.'

'Well, I guess I've been feeling a little rundown recently and, I don't know, just a heck of a lot older than I used to be. '

'We're all getting older, Bill and, as we do, we need to look after our bodies more than perhaps we used to back in our more youthful days. Tell me, what symptoms are causing you to feel this way?'

'Oh, I don't know. Palpitations, sweats, dry mouth, headaches, panic attacks, a cough…'

She tapped this into her computer

'Does the cough produce a mucus?'

'Sometimes.'

'And what colour is this product?'

'Depends really. Sometimes yellowy-green, sometimes greeny-yellow, sometimes with blood.'

'Do you smoke, Bill?'

She needn't have asked. My fingers were the colour of a Simpson.

'Yes.'

'How many a day?'

'Ten,' I lied. 'But I am trying to quit.'

'Good. You should. ' She was sterner now.

'And how many units of alcohol do you drink a week?'

Who the fuck kept tabs on how many 'units' of alcohol they drank a night, let alone a week?

'What's the recommended intake?' I asked.

'Around 21 units a week,' Dr Linda replied.

I did the old trick of halving it and adding seven. This was the way you worked out the age of the youngest piece of ass you could tap. Twenty-two for me. Imagine what you could do with that. Back to the task in hand, Bill.

'You know, about seventeen, eighteen,' I lied again. This whole open and honest thing really wasn't working out.

'And how regularly do you exercise?'

No calling me 'Bill' now, definitely sterner. Disapproving, almost. Christ, if she knew the half of it.

'If I'm being open and honest, a lot less than I used to since I twisted my knee at five-a-side last year. I do try and run twice a week at a lunchtime though.'

'Okay, thanks, Bill. What I'd like you to do next is to take your shoes off. Just leave them under my desk here, and step onto the weighing scale over by the wall there.'

Slowly but surely I was losing my clothes. We were getting there.

I stepped onto the scales and a digital display read 70 kg. I sounded like an import of marching powder.

She jotted the figures down, this time on a notepad.

'Okay, if you could step from the scales over to the wall there, we'll measure you up.'

She measured me (6 ft – just), again took a note and led me to what seemed like a higher, less comfortable shrink's couch.

'If you'd be so kind to lie back on here, Bill, I'll explain to you how we're going to use the measurements we've just taken. We're going to work out your body mass index, or BMI, which is a statistical measure of body weight based on the height and weight readings we just took. It's a widely used diagnostic that you've probably heard of and is used to estimate a healthy body weight, something which is essential to the Medi-Health Wellness Check.'

I nodded, turning the corners of my mouth up in agreement. They didn't miss a chance for a brand namecheck.

She tapped some figures into the keyboard again and rapped her black polished fingernails against the rich oak desk while she waited for the machine to whirr into work. As the screen slowly changed, she surveyed the information and swallowed. The rap of the fingernails came to a halt.

'Okay, Bill, it's telling me that your BMI is 20.9, which is just about healthy, but not necessarily just about right, for a man of your shape and size. A healthy weight is perceived to be between

70 kg and 82 kg, and as you'll have gathered, you sail close to the wind at the lower end of the spectrum. From this I can safely ascertain two things: one, you're not eating enough, and two, when you do eat, you're not eating the right kind of foods.' She emphasised the word 'right' a little too strongly.

My head dropped slightly in shameful recognition reminiscent of the time when as a 14-year-old boy my mum caught me with my jeans around my ankles and the TV tuned to the Home Shopping Network's Summer Special Swimwear show. This time I didn't have to pull my pants up, but lifted my shirt as Dr Linda talked me through the next procedure.

'I'm going to attach a series of little receptors to your skin which will send a small painless electrical impulse through your body, providing a reading of your heart's activity on the small screens here.'

What screens? I hadn't noticed any screens. But sure enough there they were to my right hand side, six previously ignored little boxes, looking for all the world like monitors from prototype computers, ready to tell of a murmur or a shudder or an altogether tick-tock-stop. The inanimate took on evil tendencies. The waves rose and fell and fell and rose and rose and fell while Dr Linda's face remained impassive and access to her emotions impossible. She didn't give the 'Oh fuck, another one bites the dust' look I would have been prone to in a position of such delicately-poised importance, but perhaps they devoted whole semesters to poker facing at medical school.

'Fine. You can pull the receptors off now. It might smart a little. I'd do it but I don't think it bodes well for my tip if I inflict too much pain on my patients.'

She'd made a joke.

'Some people like pain.' I squirmed as I said it, pulling the sticky plaster off hard and fast in punishment, thus proving the validity of my embarrassed slip.

Dr Linda ignored my quip and carried on with her business of being a £300 an hour private doctor. I'd have paid her double for a shag and taken half as long.

'You can put your shirt back on now. Unless you'd like to walk bare-chested around the centre, that is. I'm going to send you for a chest X-ray. Now, this doesn't normally form part of the Wellness Check but I think in the circumstances, with your smoking habit and incidence of blood production, it wouldn't do any harm to check you out more closely. A very important area, Bill.'

She directed me back out along the corridor to a desk where a middle-aged matronly type greeted me and showed me to some firm but comfortable seats and a coffee table of up-to-date magazines. I sat down.

A fucking chest X-ray? So this is it then. The all or nothing. The now or not-lucky-enough-to-be-never. It was like sitting in the queue at the passport office for hell. I'd only ever had an X-ray once before in my life. I'd been playing kiss chase in the school playground with some of the girls from the year above. I think I was about six or seven at the time. When I say I was playing, I mean really that they were playing, I was just trying my darnedest to join in as it beat playing marbles with my sick-down-their-nylon-sweaters, barely comprehensible male contemporaries. Remarkably, one of my peers had managed to bag himself a girlfriend. I happened to be chasing hot on her heels. How was I to know? Relationships tended to last for the length of a school day back then, which to be fair was longer than the lion's share of my sorry situations. It must have been his baseball pitch which attracted the skirt in my sights to her pre-pubescent partner, as the little fucker picked up a huge glass marble and launched it right at my head. I caught sight of it just as it cracked me on the cheekbone and the rest of the next hour passed in a fuzz of heat, sweat and memory loss. A bit like my first pill. But we'll get to that another time.

Before I had a chance to look at the latest copy of *GQ* and find out where I'd been going wrong, my name was called out by a Doogie Howser lookalike and in I went. Again I took my shirt off, but this time put my chest up against the cold metal of a flat surface while the boy left the vicinity and clicked his buzzer like a teenager on a 'Bring Your Son To Work Day' who had been charged with moving the PowerPoint forward on Daddy's big pitch. The radiation lurched towards my insides.

After a short wait I was sent back in to see Dr Linda who reassured me that all was fine enough with my vital organs, before lecturing me on the slow but irrevocable damage my devil-may-care lifestyle was having on my inward and outward glint. She saw people like me every day apparently. Guilt-ridden fuckers who, after internal debate on infernal affairs, came in at the seventh sign of spit with blood. The next visit, and the one after that, wouldn't have such an easy outcome apparently.

What-fucking-ever. School's out for summer.

'Was there anything else, Bill?'

There was one more thing before the bell rang.

Deep breath.

'There was something… but it's a little bit sensitive.'

'Go on, Bill…'

'Well… there's been a little spot on the end of my… my… penis for a while now and I thought you might be able to take a look at it.'

It'd been a long time since I'd done this without been liquored up. She filled the expectant pause with a professionalism not seen since the African prostitute I'd been bought as a twenty-first birthday present in Hamburg. I hoped the endgame wasn't the same. I may be hauled in front of the authorities if so.

'Okay, Bill, let's take a look.'

I undid my belt, clumsily unzipped my trousers and poked the end of my dick out of my pants. I did not pick a good day to wear comedy boxer shorts. This probably had something to do with the fact that I never actually bought my own pants, just kind of accumulated them from open drawers or Santa Claus. Note to self: buy better pants.

It looked like a naughty schoolboy hauled up to the headmaster's office, lying prone, almost retracting into itself to hide from crimes past and soon punishable. After a cursory glance, one of her shaped eyebrows raised, motioning me back to a more dignified position.

'Now, the Wellness Check doesn't normally include an STI test, and I'm certainly not an expert in the field but it looks like nothing to worry about to me. But I do think you should visit your GP to talk through this and your ear problem.'

Oh, the ear problem. I hadn't mentioned that, had I? Seemed a bit tame when I had a good cock story to tell.

# Chapter 4

Ever been at a dinner party with an accountant? Scratch that, two accountants? Trying to outdo each other with their incessant wittering. Did you understand a word the fuckers said? Slurping about P & Ls through a minestrone soup. Yakking about ledgers, A/R and A/P over linguine. Being wan about working for the Big Five over tiramisu. Chit-chat full of their own impenetrable idioms. In PR, we saw this and we raised it to new levels of smugness.

We were forever giving colleagues a heads-up during a sit-down or a touch-base so they could get the skinny on their radar. We sprinkled our magic on cradle-to-grave strategies for new products which we'd drill down to at idea showers which gave our clients strategic staircases going forward. We'd get all our ducks in a row to stop the grass growing too long on ideas.

And then there was the low-hanging fruit. I was all about the low-hanging fruit. In case you were ever misguided enough to want to join Satan's gang, or just wanted to know enough to bluff your way to a blowjob at a PR party, stay tuned in.

- **'A heads-up'** – To make aware of, sometimes implying some kind of inside information. As in, 'Pete, I want to give you a heads-up on the Workington account before we meet that slimy fucker Mathison.'
- **'A sit-down'** – A meeting, most likely stolen from Italian American Mafia language. As in, 'We need a sit-down to run through the invoicing for the consumer division, Carol. Capiche?'

- **'A touch-base'** – Again a meeting, but quicker and less formal than a sit-down. As in, 'Can we touch-base on the Cutler and Noble campaign? Time to get me up to speed, Jill.'

- **'The skinny'** – The most-up-to-date information. Appropriated from some bullshit American TV show mostly by the skirt in the office, but increasingly used by the sad, greying men in an attempt to seem with it. As in, 'Yo guys, what's the skinny on the social media strategy?'

- **'Radar'** – People's in-head to-do lists. As in, 'Get that feature off my fucking radar before I tie your hands and feet together, stick a pencil up your arse and force feed you ten million malnourished woodworm.'

- **'Sprinkle our magic'** – To add our creative touch to an otherwise mundane situation. Drugs and alcohol sometimes help. As in, 'I think it's time we sprinkled our magic on this eye-wateringly dull creative. Does anyone have a 50 pound note?'

- **'Cradle-to-grave strategy'** – A plan to take as much money off the helpless bozos from the moment they first sit down in our office to the end of eternity. As in, 'We need a cradle-to-grave strategy for this new cider. One that's so to-grave that in the event of a nuclear holocaust all that's left is cockroaches, herpes and this fucking money-making plan.'

- **'Drill down'** – To get to the heart of the matter, or sometimes the soles of the feet. As in, 'Let's drill down to who this fake-titted fame-hungry whore really is. I mean, does she have like a disabled sibling or some other redeeming feature?'

- **'Idea showers'** – Gatherings of two people or more, where minds are dumped, random thoughts shouted out and big ideas talked through. Also a window into the frankly frightening minds of the other fucks you worked with. As in, 'Right everyone, let's schedule in an idea shower for 10 a.m. on this new crisp. They're not fried, remember. Baked. Baked.

Thoughts around that please. Jean, can you get some *pain au chocolats* in? We're gonna really go for it.'

- **'Strategic staircases'** – Plans which moved incrementally towards their conclusion. Often had the effect of making you want to throw aforementioned strategist down a very real and very hard staircase. As in, 'It's time to lay down a strategic staircase for the Weyermakers, team. Like, now.'
- **'Going forward'** – In the future. One of the more annoying turns-of-phrase. As in, what would happen anyway if you just sat at your desk with your pants around your ankles playing 'La Marseillaise' on a kazoo. As in, 'What's our plan for the transport arm of the business, going forward?' (Go on, take it out and read the sentence again. It makes no fucking difference does it?)
- **'Get our ducks in a row'** – To systematically organise our ideas, or ensure everything was in place for success. As in, 'We need to get our ducks in a row for this Arab sheikh before he gets on his camel and fucks off to the next loose-moralled agency.' No animals are harmed in the delivery of this phrase.
- **'Stop the grass growing long'** – To avoid having lights go out on inspirational moments by actually actioning things as opposed to just throwing a ball against the wall all day shouting out buzz words just loud enough to grab the attention of the new intern over in the events team. As in, 'We've got to stop the grass growing long on the idea to get the CEO to adopt an autistic ethnic kid for the week.'
- **'Low-hanging fruit'** – An easy win, a no sweat solution. As in, 'Let's snaffle up the low-hanging fruit for this new client to keep 'em sweet before getting knee deep into the real problem.'

Yep, we'd pretty regularly litter sentences with this shit. We probably should have struck up a deal with Linguaphone to induct and indoctrinate new starters. Untainted souls who could have escaped there and then and instead devoted their lives to charity work, health care or scrubbing toilets. Anything to make a tangible difference.

So now you've got the skinny on the bullshit we said, it's worth you knowing how we bullshitted. You know, the tricks of the trade. Now, I don't mean how to knock out some killer copy or how to write a snazzy headline or how to get the best table at The Ritz without reserving. What I'm talking about are cerebral sleights, the mental manipulation that every good message-pusher used to ensure it was their way or the highway.

There were six basic steps we used which could convince people into doing anything you so desired. The beauty was in their simplicity. They were as old as time. To pass the days we'd even bet each other we could soft-arm some sucker into doing something. Anything. When there was a round of drinks riding on it, it was amazing what some of us would do. Me especially. Right, okay.

1. **Reciprocation** – Now this was Old Testament stuff; an eye for an eye, a tooth for a tooth. Or a corporate golf day for a six month campaign. Backstage at a Madonna concert for a re-launch strategy. Front row for *Les Mis* for some global repositioning. A three-gin lunch for a double page spread. If we scratched their backs, they'd scratch ours right back. Even when their backs weren't itchy. It was beautiful. Go on, do something nice for the next person you see. I'd bet my last bean they'll do something nice back for you within the week. It's how they're wired.

2. **Consistency** – Got a gym membership? When was the last time you went? A while back, huh? I bet you plucked up all your courage to go. Talked yourself in and out and in of it a million times. Got on the same treadmill you had six months before. And got the fuck out of there before anyone realised

29

how out of place you were. You didn't cancel your membership though, did you? Oh no. Because, if anyone asks, you're a member of the gym and you go as often as you can which isn't enough but you've had a busy few months and you'll always be a member as you're a consistent human being. Not boring enough to set your watch by, but certainly not erratic enough to appear unstable or untrustworthy. 'Well, this idea worked last quarter two, Mr Henderson. You thought it was a great idea then…' We'd wheel out the same shit year after year to our committed consistent customers. To change their mind would admit some earlier error of judgement on their part. And no one likes to admit they were wrong. We rarely even had to assemble the box, let alone think outside it.

3. **Social proof** – How many times have you found yourself in a huge queue for a nightclub? Everyone dolled up to the nines, faces tight with anticipation at what beholds them beyond the 'roided up coke-buckets on the door. Shiny shoes tip-tapping the floor. Cigarettes being burnt down to the tip. Chit-chat-chattering. Nervous almost. Why the fuck are these people itching to get inside? Because there's a big queue, that's why. Because every other hedonist in town wants to get in there. So you do too. Because it must be good tonight. Because it's one-in one-out. What do these people know? I want to know too. Let me in for fuck's sake! You needn't have bothered. It's not Studio 54, it's called Rumours. And it's shit. We pulled this trick on the unsuspecting all the time. We'd organise lunches where hot leads would sit next to stool pigeons who'd tell them how their lives had been infinitely better since they started working with us. You know, how their business had grown, their shareholders were happy, their wives could come, that kind of thing. Once they had it from the horse's mouth, they were just dying to sign up. I mean, everyone else is doing it, right?

4. **Liking** – To be honest, this one even made me a little bit sick.

We had a whole room full of monkeys whose job it was to socially profile our potential paymasters. We're talking anyone from FTSE 100s to leggy 6-stoners. We called it 'Department Delve' or DD for short. No stone was left uncovered. They'd search microfilms at the library. Take a fine-tooth comb to Companies House records. Track down old college room-mates. Bribe ex-lovers. Sometimes we'd bring in Private Dicks if we needed to, but hell, I think they were more ethical than some of the nosey fucks who worked in DD. By the time one of the account team was ready for the first contact, we had more prep than The Hamptons in holiday season. We'd like their football team. Our grandmas were from the same town. We took two weeks in the same château. If they were Tom Ripley, we were Tom Ripley too. Basically, we became their kind of people. And who didn't want to work with their kind of people?

5. **Authority** – Everybody likes to have a friend in the know. Someone who had their fingernails under the phoney veneer of life and peeled it back for them every now and again to let them in on the big secret. Mostly so they could relay that information to their even more sheltered friends, thus becoming the Oracle of their own circle. And repeat. Until everybody knew what nobody had known and a new, even darker secret had to be constructed. We didn't just whisper those secrets. Without us there'd be no pursed lips. Clients lapped it up. The best bet was to take a newspaper to a meeting and casually flick through it. While on first impression this seemed rude, when the clown opposite cottoned onto what you were doing, they were entranced. 'One of ours, another, oh, this one's placed by Shalter Wyverne, one of ours… see this story here, Mr Phillips? Dad of the Year, my hairy arse. Now if I tell you this, you've got to promise to keep it to yourself, trade secret, see… okay, I

can trust *you*, I can tell… see this shitty Superpops celebrity? Well I know for a fact he's been fucking his make-up boy for the past six months. When I say boy, I mean boy, if you catch my drift? And this whole cover-up campaign where he's being pictured at every god-damned amusement park in the country with his, let's be honest with each other, butt-ugly kids, has been quite, quite beautiful.' They loved hearing shit like this. Share your authority with them. Make them authorities too. When they'd wound their jaw back up enough to spill it they were back for more. And as soon as they entered your peripheral vision, the clock started ticking. And what was time? Money, my friends; dirty, filthy, beautiful money.

6.  **Scarcity** – No girl ever put out when you gave them your first Rolo. In the desirability stakes, less was most definitely more. And so it was in our world. We'd tell them we'd love to get them that Platinum Diner's Card, that holiday home, that better life they'd always dreamt of, but there were only so many hours in the day. So they'd just have to wait. Unless they wanted to speak to our accounts department who we were sure could help them out on a favourable rate for those minimal hours. Higher than usual of course, as they were so few and far between at present. But favourable all the same. They always asked to be transferred. Of course they did.

As I said before, it wasn't their fault, they were wired like it. The brain had these default settings it whirred to when someone like us wafted the mental equivalent of a tasty pie underneath it. It had to. There was too much else to think about. Super size, interest free, soy, skinny, decaf, support packages, gold rates. People needed a short-cut where they could get it. And we exploited the shit out of it.

This stuff depressed the hell out of me.

# Chapter 5

'Do you love me?'

Silence.

And then. The reply.

'I'm in love with the idea of you.'

That had been if not the beginning of the end, then the end of the beginning. We'd got together in a whirlwind of youthful freedom, cheap alcohol and the flexibility of the timetable of a Bachelor of Arts degree. The first time away from home was, for both of us, a chance for reinvention, half-read novels and sexual exploration. I fucked more times in the first week we'd known each other than I had in my previous 18 years of existence. Sure, I'd come a lot, but generally at my own hand. Absent parents and satellite television gave the teenage boy if not the predilection per se, then certainly the opportunity to enjoy it with a bon viveur not granted to all. And don't get me wrong, I had fucked before, just never in the casual-yawning-oh-it's-just-another-fuck kind of way. The previous times when girls had been kind enough to let me stick it in them had been ingrained like Kennedy assassination moments.

The first time was memorable if for nothing other than it being the opening notch on the post. I'd started dating a girl in the year below me at school. The girls in my year wouldn't look at me once, let alone twice, so I set my sights on the nubile things of Year 10. Innocent, mysterious, and best of all ignorant to the fact I was a social retard. Well, at least until I opened my mouth. Which didn't seem to matter for Laura Stanton, who, when she wasn't shoplifting mascara, was actually a very sweet young girl. Or so I'd assumed. She was the only one who'd ever spoken back to me. About nothing in particular you know. How many fags we'd smoked that day. How many gigs we'd been to. How we'd watched loads of 18-rated films. And with my age advantage, I had a whole 12 months more to bullshit my way to some form of twisted teenage desirability. The girls in my year would never have believed me.

While Laura's parents sat in the lounge watching soap operas most weekday evenings, little did they know of the drama unfolding in the back room. We'd heavy-petted for months under the guise of my schooling their middle-born child on the whys and wherefores of GSCE German. When The Stantons, or Ralph and Val to me by then, finally did leave the house for the first time since their honeymoon for lasagne twice at the local Trattoria, the sexual encounter that took place in their two-up two-down wasn't pornographic, but awkward, embarrassing and over before we knew it. But the fact that it was over meant it had begun and the fact that it had begun meant that it had happened and I was off the mark and no longer a virgin and a man of the fucking world.

Take two I had less to do with. Everyone had a friend of their mother's they fantasised about. It was a rite of passage for all young men, like being sick off cheap liquor or growing a particularly bad bum-fluff moustache and thinking it added years to your age when in reality it gave you the look of the Saturday boy at a dusty Mexican filling station. You know, *the* friend, not the one who baked succulent cakes or organised the Parent Teacher Association.

The one whose look would linger on you a little too long as you brought her an ashtray as she drew on a cigarette at your mum's Tupperware party. Dark red lipstick framing the trail of smoke. Well, it wasn't her. But by Christ I wish it had have been. Instead it was Rosie Jenkins, who lived four doors down from our house and was a pretty big wheel on our Neighbourhood Watch committee. There had been a party at The Jenkins' house to celebrate their eldest daughter Sylvia getting the grades she'd needed to go to Oxford. They were that kind of family. Well all apart from Scott, who was a year younger than me, and highly impressionable. The party, if you could call it that, had been Dullsville 5000. Proud uncles. Goofy kids. Local busybodies nosing through the kitchen cupboards. Lame with a capital L. Until I told Scotty that drinking whisky put hairs on your balls and that he should see what his daddy had locked away in the cellar. To really lay it on thick I pulled out a pube. Social proof. Sure enough he returned with a 3/4 full bottle of Glenfiddich and 5/6 later I'd passed out under the coats on the Jenkins' matrimonial bed.

Now Mr Jenkins was a dog and had his eye on my mother that night, trying to impress her with his tales of Indian railway rides and his insight into Hemingway's short stories, moving just a little too close to hear her reaction on the Calcutta to Bombay Express. When she tried to escape him, leaving the marquee they'd erected to mark the special occasion for some fresh air and a menthol cigarette, he'd followed, cigar cutter in hand. Not being much of a drinker herself and unable to see her husband, Mrs J retired up the wooden hill, thinking it best to leave the rest of the night to Sylvia. It was her night after all. Moving the Barbours to one side to find a body in the bed, she whispered,

'Come on Albie, let's do it like old times. Our little girl's all grown up and going to college...'

And so I let her ride me. I had a raging hard-on from dreaming about Mrs Brannigan, my mother's friend with the dark red fuck-me lips. We'd been doing it on a craps table in Vegas, while a crowd of ice-blonde Russian double agents and Texans in 10 gallon hats watched on aghast but aroused. Coming round to being mounted by a 40-something plump lady, while initially disconcerting, was still as rare as hens' teeth for me so I kept as quiet as I could. The old girl didn't usually hit the sauce and was so gone on Babycham and gin she didn't seem to notice. I managed to last longer than with Laura, which I think I have the whisky to thank for. She soon tired, rolled off and started snoring. Sobered up mentally if not physically, I got the hell out of there. The party had died down by then and I managed to escape unnoticed. I even managed to knock one out thinking about the Vegas situation when I got back. Right in Ivana Kickarlakov's apple martini. I was getting better at this.

Ever since that night I kind of took Scotty under my wing, making sure he wasn't picked last on street football teams, that he didn't catch hell off the kids on the school bus. Apparently his old man hit the fucking roof about the missing whisky but it was Sylvia's then-boyfriend who got the blame. They never did think he was good enough for her anyway, what with her going to Oxford and all. There's a lesson for Mr Jenkins in there: try to fuck my mother, I'll fuck your wife. And drink your whisky. Not a bad mantra to live by, that one.

Third time was most definitely not lucky. After the incident with Mrs Jenkins I'd gone through a bit of a dry spell. Which for a 16-year-old who's just been introduced to the reality that other people could help you get your rocks off is a bit like telling a dope fiend they've won a muffin factory in a raffle and then hiding their ticket. It was tough. I figured the only way anyone was going to have sex with me again was by investing the time in a girlfriend. The lucky fuck I'd had was like a lottery win, albeit one in a developing country. Finding a girlfriend wasn't going to be the easiest task for a spotty little smoker like me. Sure, Laura had gone for that routine, but she was pretty wild. I don't mean sexually, just in her outlook. What I needed was a nice girl. One to take home to my mother, which I certainly couldn't do with Mrs Jenkins.

I was clearing about ten fags a day now, and was struggling to pay for them through my measly pocket money and occasional gifts from well-meaning aunts. There was a particularly sharp card racket being led on the 512 bus by an entrepreneurial kid by the name of Tony Bonano, but my hand rarely came up. So I got myself a Saturday job at the local pet superstore. Petsworld: Where Pets Are Friends.

The first time I saw Trisha she was in the dog grooming parlour, wearing a red all-in-one shell boiler suit, blow-drying a particularly vicious poodle. She remained patient. She was caring. She seemed kind. A giver. Just what I needed. I'd yet to realise that these qualities in a 16-year-old girl equalled frigidity.

We endured what my grandfather would have referred to as a long courtship. If I'd have been a fish I'd have wiggled my tail so much my scales would have fallen off. But I wasn't. I was a cashier at a large domestic animal emporium. The equivalent of my waggle-dance could be finding the price on a tin of dog food, giving her the coppers from my float or dealing with difficult gay couples returning dog chains with guilty faces. Anything to build up enough good will for some form of physical contact. I had to be her work bitch for six whole months before she'd even see me outside of my yellow uniform. Oh, and not like that. Not out of my clothes, just in a non-work situation. Where the same routine picked up. For dog food prices see helping with homework, for float fiddling see walking her home from work, for rent-boy refunds see chaperoning to awful fucking chick flicks.

But good things come to those who wait. That's what decades of Guinness advertising taught me. Unfortunately, while Trisha looked good in the glass, the drinking certainly wasn't quite as good as a pint of the black stuff. Similar iron content, but mostly from the blood that seeped out of her pussy, down my legs and all over my boxfresh Adidas Trimm Trabbs. They were ruined, and so was she. It was her first time. As someone with two stripes on my shoulder already I'd quickly become unsympathetic to the traumas of the newly christened. 'Doing It' hadn't turned out to be what Trisha was led to believe by glossy magazines, late night shows and sluttier friends. And after becoming a virtual pariah to get a fuck, I now couldn't give one. Next.

Anyway, enough of those early scores and back to the one who actually meant something once, somewhere in the deep and dark distant past. Her name was Deborah. The three year honeymoon period afforded by a slack degree and slacker attitude to knicker elastic had been glorious, but as with all good things, I had too much, too soon. A weariness snuck in, a plateau had been reached. After the Kodak moment of throwing our caps in the air on the steps of some ancient limestone building paid for by the slave trade, a very real, tax-paying, putting the bins out on a Monday existence had had to start. No more 2-4-1 nights, no more long lazy naked afternoons. The honeymoon had become a retirement cruise, only with less buffet lunches. Like meeting up with a holiday romance who seemed less exotic when the backdrop shifted from palm trees to pallid streets, once removed from the carefreeness of college, our relationship seemed a trick. This wasn't what I signed up for. I was just glad of a shag, and got carried away. I always get carried away.

When the rat race replaced the sack race, we had excuses to see each other less and less. Carving out some kind of crappy career got in the way, but frankly work became a welcome reason to keep out of her way. Take away the fucking – which she was – and the girl who'd helped me hit my sexual stride was boring, staid and dull dull dull.

Fun was a box-set. A new recipe. A farmer's market. A visit from her parents. As a 20-something, I still wanted my life to be ripe with recklessness to feed my inner raconteur. Not a patchwork quilt, Pecan pie and E fucking R. One day. Perhaps. I'd rather drink in the pub, making friends with strangers. I'd climb into our bed later and later, with no explanation asked for or offered. She'd resigned herself to not wondering what we were doing that weekend. She already knew. She was sitting in, alone. I was out, somewhere, anywhere but there. Crawling from park bench to party to strange beds to her. We were in a circle so vicious it had teeth. Something had to give.

And that was when she asked me the big question. My answer confirmed what 12 months of Byronesque behaviour had illustrated. I was in love with the idea of her. I was also in love with the idea of the three day week, free bars and blow-jobs on the National Health Service but often the 2 + 2 of the ideal and the reality made 76. I couldn't face the months of perpetual groveling and not being myself that was the by-product of easing the conscience after an indiscretion. Which would inevitably lead to others. It was time for a spring-clean. This, for a messy fucker like me, was damned hard work. Luckily, cleaning of any kind was not high on the agenda in my new place of residence.

After leaving Deborah I'd floated around on stained sofas and friends' floors for a while until I took a room with a couple close to the Turkish part of town. Now, I don't mean that it looked like Constantinople. More that every other shop front showed off a grotesque picture of a doner kebab. The area was less up-and-coming, more been-and-gone. I'd met Craig and Connie in one of the many pubs I frequented and they'd seemed idealistic, environmentally aware, in love and short of cash. Fuck knows why they thought I'd make a good housemate but the pursuit of money pushes people into very strange situations. I'd thought that for a couple of hundred a month I could perhaps learn something about relationships from them. Either that or split them up. One of the two. Time would tell.

The house was from the Victorian period and retained much of the era's ambience. The living room was very well lived in, the walls and upholstery taking on a nicotined hue that could well have been a desirable shade had Keith Richards been an interior designer. A barefooted walk on the carpet was a lucky dip with prizes of burnt roaches, ring-pulls or pizza crusts. The *piece de resistance w*as a poster of a ginger cat clinging by its claws for dear life from a broken branch, underneath the bubble-written advice to 'Hang On In There'. Sitting on the sofa and looking at it felt like being in a post-apocalyptic Athena.

My bedroom would certainly never fall foul of the Trade Descriptions Act. It was a room, with a bed, and no space for much else. This spartan approach to my quarters felt like a well-earned penance for leaving my cosy flat and cold girlfriend behind. Who needed Ikea side tables, feature mirrors and retro lamps anyway? Just more stuff to throw in the heat of an argument. It was fair to assume that it was best if I kept the lights switched off when bringing company back.

The bathroom had the unusual feature of a secret passage, which led downstairs. Although it wasn't so secret. There was no need to pull on a dusty tome on a bookshelf for it to be revealed. At the toilet's three o'clock was a gaping big hole which looked out directly over the kitchen sink. This made shits perhaps more interesting due to the conversational possibilities on offer, but certainly more self-conscious. The stench caused by my body repelling the red wine and Guinness I saw fit to constitute lunch wafted down to the kitchen, rarely being drowned out by the smells of the cheap nutritional non-entities those poor fucks I lived with served up each and every night. It was a wonder the three of us didn't catch scurvy.

# Chapter 6

'Carter Road… number 35. Which side is that? On the right? Ahhh. I used to see a girl who lived in the first road off there on the left. When I was in University, that was. Cracking girl. Cracking girl.'

He looked wistfully to his shelf of certificates and family portraits.

'Never did know what became of her. That was way back in the seventies.' He looked at the records on the computer screen. 'Before you were even born, lad. Anyway, what can I do for you?' My eye scanned the room and rested upon his shelf. Old medical prizes and photos of kids, horses, holidays. One photo looked at me. 1976-2004 read some gold lettering at the bottom of an Olan Mills style portrait. I looked back to Dr Edwards. Same wavy hair, but greyer. Same apple shaped head. Same monobrow. Fuck. If the son of a practicing medical professional could peg it before thirty, what chance did I have?

'Anyway, lad, what can I do for you?'

'Well it's a bit of a delicate matter to be honest, Doc…'

'Come on lad, my business is delicate matters. There's nothing on God's green earth I haven't seen twice in this room.'

'It's to do with my…'

'Penis? Your old boy?

'Erm… yes.'

'Right, well let's have a look at him then. Come on, don't be shy. Mrs Walters is waiting to see me next and the poor old girl's got chronic bronchitis. Over on the table there….'

41

'Okay.'

I'd never before undone my belt under the watchful eye of a moustached middle-aged man. It was all very procedural. I imagined this is what being bummed in public school was like. Very matter of fact.

'Ah, there he is. What seems to be the problem with him then?'

'Well, I've had a woman look at it. A woman doctor I mean. And she thinks I may have a genital wart...'

He took my cock in his cold left hand, the silver of his wedding band sending a chill through my nervous bell-end.

'It's hard to say for sure as these things come and go without ever really going. And strictly speaking you've come to the wrong place, but I'm never averse to checking out a little fella. You really should go and visit the specialist genito-urinary medicine clinic over at the hospital. But what I can do is give you a referral so you won't have to queue up for too long.'

I put it back in my pants while the doc scribbled out a slip for me and then pressed it into my palm, his hand warmer this time.

'Thanks,' I said.

'Glad to be of help, lad.'

As I left the office I could hear him muttering 'Carter Road' over and over under his breath. He laughed to himself as I shut the door. Mrs Walters gave me a stinking look.

My email account was a magnet for electronic missives that ranged from the banal to the biting to the bizarre. If it wasn't Miles demanding a forward planning meeting on the Brompton account, or Carol after inspiration for a strapline for a new brand of hand lotion, it was Jill telling me what a cunt she thought Miles was and asking if I agreed, or messages from a Ukrainian blonde declaring her desire for a strong man to start a big family and make long love. I don't think it helped that I clicked through on these ones.

Every now and again though, Trent would mail me the CV of girls who'd applied for a job with the company, sadly thinking that working with us could be their first step on the ladder to a meaningful career in the media industries. Delusion. Now, as you've probably already guessed, I wasn't part of the recruitment team, God forbid. How Trent had got the gig was beyond me. But there was fortitude in Trent's forwarding. Pressing 'send' meant I could search the young hopefuls on Facebook and we could compare marks out of ten and work out whether or not we'd need to shave/iron/not smell of booze on the day they'd come in for a grilling.

Trent's real name was Kevin Fisher but he'd changed it by deed poll because he thought it made him sound more Hollywood. He had aspirations of becoming an actor but with a portfolio that boasted two kitchen cleaner commercials, a callback to play bus driver #2 in a television dramatisation of the 7/7 London bombings, and five long empty years of lounging on his arse, we all knew Trent should change his name back to Kevin and be done with it. But the guy loved tail and talking about tail, and for this I tolerated him. It was better than writing punch-myself-in-the-face press releases. This morning's inbox contained one of those 'now and then' moments.

---

From: trent.rogers@morgan&schwarzmorgan&schwarz.com
To: bill.mcdare@morgan&schwarz.com
Subject: The new project

---

### Christy Kelkin
Tel: 07723 765678
Email: c_kelkin@gmail.com

**Personal statement:**
Highly efficient administrator seeking positions vacant. The

43

position should allow the application of organisational skills. Highly motivated and able to take the lead in achievement of the business' vision and mission. Ready to use report writing and project presentation skills for the advancement of the company.

**Educational Qualification:**
- Diploma in Business Administration from the Miller School of Business in 2011
- Certificate in Secretarial Studies from the Lee Community Secretarial School in 2012.

**Other Qualifications:**
- e-Type Touch Typing Award
- Japanese GSCE.

**Work Experience:**
2012 – 2013 Administrative Assistant at One Voice Music Enterprise
- Organised company functions and events
- Kept records of the company's events and progress
- Organised and kept schedules for managerial team
- Met with clients and ensured that they were well informed on the company's policies
- Provided information to prospective and current clients
- Assisted in the preparation and presentation of reports.

**Achievements**
Assisted in the development of a new and innovative record keeping system software.

Interesting. Well, ish. She had a foreign-sounded name and seemed practically teenage. Good fucking Lord. I logged onto the internet, found Facebook and tapped the name 'Christy Kelkin' into the search bar. Not surprisingly, there was only one.

---

**Christy Kelkin...** is laughing. To herself.

---

| Gender | Female |
| --- | --- |
| Birthday | 15th February 1990 |

---

## Basic info

| Siblings | Joe Kelkin | |
| --- | --- | --- |
| Relationship status | It's complicated | |
| Political views | Look after yourself, they won't | |
| Religious views | Ha | |
| Bio | Whatever people say I am, that's what I'm not | |
| Favourite quotations | There has been much tragedy in my life; at least half of it actually happened – Mark Twain | |
| Likes and interests | Music | Nirvana, Nick Cave |
| | Films | Disney |

These days, you could tell more about someone by trawling through the open-hearted hooey they saw fit to share over the World Wide Web than you did by sleeping with them. Sure, you'd swapped bodily fluids and made her call you daddy, but did you know that her favourite novel was *The Bell Jar*?

So, what of this one? Well, she seemed just like the kind of teenage car-crash that would have the office's alpha males turning hard at the mere thought of her vulnerability. These were the kind of girls guys in our industry preyed upon. Young, appreciative of dark, heartfelt music, impressionable, damaged.

But what of her marks out of ten? Well, it was pretty difficult to assess a piece of ass when she hid behind a Hallowe'en mask in her profile picture. Bringing down the office sport like that. Trent would be disappointed.

It wasn't long before we got to see behind the mask. Trent had discovered she was booked in for an interview with Miles in two days' time. The company was in desperate need of a new receptionist after what happened to the previous incumbent of the front desk's red swivel chair. The incident had become known as '*Die Dina Debacle* . Not because Dina had died, but because Jill, the septic source of much of the office's trash talk, had spent two years as an au pair in Bavaria and was a sucker for alliteration and the unnecessary use of foreign words.

Dina was a nice well-meaning young lady. Her wholesomeness rooted in her rural upbringing. The only daughter of a widowed down-at-heel dairy farmer, her self-sufficiency and strong moral fibre made her the perfect filter for the trumped-up businessmen, tricky callers and time wasters that swam to our switchboard each and every working day. She'd ask for names and numbers as a rule, tell phone spammers we were stuck in strategy meetings, or solve problems herself with a wherewithal and wit that were rarely seen – but highly desired – as the front-face of an organisation like ours.

But then along came Trent. He'd email me on an almost hourly basis how Dina's ruddy cheeks rubbed him up the right way and what he'd like to do to her given half the chance. But the problem was, unlike most of the girls who slid in through our swing door, she wasn't giving him even half of half a chance. She was dedicated to her work, not swapping fuck-me looks with the account handlers. Trent realised he would have to up his game. While most men faced with unrequited lust would work hard to woo a potential lover with poetry, posies or platitudes, Trent took a slightly different approach. It was the tradition for non-married members of the office to share a few drinks on a Friday night before heading off to a weekend of whatever lay ahead. Car boot sales for Pete, a one-way ticket to cirrhosis of the liver for me. Different strokes for different folks. After months of spurned invites, Trent realised the object of his affections was going to have to be fished with a more wholesome bait. It was on a Wednesday when his evil plan became apparent. Carol walked over to my desk, clutching an A3 sheet of paper in her hand.

'Have you seen this, Bill?'

'I can see it, Carol, but I have not seen it.'

'Very well, Bill. Literal as ever. Well, it's Friday night's drinks, they're going to be in aid of Save the Children. It's the big fund-a-thon day on Friday, you see. Apparently we all have to wear one yellow item of clothing and…'

'Just the one item of clothing?'

'Golly no, Bill, let me finish. One item of yellow clothing and donate a fiver. To give a little back to those poor kids. It was Trent's idea. It's nice isn't it?' Nice wasn't the word which immediately sprang to mind. Nefarious was. Trent knew Dina was never going to be interested in going to the pub just for the pints and peanuts. But by appealing to her good nature and plying her with toasts to the downtrodden and Downs Syndrome he was banking on the Trojan Horse of charity donation leading to a Trojan of a very different kind.

'Very nice, Carol, very thoughtful.'

As if forcing enough alcohol down the poor girl to tranquilise a horse wasn't enough, Trent managed to finish the job while Dina was distracted by Pete's inane chat about premium bonds or the price of a barrel of oil. Ketamine, slipped right into her drink. Being from the countryside she had no idea what a Mai Tai tasted like. He could have got away with lacing it with arsenic. As the group broke up in numbers and Dina broke up in body and mind, good old charity-champion Trent rose to his feet with the declaration he'd drop her off in a taxi.

'It's been a long week, she's tired.'

'I'll jump in.' said Pete. Trent had banked on this cover. Pete always wanted to go when people were splitting a cab, it appealed to his frugal nature. And the best thing? Pete lived closest to the pub, meaning he'd be first out. Sadistic, but systematic. You couldn't fault Trent for that.

Poor Dina didn't stand a chance. The key-load of ket had seen to that. We never saw her in the office again, her irregular correspondence with Carol our only update. The last we'd heard she was living out west as part of a breakaway group from the Seventh Day Adventists. It was rather sad the lengths she had to go to to forget that night. We couldn't help thinking she only wrote to Carol due to a healthy commission on offer for enlisting new recruits. And Trent? He didn't bat an eyelid. It was all in the game for him. All in the game.

A new phase of the game's play began the day Christy walked into our often wired, always warped little world. It was the month-end, which meant the atmosphere in the office was tauter than usual. The tension emanated from the Finance Department, who for the other twenty or so working days of the month were treated with the pity and contempt it was felt grey-suited penny-pinchers deserved from a cluster of 'creative' coke-heads. But come the time of the month someone responsible had to monetise our hair-brained, half-cut ideas they ruled the roost. And every one of us who enjoyed the comforts of warm clothing, the Taste the Difference range and a roof over their heads damned well fucking knew it. It was like the role reversal of the bullied becoming the bully. And the asexual abacuses loved every minute of it as we scrambled around to try and come up with a list of outputs worthy of the inflated sums clients paid us on the second of each month.

Every month, when the figures were being collated and the activity interrogated, a shadow of doubt crept across some members of the team as we realised the game was up and the last days of Rome upon us. Jill could sometimes barely talk, which was a fucking godsend, but even she broke out of her nervous nihilism to comment on the stranger in our midst.

'I imagine that's the new girl, then,' she said to no one in particular. Welcoming the break from my screen, I replied 'Where?' but before I could get the word out I'd realised exactly where, what and whom she was referring to.

It was her red red hair which punched me hard in the heart from the off. She was in Miles' office, which perched above our factory floor like a dictator's palace peering over a favela. Surrounded by his Barcelona chairs and misjudged modern art chosen by his overbearing Japanese girlfriend Kira, she was still a good twenty yards from where I was now ignoring Jill. But that didn't dull the effect. Ruffles and ruffles gushed from her head the colour of dried blood and served to stir mine. Flame-haired broads stoked my coals. Not only did their colouring speak of passion, of love, of danger, but the women who wore it often burnt brighter after a childhood of piss-taking from shitty, spotty little sheep who knew no better than to flick rubber bands at the ginger girl because she was 'different'.

But she stood out for me for different reasons, and I felt a wave of nausea come over my body at the fact Miles was first in to bat.

Miles was our boss. He was the kind of guy who'd walk into a bathroom, unzip his fly and go right ahead and piss in the middle urinal. No hiding off to the side for Miles. It wasn't that he *actually* had a big dick (far from it if you were to believe the stories that did the rounds following the industry awards' party back a few years ago). As with most things at Morgan & Schwarz, the truth didn't matter. He possessed an absolute blind faith in the fact that he did, and did a hell of a job in making others believe the same. Whether you were a clerk at his bank, his ex-wife's mother or some starlet who'd chase him all night at a Bellini and bullshit function, you didn't have a dealing with Miles Carter without coming away with the unwavering knowledge that the dude packed heat. He had a confidence others weighed out in Peruvian lines and a clarity that came from being teetotal for 12 years. And that's why he was the big man on 120k a year with an expense account that rivalled a small nation's GDP. I hated him from the pit of my stomach and respected him from the depths of soul.

Miles often took the time to welcome new starters with a brief but courteous greeting in his office before setting to his big important boss stuff. None of us were really certain of what this consisted, but we were scared sure the place would be washed into the sea if he wasn't left to it.

The business of the first dayer's orientation was led by Pete, as was the case with most extra-curricular activities: a caring and competent First Aider, a no-one-dies-on-my-watch Fire Warden, a by-the-book Green Champion: logistically, administratively, environmentally, pastorally, Pete ensured no stone was left unturned, unconscious, on fire or switched on overnight.

We'd all had the pleasure of Pete's thorough introduction and now it was Christy's turn. He'd welcome her to the building, recite the Morgan & Schwarz story by heart, before unleashing a policy blitzkrieg: sickness and absence (you're dead or at your desk), internet use (let's not bring up what happened with Greg and his 'research'), holidays (you'll need them), ad infinitum.

It was during the Health and Safety supervision that Pete entered what athletes commonly referred to as 'the zone'. The beady eyes of the office got ready to climb on their stalks. This phase of the induction gave its tutor the chance to flex the Three Ps (practicality, power and a physical). It gave Trent and I the One P (the opportunity to perv). Christy had followed Pete out of the boardroom, through the floor and to the other end of the office where printer supplies were stored. With our itchy trigger-fingers always poised to ignore the advice in our email signatures and print off things which we really didn't need, ink cartridges and paper were kept not in store cupboards but near the printers. Their out-in-the-openness saved Pete from being in an awkwardly close stationery cupboard situation with an unrelated female, and their relative light weight made them the perfect boxes with which to demonstrate the perfect bend. Never before has a man been so unaware of how plum his job was. As Christy Kelkin bent her knees to pick up a box of ream-wrapped 80gsm office copier paper, using her leg and buttock muscles to lift and correctly not twisting her body, she twisted a grip around my heart like I'd never felt before.

Now, I know what you're thinking. Lust at first sight. Which, okay, it was. But it wasn't just that, it was more than animalistic desire. Where the fuck was this coming from? It was something deeper, something different, something new, an urge to look after, to protect, to keep warm, to keep safe.

Turns out I wouldn't have to wait long to fulfill my new perverted paternalism. I heard a sharp cough and about-turned to see Pete, clipboard under arm and pen poised, and Christy, all red and warm and blurred. My eye focused. Pete cleared his throat.

'Bill, this is Christy Kelkin, the newest recruit to the good ship Morgan & Schwarz.'

'Hi,' I said, standing and offering a hand. It hung in the air for what seemed like minutes before her small, purple nail-varnished fingers reached out to shake it. Awkward. My shirt had tucked out of my trousers. I was very aware of the stale cigarettes on my breath.

'Hi,' she mustered, with a nervous smile.

'Bill's your new "buddy",' Pete chirped. 'I mean, we'll all be your buddies soon enough, but Bill here is your buddy in a more formal sense of the word. It's a scheme we operate here at Morgan & Schwarz through which a long-serving employee is assigned to a new starter to answer any general questions they may have about the company: anything from coffee breaks to, ooh, I don't know, our company pension scheme. Now, everything will be covered in your orientation today but Bill will be on-hand throughout your probationary period to mentor you and sort out any questions, queries, quibbles or, umm, quizzical thoughts you may have. We find the scheme works ever so well in helping integrate newbies and in ironing out any cultural creases. Most people tend to have a weekly catch-up in order to maintain structure, but of course the very nature of the arrangement means questions can be fired Bill's way at any time.'

Christy and I nodded in approval at Pete, intermittently stealing apprehensive looks at each other.

'Right, off we continue on the floor tour', Pete said. 'Next stop, the bulletin board.'

# Chapter 7

Generally at around one o'clock, I went somewhere quiet. Somewhere far away from the social media strategies, the thought showers, to take a deep breath, gather my thoughts and prepare for the afternoon hawking propaganda to some equally tired hack. But every once in a while, I felt the urge to brush up against the crowds of people to prove I was still alive. To feel their buzz, their hope, their expectation at the endless possibilities a day in the big city presented to them. Today was one of those days.

Central Station must have seen tens of thousands of pairs of heels each and every day. Heels going north to visit cousins, heels heading south to take in some fishing, heels kicking themselves at missing the 13.42 out of town. But from my infrequent visits to the terminal, I'd come to know the grafters and grifters who worked the station floor. There was the phoney Hare Krishna in his orange shawl and too-new sandals who duped travellers out of small change for flowers, before picking discarded ones from the bin and reselling onto the next vulnerable small-town face. And the cup and ball con man who still managed to swindle passers-by with the oldest trick in the book through some animated stool pigeons and a mesmerising handlebar moustache. But today, another figure not only caught my still-sleepy eye, but damn near pulled it out of its socket.

From a distance, he looked like one of the doom-mongers you sometimes saw holding 'The End of the World is Nigh' placards. But as I moved closer and into focus I could see that he wasn't proclaiming the end of days. His sign read: 'Sister Gina. Fortunes told. Ten pound Bill. 182 Worcester Street'.

Great. More pyschobabble. I'd had enough of that for one week.

I stood about five paces away from the man, trying to process the scene. The sign he clung to was a half taller than him again. His clothes were unremarkable; he wore the typical kind of duffle coat you saw all the old folks of his age wearing on the estates which sprawled across the city's east side. His thick black-rimmed glasses framed two content and confident eyes which stared straight ahead to where the light fell from sparkling glass windows. I'd seen him before. The yellowed nicotine-stained fingers of my internal filing system flicked through snapped scenes, muddled memories, and boozy bites of conversation to place this man. Where had I seen him before?

'Do I know you from somewhere?'

'We all know each other, brother man.'

'Oh great, not you as well.'

'All of us, brother man. We're all in the same boat. Paddling furiously along life's little stream, one stroke forward, two strokes back. And sometimes the water seems to be getting into the boat, doesn't it, brother man? And your little hands just can't scoop it out quick enough, can they?'

'You could say that.'

'I did say that, brother man. I've been waiting for you to come and see me, you know.'

'We have met, haven't we? But where?'

'You could say we've always known each other, brother man.' It was then that the words he held jumped off the page. 'Ten pound Bill'. The b of Bill was capitalised. Like in my name. Bill. Billy. Bill. This sign was made for me.

The serendipity of the scene must have dazed me because as I refocused, he'd vanished. I slapped myself in the face, hard, and hit my heels to 182 Worcester Street to find out just what the hell was going on. As I ran out of the concourse, trying my best to avoid tripping over suitcases being pulled in every direction, I was hit by the natural light of the bright sun. I headed north for a block or so, weaving in and out of newspaper vendors, window shoppers and camera-clutching tourists until I realised I wasn't actually sure where Worcester Street was. I came to a stop, pulled my phone out and tapped the address into the GPS. These Flakberrys Morgan & Schwarz grafted to our palms did have their uses. Three blocks east, one block north. Or vice versa. Such were the wonders of a well-planned central business district. I'd walk the rest, that running had fucked me. Dr Taylor would be most pleased with the exercise. I lit a cigarette to celebrate.

As I strolled the short distance to my destination I asked myself: WTF was I doing? Psychics were the kind of people I actively avoided and now I was going to pay somehard-earned money to keep one of them in hoop earrings. The only thing that didn't surprise me was my lack of surprise at this strange twist of events. Sometimes I found myself flung into situations which seemed to belie my very being, generally at the behest of those fuckers who fed and clothed me,but this one was all of the universe's doing. It wanted me to go to Sister Gina. Who was little old I to step in and turn the other way? Anyway, it beat a conversation with Pete in the staff room on the Middle East crisis or the benefits of subscribing to *National Geographic*.

I spun onto Worcester Street, and slowly turned my eye to finding the numbers on the unassuming bricks which put together the buildings. Sure, I knew exactly where 182 was from the GPS, but my generation had the misfortune of being born on the cusp;

neither able to live without technology, or able to live solely entrusting it. Better than a World War or two granted, but an annoying-enough anomaly dictated by age.

Number 182 wasn't marked out by lamb's blood or other such witchcraft, but by a list of apartments and names aside round gold bells. So far, so conventional. And next to number seven, in red ink, was the name 'Sister Gina'. As I rang the bell I resisted the inner urge to think 'if she knew I was coming she'd have been at the door with some *te de menthe*', but realised that joke was straight from Pete's A-list material.

I waited for what seemed like minutes but was likely some strung-out seconds. I was nervous. Fuck fuck fuck. I rang again. Longer and harder this time. There was a distant noise, before rays of light brightened the corridor that was visible through the glass of the door. An almost impossibly small, old woman came into half-sight. As she moved slowly closer, small step by small stick-supported step, she took the form of an ancient but elegant babushka. Her stooped head was covered in an intricately woven headscarf, her long skirt almost swept the floor as she came closer to me. What did this woman know? Why had I been drawn here? She pitched her stick in front of the door, steadied herself and edged it outwards. I took the slack and pulled it wider.

'Xschuse me,' she said in a shrill voice, pushing me out of the way with a strength that didn't previously seem possible. She scurried down the street. That was that.

I turned to walk away when a crackle came from the intercom system, 'tssssshhhh... cccchh... hello... who... tschhhh... is... it?' The noise came from buzzer number seven. I pressed the gold button again and spoke, 'I, uhh, saw an ad in the, uhh, station and...'

'Come on in. It's at the top of the stairs.'

The door clicked open. I pushed, and entered, not knowing quite what I was getting myself in to. The stairs were through a closed door on my right hand side. Darkness descended as I entered. My heart raced. I felt my way through the blackness for the first step. I reached out for a handrail, but found nothing. My hand opened and stuck to the wall as my feet edged their way upwards. Every five steps or so the darkness was pierced by shards of light from small, barred windows which marked the end of each flight. The steps came to an end, and I pushed open the door at their top. Light hit me. If I'd have known this was the end of my tunnel I'd have stopped for a pint or three first.

I walked along the corridor to number seven. I knocked and nearly fell through the ajar door. I felt like a mole at a laser show; my perception was fucked.

'Welcome.'

I rubbed my eyes and focused on the form in front of me: Sister Gina. She was a lot younger than I'd expected but about as short. She had an unremarkable enough appearance, one you'd pass by on the daily commute to a life sentence job without clocking even once. When it came to looking like you had a direct dial to the other side, the babushka won hands down. Gina looked so fucking normal. Like a bistro waitress, your kid's teacher, or a functional secretary. Blink and you'd miss her. What could you expect for a ten-pound-bill I suppose?

'Hi.'

She turned and beckoned me to follow her. As I did, I tripped over a living, breathing foot-rest that nearly bit my ankle off.

'Fuck!'

I felt I'd spoilt the atmosphere already.

'Please excuse Mr Sheridan.' I looked at her blankly. She elaborated. 'The dog. And, please, no foul language here.'

'I'm sorry. I had a shock, was all.' I hoped it wasn't to be the first of many.

'You are forgiven.'

We walked through to a regular suburban kitchen. No incense.

No crystal ball. It was just like the kitchen your older sister had when she moved to the big city and lived in a slightly shitty apartment in a building long overdue a good lick of paint. We sat down at a pine kitchen table that had like it'd seen one takeaway too many. If it was my great calling to come here this lunchtime, my life really was as shit as I'd come to expect.

'So, thanks for visiting Sister Gina, midtown's most economically priced insight.'

'A pleasure.'

'So, what are you here for?'

'Well, I was kind of hoping you could tell me that.'

'So, I can look deep into your future with a full deck reading for fifty, can positively align your chakra for twenty…'

I hadn't realised she'd been talking administratively.

'Look, sister, I'm here for the ten pound fortune. Nothing more, nothing less. Lord knows why I'm even here for that. Pardon my language.'

If she was upset by my reluctance to be upsold she didn't let on. She needed a few months with Morgan & Schwarz. Our sales scams would have doubled her profits in no time at all.

As she took my hand, something happened. Gina's eyes glazed over like she'd been smoking premium strength weed since before she pushed the duvet aside. The nondescript had turned spooky. Rather than examining the crags of my hand for a red flag which screamed Dead By Forty, she held it in a ritualistic way, as if to ground herself in case of an electric shock. Her glassy look focused on the middle distance of the frayed wallpaper over my left shoulder. I'd wanted to think that she'd know I'd become a daytime TV host, would travel the world on the back of a donkey and have my kids go to Ivy League schools just from looking at the lines on my hand, but it seemed it wasn't quite going to play out that way. There was a silence. A strangely comfortable silence. The dog barked. I jumped. She tightened her grip on my hand.

'Why do you always worry about heart disease?'

Her question knocked me for six. Three months ago, my dad died of a heart attack. Or a broken heart. Either way, he was dead and gone. I tried to regain composure.

'Doesn't everyone?'

'Not like you.' She was right. I'd give myself palpitations over palpitations, losing sight of whether they had existed in the first place or were my Frankenstein. She knew she'd hit the bullseye.

'Well, look, don't worry yourself about it. It won't kill you. You'll live until you're grey and old.' If it meant I'd look like George Clooney, I'd take that now.

'You work in some kind of office, yes?' I didn't show agreement.

'Some kind of fancy office, yes? Well don't let those people take advantage of you. Value your ideas and don't let the fat cats get rich off your blood. Money will come, money will go. You've got to hang on in there.'

Gina started to waffle a bit after that; something about a mysterious stranger and a girl, but by then my mind was wandering back to the earlier talk about my ticker.

'You can do great things. You will do great things. You've just got to hang on in there. Hang on in there.' Sure, hang on in there. I wasn't going to die of heart disease. Repeat, I wasn't going to die of heart disease. This was a fucking revelation. Bullshit, likely, but my kind of bullshit.

# Chapter 8

When I wasn't spending my lunchtimes visiting mystics, I had another regular appointment. While colleagues Skyped distant friends and relatives, shopped for educational toys for their children or went and worked out with Brian from Human Resources, I'd go and sit on the bench right outside our office and drink cheap cider and fortified wine with the local pissheads. The beauty of the plan was in its audacity. Most problem drinkers hid their shameful secret from sight, sipping on the odd bottle of gin from their bottom drawer when no one was looking, or slipping into the stationery cupboard for a quench of a quart hidden in with the box files. Not me. My raging alcoholism would remain latent, at least in its delivery, thanks to my woods for the trees approach to the mid-day blues. I'd leave my desk with a kit-bag under the purely aspirational auspices of jogging in the park. I'd ride the seven floors down to the ground and exit our building, always being careful not to get in step with an errand-running or lunch-grabbing colleague, before taking a sharp left to an alleyway which was filled with large industrial bins, used by the kitchens of the mostly Asian restaurants that backed onto the narrow path. There, among the leftover bones, hidden from the main thoroughfare, I'd change out of my luxury merino wool suit into paint-splattered jogging bottoms, a charity shop woolly knit and, the piece de resistance, the chaser to my pint, a full face balaclava. They never suspected a thing.

My fellow winos and wasters – it was no good kidding myself I was a tourist – assumed the balaclava hid some third degree burns picked up in the Iraq war. I did nothing to dispel this myth, regaling them with tales from my days with Royal Welsh 2nd Squadron out in Basra. Maybe I planted the seed from which this crooked tree grew, but a good PR man was never going to leave his fingerprints on the sapling. They particularly liked the one I told about the grenade that was lobbed into my armour-plated vehicle. Sometimes I caught it in my mouth before spitting it out and throwing it out of the window. Other times my hard but fair lesbian co-driver and I jumped out of the door and took cover under the body of a dead insurgent, while the car blew up like something out of a Jerry Bruckheimer movie. They didn't notice the details changed every time we talked. I think they wanted to believe. Either that or they were too smashed to register. The way I told them, I often kidded myself I'd done a tour of duty.

It's fair to say that these guys killed me. Not literally, although some of them looked as if they could be the catalyst for my grisly end. It was my emotions they killed. Why were they out here while I was (barely) in there? What fork in the road did they take that I didn't? The one signposted depression, dependence, disease and deathly cold? But sometimes the signpost got spun around, Wile E Coyote style. Who knew where our decisions or indecision would lead? No one, really, but we could load the dice. It was probably time I stopped loading them in the dealer's favour. Soon, anyway, sometime soon.

One of the men, Sid, lived up to your usual trampy stereotypes. Wild beard? Check. Ragged clothes? Check. A stench of stale piss and a taste for industrial strength turpentine? Check. But from his red, flaky face shone two bright childlike eyes which looked like they viewed each new day with wonder. It was only unfortunate that each new day was full of the filth and fury of the fucked up streets. Not quite the first awakenings of life. Poor fella. I'd often fantasised that I'd make a hobo a cut above the average. No sitting in the rain for me. No sir. My days would be spent in the warm, safe haven of the city library, learning, questioning, bettering myself. None of this putting up with the cold and constant precipi-fucking-tation of this place. I'd be off on the railroad, travelling with the cargo, hiding in the washrooms, under seats, over mailbags, always moving, always searching, always getting closer to that better life. What this romantic, rolling-stone-gathers-no-moss vision of life on the road didn't bank on was the high propensity of dangerous addiction. An addiction which was worn well into the faces of those who surrounded me. Sometimes one of the faces would linger on me for too long when I finished a tall tale of derring do on the battlefield, and the others were creased over laughing, lost in their mind's eye or pulling hard on some much-needed nicotine. His face was the most ravaged of the bunch, and in a way the saddest. These dark eyes weren't childlike, but knowing, insightful and accepting. They smiled sadly. They belonged to a man whose age was hard to fathom. They say the streets put years on you, a bit like with TV and pounds on the waistline, but without the ability to be shaken off by hiring a queer stylist with a penchant for vertical stripes. Regardless, he wasn't a young man and his gaze told of a life that had known more than this; known warmth, hot food, self-respect, love even, whatever that means. But not now, not anymore. That was old news, better off boxed away somewhere. The key was in his stare. He gave me the heebie-jeebies.

The balaclava was a voyeur's best friend, allowing me to eavesdrop unmolested on the mundanities of the midday break. Jill on the phone to her husband calling Miles a cunt, me a cunt, him a cunt. Pete haggling energy suppliers. Miles speaking pidgin French to some no doubt knock-out broad. So far, so expected. On this particular day, Carol and Pete ambled in front of me and my drinking buddies on their way back from the coffee house. They were giving an airing to the *topic du jour* at Morgan & Schwarz: Christy.

'Well, I think she seems like a very responsible young lady,' said Pete. 'If a little risqué at time. I'm not sure the skirt she had on yesterday was entirely appropriate office wear.'

'She certainly adds a little colour,' said Carol.

'Indeed,' Pete said through a steaming latte. Pete didn't usually spend money on boutique beverages, not when there was a kettle in the kitchen. He must have been feeling particularly frivolous today. This was unlike him. Perhaps he knew Carol had the latest gossip. He could be surprisingly perceptive at times.

'It's a wonder she's here at all,' said Carol, 'considering everything she's been through.' Pete stopped slurping and urged Carol to continue with a nod of the head. 'I mean, bringing up her brother all on her own at such a young age and her dad leaving them and all that nasty business. Sounds like the best thing he could have done for them anyway.'

'I don't quite follow, Carol.'

'Oh, sorry, Pete. Christy came through the Positive Pathways scheme. You know the one that places young people from underprivileged backgrounds into the workplace.'

'I see,' said Pete. 'Sounds like you really bonded.'

'Well…' said Carol.

'Well what?' said Pete.

'You could say that,' said Carol. 'Or you could say I accidently stumbled across her file when looking for something for Miles. I couldn't help but read it.'

'Carol, what are you like?' said Pete.

They laughed.

'Show us your minge! SHOW US YOUR MINGE!'

Carol shrieked. Pete defensively stood in front of her. One of the tramps had lost the plot again. Spider was no good around women. Part of the reason he was out here. He rubbed his legs and salivated at the short, unattractive middle-aged woman in front of him.

'How dare you?' said Pete, and they scurried away through the revolving glass doors of the office.

I really did need to watch the company I kept.

I'd always go back to the office. Someone had to pay for my booze so it might as well be PRWire. Com's 4th Best Agency of 2013. I felt a bit like the tramps' envoy on the other side. The UN ambassador of an embittered tin-pot nation, stating their shaky case to the suits, squares and continent. This afternoon in the office had the potential to be massively awkward and embarrassing. No, I hadn't left my fly undone and asked if anyone was thirsty again. It was the first of my buddy sessions with Christy. Christ alive. Daytime drinking usually sharpened me up, or at least levelled me out, but with the ACME anvil of this afternoon's session hanging over me I felt nervous, edgy and ill at ease. Maybe this was nothing to do with the booze. Maybe these were real life feelings. Imagine that. Time had conditioned me so the only emotions experienced during office hours were apathy or hatred. This was new. I felt like I was preparing for the most disappointing first date ever, one where the off-chance of oral sex had already been ruled out before I'd even washed my knob in the sink and rushed out of the door.

'So, erm, these things are meant to be so as you can ask, erm, where the washrooms are, and, erm, when the weekly fire alarm goes off, who the biggest douche in the office is and if you're ever going to enjoy working here,' I said.

'Great. They're down the corridor, second on the left, 2 p.m. on a Wednesday, Miles has taken an early lead and the jury's still out,' she replied.

We were sat facing each other in something that looked like the interrogation room for the Nuremberg Trials, if a daytime cable TV interior design celebrity had been in charge of soft furnishings. Try as it might, the ambience was still more Hermann Göring than Gentle Lavender.

She looked at me, deadpan, for what seemed like an eternity. I looked straight back. She laughed. I followed. The reciprocation rule.

'So, how are you finding it?' I asked.

'Well, you know, okay. Really, umm, quite okay,' she answered.

'I did know.'

'What?'

'Oh, nothing… anyway, so do you have any questions or anything? I think this is what these things are meant to be about.'

'Well, not really, Bill. Pete's orientation didn't leave a stone unturned, and I've managed to find the bathroom all by myself.'

'Yes, Pete isn't allowed near the Ladies after the incident…'

'What incident?'

Should I wink? Should I wink? I fucking winked.

'Have you got something in your eye?' she said.

Oh dear. Oh shit.

'No, I was trying to denote there was no incident. It was an attempt at a joke,' I said.

'Ah, of course, there would be no incident with Pete and the ladies would there? He's very thorough but doesn't quite strike me as the sex offender type.'

'Na, he's too busy tending to his desk tidy for any of that funny business,' I said. I reached for my mug and cupped it with my hands. It was still hot. I swirled the tea inside around a couple of revolutions, lifted it to my lips and blew on it. Her red hair seemed to sway a little in the breeze. Maybe this was in my head. I drank, as ever glad of the crutch appropriate to the situation. Christy broke the silence.

'It was funny, you know.'

'What?'

'The joke, your joke about Pete…'

'Oh, that, it was, uh…'

'…funny is what it was. I'm sorry, Bill, I'm a little bit slow on the uptake at the moment. I've been listening so carefully to every word … from Pete, from Miles, on the calls to the front desk … I'd almost forgotten to look for a subtext.'

I smiled. She relaxed.

'Pretty full on, huh?' I said.

'Yeah, you could say that. I can't say I ever thought I'd end up in this industry, but you know, it's certainly an eye-opener and I'm learning.'

I nodded.

'So, what about you, Bill? How long have you been here?'

'Longer than I care to remember or realise,' I answered.

'It can't be that bad.'

'Which? The job or the time passing?'

'Either?'

'I wish it were neither,' I said.

She looked less comfortable now. I was scaring her off. 'But it's not so bad really,' I said. 'You know, once you get used to it. And hopefully these buddy sessions can help you, you know, settle in.'

'Buddy sessions?' She laughed. 'I don't think I've ever had a 'buddy' before.'

'Me neither,' I said 'Friends? Maybe. Acquaintances? Definitely. Family? Unfortunately. But never a buddy. It is a bit like organised fun, isn't it? Like our parents are friends and they're forcing us to play together. Christ, if Miles were my dad I think I'd poison myself.' Her eyes glassed over at the mention of family.

'My dad's dead,' I blurted out.

'Mine's as good as,' she replied.


We quickly changed the subject. The rest of the session was spent talking about Nirvana. Thank god for Facebook stalking.

# Chapter 9

I was running down a narrow, winding cobbled road, barefoot, scared and sweaty. I looked over my shoulder to see the progress of my aggressor; he was gaining. He, or it, was a giant, red, fleshy tomato and he looked mad. Maybe all giant red things look mad by sheer dint of their genealogy but I wasn't taking any chances. I didn't particularly like eating tomatoes, let alone being eaten by one. Keep going, Bill, towards the light, towards the light.

I tripped.

Fuck. Ouch. Fuck. Blood started to seep out of my shin. Pick yourself up, Bill. The blood had seeds in it. I put two fingers hard against the wound, to stem the tide, and lifted them to my mouth. Tomatoes. My bloodstream made up of vine-ripened sun-blushed tomatoes. I'd deal with this later. He was gaining. And he looked pissed. To the light, Bill, to the light. The sun was breaking through the end of the snaking street. I was nearly there. I looked over my shoulder. He was right on my heels now, panting, grimacing, menacing, gushing tomato juice. I ran into the light.

Something hit me hard and wet on my right temple. A horn sounded. There were bare chests and goggled faces for as far as I could see. All throwing, all dodging, all screaming. Tomato flesh was everywhere. The gutters ran red. I sank to the cobbled floor and the juice washed over me. It tasted familiar. My body sank. Underneath the liquid, I could hear a knowing, vindictive laugh.

The alarm went off. It was 7.01 a.m.

It was the weekend, which meant I didn't have to drag my bones out of bed and try to revitalise myself with a cigarette in the shower (there was a knack to it, trust me), before heading off to massage the truth for money. Oh no, today brought a different walk through the valley of the shadow of death: a visit to my mother's house. Well, not strictly just my mother's house. My mother and Barry's house. Their little shag-pile-carpeted, feature-fireplaced, trinket-strewn love nest. You'd think I had other affairs to attend to on my day off; correspondence to catch up on, petunias to prune, a sedan to wash, wax and polish, or a church hall bring-and-buy sale to co-ordinate. Well, I'm afraid all that was going to have to wait. It was their third wedding anniversary (denoted by leather, I dread to think of what they bought each other) and I had to go and bathe in their second-marriage smugness. I had to. There was no getting out of it. Was there? Could I not concoct an excuse? An embarrassing ailment that called for careful quarantining? No, I said I would go. I'd been a disappointment enough. I said I'd go.

My mother and Barry lived in an anodyne, soulless suburb. It was the kind of place social climbers moved to be away from the foreigns and the traffic and the late night noise and the drugs, but all they were left with when they got there were shit CD collections and each other. It was the home of pooper-scoopers and swinger's parties, right-wing newspapers and patio heaters. It was everything they thought they'd ever wanted, all those years ago in the dark, damp rooms of their distant youth. This was progress. This was each generation doing better than the last. Evolution needed a revolution or we were all going to be watching a Blu-ray in surround sound or at a cheese and wine party when the computers finally took over or the aliens came to fuck us up, whichever comes first.

'How's that lovely couple you live with, love?' said my mum, flicking the bangs of her too-young hairstyle behind her ear.

'They're good, Mum, really great,' I lied.

'Must be a bit queer living with a couple mustn't it, Bill?' said Barry. Fat-faced, receding hairline, no soul, spawn of Satan, Barry.

'Well, I lived with my mum and dad and they were a couple, Barry.'

'Don't be smart, son,' said my mum. I bit my lip. 'I wish you could find something like that.'

'I do most nights, Mum.'

'Oh, Bill.'

Barry bounced off his stool and strutted around the kitchen island to the ice dispenser in the fridge door, like a cockerel with rickets and a paunch. He wore black jeans, far too tight for his figure or age, and a black vest which revealed formerly muscular, currently flabby, hairy arms. Colour was provided through peroxide flecked liberally throughout his gravity and fashion-defying spiked haircut. His bouffant had been eroded on both sides by the wash of an existence in the lowest common denominator 'entertainment' industry, leaving a sad spit of hair on the top of his head.

'Do you want some nibbles, love? We've got some of that hummus in. Barry can't get enough of it. He's got such an exotic palate.'

'I'm okay, thanks, mum. I wouldn't want to spoil the roast.'

Vasco de Gama would turn in his watery grave if he saw my mum's cupboards. Their shelves stocked not a sniff of a spice or a hint of a herb. My mum was a somewhat simple but effective cook, steeped in the tradition of stodge. Barry had designs on a higher station but, as with everything he tried, his voyage to the vanguard of cutting-edge cuisine came to a halt about 10 years before the present day. Hummus? How retro. We wouldn't have fed that to the Morgan & Schwarz dog.

'Okay, love. We can go into the posh room if you like, seeing as how it's a special occasion and all.'

'Of course, Mum. Did your card come in the post?'

'No, love.'

'NO? I could bloody throttle my secretary. And no flowers either?'

'No, love.'

'I expressly told her to… oh, look, it doesn't matter does it, Mum? I'm sorry.'

'It's okay, love, I know you're so busy. The fact you're here is all that counts.' I'd post a card on Monday.

'I know, Mum. We're so slammed in the office at the moment that I'm working most weekends.'

'Well, I hope they're paying you double-time, love.'

'Something like that, Mum.'

'It really is a shame you can't make it tonight, love. Barry's booked a Motown tribute act – The Four Degrees. There'll be five when you get up with them won't there, Barry, love?'

'I'm not sure about the equipment and acoustics in the club, babe, but I'll give the old lungs an airing after a few shandies, no doubt. Just like old times…'

Now don't be drawn in by his nostalgia bullshit. Old times, my fucking arse. Costa Del Sol karaoke bars still looked shit in sepia. That was Barry's Everest: running five-time weekly sing-along sessions in the sun, playing the Sonny to a revolving saloon door of desperate divorcée Chers. Which, yes, as you've guessed, was where he met my mum. Four years ago today. They married 365 days later. She'd been drawn in by the glamour, the attention, the chance to be in the spotlight and on the stage. My dad had barely put her on a bus. It's hard to know if they were *over* over when she fell for Barry's bum notes. In truth, they'd never even got started. My dad was distant and drunk, or drunk and distant. After a while it was better for him to be the latter, Mum and me got along just fine when he was out of the picture. The house was better without his brooding, boozing time-bomb around the place. You never knew when he'd be back to explode. He didn't give warning calls like the IRA. When I thought about it, really fucking thought about it, you know, objectively, I suppose in some ways Barry was better for her. Probably. At least he was there. And when he was there, he wasn't out of his head.

But I hated him.

Why?

He made my mum happy, something she'd only known fleetingly before. I hated him because – without getting all Holden Caulfield on you – he was a phoney. He had one dogshit song in the charts 40 years ago, and then pressed play on a tape deck and hogged a mike until his crow's feet kicked in. To call him a failed rock star would be a disservice to failures. But at least he tried, I suppose. My dad was trying, but he never tried, not at anything worthwhile. Maybe I hated Barry because he wasn't him. And, slowly, little by little, I was.

My mum went back into the kitchen. I looked at Barry. He looked at me. She reappeared with three glass dishes. This wasn't a roast.

'Now, I know you said you didn't want to spoil your roast, but I've done a prawn cocktail. I know how you like prawns.' Christ, she was doing her Christmas menu. She'd bring me in some socks and a body spray and shower gel gift-pack any minute now.

'Thanks, Mum.'

'You're welcome, love.'

The silence we ate in was broken only by Barry's chewing. Some Thousand Island dressing dribbled onto his chin.

'Remember Jessica Jennings, love?'

'Who's that, babe?'

'No, not you, Barry. Bill, remember her, love?'

'Vaguely, Mum, vaguely.' I remembered her alright, she lived on our street. She was fat and ugly then. She'd be fatter and uglier now. Time was no one's friend.

'Vaguely? Gosh, Bill, you practically grew up with her. Well, she's coming tonight. She's been teaching English in Japan you know. She doesn't even speak Japanese.'

'Don't get me started on the Japanese, babe. Do not get me started. Mean, horrible little gits. Pardon my French. Very cruel people. Very cruel. They were heartless in the war, and they're heartless now. I mean, what's a bloody whale ever done to them?' Barry finished, and stuffed a prawn in his mouth.

The rest of the meal passed without much more incident. Mum trying to fatten me up, Barry playing the ageing glam rocker flirting with the far right, me just being, well, not me. I left the table and took a walk up the stairs. I still had some things, old books and records mainly, that were stored in their spare room. It was comforting to thumb through old things: a song, a sentence, a sentiment could take you back to another time, another place, another life. I liked it. Maybe needed it.

From the top of the stairs I could see their bedroom door was open. It might as well have been Pandora's Box. Silk sheets and tiger print scatter cushions. I couldn't help thinking this was a house where old people had sex. I was sick a little in my mouth. A prawn swam in the bile. I went into the bathroom, spat it down the plughole and rinsed my mouth out with water. The toilet seat called me. A shit. That's what was needed. There was something comforting about shitting in your mum's house. It felt like childhood. Not the fact that she was there to wipe your arse if needs be. Just the fact that she was there, and you were taking a dump, and she didn't give a fuck or judge you because you used to live inside of her stomach. After that, anything went. And the toilet paper, unlike at Craig and Connie's, didn't feel like it could take a coat of paint off the door.

I had some of my most meditative moments while sat on the

can. The porcelain provided an escape from the maelstrom of modern life. Some much needed me time, which admittedly was used mostly to read shampoo bottles. With the diet I enjoyed, it was best not to look down at my work. Think Jackson Pollock goes New England autumn. I clocked off the job, washed my hands and stared at my reflection in the glass cabinet. Why did the smell of my own shit not make me puke? The scent was reassuring, alluring even. Maybe that's why my life was spent trudging through my own shit. I needed a new fragrance, and quick.

I opened the left hand side door of the cabinet. A head made up of half a bloodshot, bags-under-my-eyes face and half a collection of pills and potions sprouted off my neck and stared back at me. It was as if the mirror had X-ray specs and saw through my skin into the substances that whirled around inside. I slammed the door shut. Even my weary expression was better than some sci-fi vision of my insane inner workings. The apothecary belonged to Mum. She'd been a med-head for as long as I could remember. Life with Dad had written a prescription as long as the weekly big shop list. I snatched a foil packet. The label read 'Citalopram'. I popped two little white ones. I could have done with a few Thin Lizzys before coming to visit love's middle aged nightmare.

As they waved me off, I felt a pang of guilt about pinching the pills from my mum. She was going to need a fucking shipment to get through tonight.

# Chapter 10

'Gold. It's a great thing to have in your portfolio, especially in times of crisis. It really is the most tangible thing you can trade at the moment. But what do I know? I'm only listening to the so-called experts. So, there I was in the jewellers the other day trying to value some of Mother's old rings. You know what the lady in the shop told me? Buy a sovereign, put it under your bed and forget about it for a couple of years. It's a very sound investment right now, if you've got the money, that is.' Pete was in microeconomic mode. The only sovereigns under my bed had fallen off the fingers of the single mothers I'd fucked from the rough side of town. Quite why Pete was advising me on investments was anyone's guess. I didn't have the money. Or at least I would have had the money if I didn't blow it all on the weekend. I'll have the money again on the 28th of the month. And the 28th of the month after that. And after that. But I'll never *have* the money. Not for comforts like that. Gold. Stocks. Shares. Holiday homes. Retirement funds. Nest eggs. Nothing for a rainy day. How do you save anything for a rainy day when it's always fucking tipping down?

Something tells me I could have done with an umbrella for this afternoon's session with Christy. I could barely tie my shoelaces, yet I was being entrusted with the pastoral care of an over-the-top attractive life-damaged girl. I didn't know where the nearest fire exit was, or how best to contact Human Resources, and I was definitely not equipped for issues and tissues. If anything, the fact I had been charged with Christy's care was recognition of the fact

I managed to just about hold it together in front of the other drones. That, or there was a rota. But I was going to take all of the positives out of this that I could.

Christy, Christy, Christy…

'Yes, Bill.' Damn, no inner monologue.

'Oh, hi Christy. Good to see you again.'

'I saw you earlier, Bill.'

'You did?'

'Yes, I was on reception, of course….'

'Because that's where you work,' I cut in.

'You got it. You kind of shuffled past at nine-ish. You said hello but looked a bit distracted.'

'Ah, sorry. I was…'

'Late? stressed? hungover?'

'All of the above,' I answered.

She laughed.

'I can see this is the kind of place that can get to people. You know, stress them out. I don't know if Jill's going to bite my head off or stroke my face. And I was sure I saw Pete counting grains of sugar onto a spoon yesterday afternoon.'

'The pressure of working at one of the city's top public relations agencies can affect us all in very different ways.'

'I suppose,' she said. 'But more than anything it makes me laugh.'

'They say it's the best medicine,' I replied. 'It just makes me angry.'

'I'm not taking it that seriously, Bill.' *When you ve been through what I ve been through*, she didn't add to the end of the sentence. Her red hair was tied back today. With her fringe out of her face, and her bangs behind her ears, her eyes took over her face, big and smudged black with make-up. They looked like they'd seen more and lived longer than the taut skin that clung to her cheekbones. Experienced beyond her years, but not necessarily in a nice way. Plus she looked like she'd been up half the night. And I should know what that looks like.

'And so you shouldn't. There are more important things in life,' I said. Unfortunately I was still struggling to find them. 'But anyway, this isn't about me. You're not my buddy, erm, well I hope you are, can be, but I'm your buddy, so I'm, erm, meant to be helping you, not you psychoanalysing me.'

'Were we psychoanalysing you?'

'Well, I kind of was,' I said.

'Well, you got to the heart of your feelings about this place a lot quicker than any of my previous experiences of that crock of shit.'

'Go on…' I said. This I wanted to know about. What had she been through? Could I help her? Could she help me?

'No, it's boring. Look, can we just get on with this? I'm tired.'

'Late night too?'

'Yes, it usually is, but not having the fun it looks and smells like you had.' I smelt myself. I stunk of gin. I knew that had been a bad idea.

'Sorry, I didn't mean that. It's my brother, he's not sleeping so well. He's been having these night terrors. They really upset him.'

'I dreamt I was being chased by a giant killer tomato the other day. Maybe I could talk to him.'

'No, it's fine. We're fine. God, why am I even telling you this?'

'Because it's better than talking about work,' I said. Because you want me in your life, I meant.

'Is it? Work's an escape for me.'

'So are things with your brother that bad then? Can't your parents look after him?' I was fishing. And using a ton fucking weight as bait.

'Sorry?' She looked peeved. 'I've already told you my dad's as good as dead. Well, to us at least.'

'I'm sorry. And your mum?'

'She is dead. Actually dead. It's always just been me and Joe. Even when Dad was around. It was so much better when he wasn't.' I looked out of the window of the interrogation room. Through the Venetian blinds I could see Miles perched on the end of Carol's desk. He had a hacky sack in his hand and was throwing it skywards with his right hand before catching it with his left; his platinum bracelet, a gift from Kira's latest modelling assignment in Tokyo, catching the light. Carol was doing all she could not to flinch every time the ball was thrown into the air. She wasn't facing us but you could see it in her shoulders.

'Can we just talk about work?' Christy said.

I didn't want to talk about work. 'I know how you feel,' I said.

'What, tired?'

'No, with your dad. I told you mine was dead. He died recently. Not long ago. Well, that's when he was pronounced dead, but his heart stopped a long time before that.' I looked up at those huge eyes to see if this was too much or out of line. She didn't look like she pitied me. Or was scared of me. This was a rare occurrence. I went on. 'He was a lot like your dad sounds. There. Not there. Not there. You being glad he wasn't there but scared shitless that he'd come back.'

'That sounds about right.'

'I'll never forget one time. I was about seven or eight. Young. But old enough to sense an atmosphere, to know when things weren't right. I was in bed but didn't sleep well in those days. Well, I'd yet to discover a few drinks before bed. I could hear this commotion downstairs. Nothing too sinister, just raised voices, familiar voices. I got out of bed and crept towards them. I didn't want them to stop, I wanted to know what was being said, what was going on; maybe this would answer why things had been weird recently. I tried to edge the door ajar slightly so I could hear a bit more. They seemed to be talking about a woman called

Maria. I didn't know any women called Maria. There was a girl in my class called Maria, but why would they be talking about her? The door creaked and the voices got louder and directed towards me. I looked up to see a missile coming towards me and my dad's face all screwed up and red. Really fucking red. I managed to dodge it but hot tea scalded my leg through my pyjamas. A commemorative Charles and Diana china mug had scattered around me into a hundred pieces.'

'Oh, Bill.'

'Why she never threw him out there and then I'll never know.' But I did know. He was hard to shake. And when she did shake him for Barry, I resented her for it. Poor old Mum couldn't win.'

'That's terrible, Bill. Are you okay?'

'I'm always okay.'

'So this is what buddies do then?' she said. It felt like a support group for two. Hello, my name is Bill and I've been fucked up for about, phew, well let me see, 29 years now. Maybe we'd get to hug later.

'But everything else aside, you're settling in okay?' I asked. I thought it was time to change the subject. She bit her bottom lip. She seemed wrong-footed.

'Yes, I, uh, suppose I am. Everyone continues to be,' she paused, if not for effect, for thought, 'interesting?'

'You could say that.'

'Trent is a friendly one, isn't he?'

'Again, you could say that.'

'I don't think anyone's ever started calling me "babe" after so short a time.'

'He's probably forgotten your name. I wouldn't take it personally.' She ignored that.

'And he keeps offering me a lift home in his car. I've told him I'm in the middle of a page-turner and like to read on the bus and that it really isn't the weather for a soft-top anyway.'

'If he bothers you again, let me know.'

'I can handle it.' Is that all you've got Trenty boy? Is a ride home the new roofie? Think again, fuck-face.

'But sleazeballs aside, everything at Morgan & Schwarz is good? No work-related queries for your best buddy?' I cringed as I finished the sentence.

'Well, the handover from the last girl – Dina was it? – was patchy to say the least but I'm picking it up, little by little.'

'Yes, Dina did leave in rather a hurry. She was in a rush to save to her soul.'

'Sorry?'

'She joined some religious cult out west. Thought she had a few sins she needed absolving of.'

'What bullshit,' she said.

'Amen to that.'

'You're born, you live, you die. The concept of any kind of afterlife is just a fairy story,' she said. 'Probably gave people some comfort of something better to come during the dark ages but now we've got hamburgers and TV, how could heaven compete?' She paused, and trained her dark eyes onto mine. 'What about you, Bill?'

'Heaven? Fuck that. I don't like heights anyway.'

# Chapter 11

Since the meeting with Sister Gina, the hacks of *The McDare Mercury* had taken on a new, more positive brief. The imaginary newsroom was a nicer place to be, pumping out propaganda to the masses of my mind like *The Daily Planet* on happy pills. The front page flashes of personal apocalypse had been turned around to semi-heroic hubris about my recent bravery. Headlines ran: 'McDare Saves Girl, Dog, Civic Pride', 'Bill: My Healthy Living Regime – Sex, Drugs and Sausage Rolls'. I was, if not invincible, or scared of Kryptonite for that matter, certainly not knocking at death's door. Well, if Sister Gina was to be believed anyway. And why wouldn't she be? She'd just become the newspaper's horoscope columnist.

The fortune of my most morally reprehensible colleague – Trent, if you hadn't guessed – would have read something like this at present: 'Your suspicion is aroused by workplace tête-à-têtes which may be more than the sum of their parts. Calm your mind, centre yourself and the inner strength to confront the culprits will come. Tread carefully, and beware black cats on Tuesdays.'

Now, the email which pinged into my inbox after my post-buddy session smoke break could hardly be filed under 'E' for 'egg-shell walking', but then that had never been Trent's style.

From: trent.rogers@morgan&schwarz.com
To: bill.mcdare@morgan&schwarz.com
Subject: The new project:update

William,

It's come to my attention that you've been spending a lot of time working on the new project. While your commitment to the cause is to be admired, it does seem that you've somewhat neglected your other responsibilities to clients and colleagues.

Please debrief me on progress as soon as possible.

Best regards, Trent


From: bill.mcdare@morgan&schwarz.com
To: trent.rogers@morgan&schwarz.com
Subject: Re: The new project: update

Trent,

What the fuck are you on about?

Regards, Bill

From: trent.rogers@morgan&schwarz.com
To: bill.mcdare@morgan&schwarz.com
Subject: Re: The new project: update

Billy boy,

Don't play hardball with me.

Have you tapped that ass yet?

T

From: bill.mcdare@morgan&schwarz.com
To: trent.rogers@morgan&schwarz.com
Subject: Re: The new project: update

Trent,

Fuck you.

Bill.

It was best to give nothing away to Trent. Not that anything *was* going on. But any scrap of extraneous information surrendered to him could be used to inform the planning process of his next forced sexual activity. I wasn't going to fluff the fucker. Trent was unbearable to be around when you had something he wanted, however small. Whether he was after your last Rolo or your sister's cherry, he boasted an unbelievably thick skin, astonishing ignorance and a huge sense of entitlement, giving him an ethic of perverse persistence. To use the parlance of the profession, I was getting Trent well and truly off my radar, for now at least. This left me with pretty slim conversational pickings in the office. Sometimes I felt I'd have had richer dialogue in the hole of a Turkish prison, interacting with sadistic guards through just a smattering of self-taught phrases, a compliant nod and a low pain threshold. Maybe I was laying it on a bit thick. I'd go talk to Jill. Jill always had something to say.

'Hey, Jill.' I was stood behind her swivel chair. Over her shoulder pad I could see she was tapping out a press release. The headline read: 'Disabled Youth Get Chance Thanks To Workington Wads of Cash'. Hardly subtle. Just like Jill.

'Jill,' I said, louder this time, 'what's going down?'

The patter of the keyboard stopped and she turned to face me. I moved to her side. Jill was wearing a trouser-style suit stolen from Annie Lennox and had a mop of ashen blonde curls that were more Sideshow Bob than Shirley Temple.

'What do you want, Bill?'

'Ah, you know. The skinny, the QT, the 411. What's going down?'

'Oh, I don't know. You on the new girl?'

Jill was rarely off target with her gossip. Unfortunately, today her sight was not set on the bullseye.

'Fuck off, Jill.'

'Drink making you tetchy is it, Bill?'

'No.' Unlike most at Morgan & Schwarz, Jill could always tell when I'd had a sup.

'You ought to watch it, you know,' she said, 'because Miles is onto you'.

'Because you write everything you think you know on the toilet door?'

'Maybe because Miles is a perceptive human being.' She'd totally fallen for the 'Miles has a massive cock' yarn.

'Well thanks for the heads up, Jill.'

'All part of the friendly service.' Perhaps Jill wasn't my best bet. I looked around the office. People worked on engagement strategies on Apple iMacs sat boastfully on sleek desks. Photo-shoot briefs were thought out to the beat of designer heels tip-tapping on the parquet floor. In the distance Miles' outline could be seen against the horizontal blinds of his glass box of an office. Even his silhouette was convincing. It was a toss-up between Carol and Pete. Both had their drawbacks. According to a selective group email Jill had sent earlier this morning, Carol was on her period and while this didn't make her aggressive, an emotion uncommon in her 5-foot frame, it did make her acutely emotional and if I had to chair any more counselling sessions with Morgan & Schwarz-esses today I was going to have a strong case for sticking a roll-neck sweater, a pipe and a chaise lounge on expenses. And if I was going to keep sneaking the odd bottle of 15-year-old scotch through on the 'sundries' column of my claims spreadsheet, it would be best not to draw undue scrutiny.

Pete it was, then. I walked over to the side of the office where he spent his nine to five. Never earlier, never later. Pete was a stickler for routine. His desk looked like it'd been airlifted from a show room in Ikea. The papers were very neatly arranged. A stationery tidy housed his pens, stapler and rubber bands. Unseen ties kept cables hidden from his ergonomic keyboard. Dark wood framed a couple with a mock happy, blank expression. They looked like the kind of soulless people who existed only in the sample pictures supplied with off-the-shelf photo frames. They were Pete's parents. Pete was on the phone.

'…but as I say, it really is a super project. Just super…' Pete was selling in a story, 'you know, I've been around, oooh, let me see, five, ten, fifteen years now, and I've never heard of a corporate giving this much back. It really is super to see. The blind school are overjoyed.' Pete looked at me like I was a distraction. 'Right you are then, I'll send the story your way. Good man. All the best.' He put the phone down and sucked his teeth.

'Bill, how are you?'

'Surviving, Pete, surviving.' I picked up a rubber band from his desk tidy and started twanging it between my fingers. I knew this would grate on him.

'Jolly good,' he said, if not meant. A sudden look of realisation came over his face. The glasses on the end of his nose twitched ever so slightly.

'It's fitting you came over actually, Bill. There was something I wanted to ask you about,' he then lowered his voice, 'but it's a bit personal. Do you think we could perhaps go into the kitchen to chat?' I nodded.

'I'll follow you in,' he said.

I leaned against the mock marble worktop. Now just what could the sad fucker want?

'Tea?' Pete offered. He knew how to push the right buttons.

'Always,' I replied. Pete flicked the switch on the electric kettle.

'Fresh water please, Peter.'

'Oh gosh, sorry, Bill. I forgot for a moment there just how particular you are about your tea.' I was more pedantic than a man who ironed his socks.

'So what can I do for you then?' I nudged. 'What counsel can I offer? I'm becoming quite the shrink around here.'

'Oh it's nothing like that, Bill.' Pete looked flustered. His cheeks reddened. 'But it is, umm, it is, personal, in a manner of speaking.' Pete didn't have a personal life. Pete creosoted fences to the musical version of *War of the Worlds* in his spare time.

'Go on…' I said.

He handed me a small business card and looked sheepishly at the floor. The design was discreet. A small swirling typeface read:

## *Brief Encounters*
## *Modern Mating Services*

'Pete, this sounds like a brothel. I didn't think you had it in you, you old dog.'

He looked at me with disgust.

'Bill, how dare you. I would never be involved in such abhorrent activities and find it frankly insulting you would suggest otherwise.'

'Jeez man, take a chill pill.'

'I won't be taking any pills either, thank you very much.'

'Okay, Pete. No sex or drugs. I got it. Are you going to shed any further light on this?'

'Well, if you're going to be sensible…'

'Very sensible.'

'Good.'

'Great.'

'Okay then, it's a, umm, evening where you have the opportunity to meet like-minded people…'

'A singles club?'

'No, Bill.'

'A gay club?'

'No, Bill.'

'What then?'

'It's a speed dating evening,' he revealed. Now, I'd dated on speed before. I had a feeling Pete's night would be slightly more sedate.

'Speed dating?'

'Yes. Speed dating. It took me a while to get used to the idea, but you know, I'm cash rich, if I say so myself, but time poor. I'm not getting any younger, Bill. And neither are you.' I'd worked with Pete for longer than I care to remember and this was the first time he'd shown any suggestion of a sexual need. A Ken doll had more meat in his seat.

'Well, Peter, the Lord moves in mysterious ways. I certainly didn't think this is what you wanted to talk about. Actually, what was it exactly that you wanted to talk about?'

'Well, I was thinking that maybe we could go along to one of the evenings together. You could be my wingman.' And then he winked at me.

'Christ, Pete, it's not *Top Gun*.'

'I know, I know, but that's what lads do isn't it? Help each other out, back each other up…'

'What the hell has gotten into you?' The kettle whistled. I gave Pete my best 'this-situation-calls-for-tea' look. I had this down to an almost involuntary raise of one brow line. Pete took the cue and set about the elaborate tea-making routine he knew it was wise to follow in moments such as these. He tried to explain himself as the leaves brewed.

'Oh, I don't know what's got into me. A sense of urgency? Because, God knows, excuse the language, I need it. A bit of life? Because I'm not sure I've been living it. Isn't it meant to be for sharing?'

I was quite sure I was witnessing a mental breakdown first hand. No need to read about this 'Office worker realises life is vacuous and guns down colleagues one Tuesday morning' story. I was front and centre. And quite certain he'd turn the two barrels my way first. Oh well, what will be will be. There might be the chance to chase some tail in the meantime. Pete was looking at me with a sense of anticipation.

'Pete, the tea.'

'Yes, sorry, Bill.'

'You know what? You're right. Life *is* for the living,' I said.

'Exactly! What was it Robbie Williams said? No Regrets?'

'I have absolutely no idea, Pete.'

'But you get my meaning. It's time to grab the bull by the horns…'

'Steady on, Pete.'

'Sorry, I'm getting carried away. It's just been a while since I've done this kind of thing.'

'What kind of thing?'

'Been in the dating game.' I dry heaved.

'So we're on then?' he said.

'Okay, Pete, we're on. When is it?'

'Well, there's one on tonight.' He gave me an expectant-dog look.

'Tonight?!'

'You're not busy are you, Bill?'

'No, Pete, I am not busy.' I could put off pleasuring myself with a bottle and the internet until another time. Who knows? I might even find someone else to do it for me.

'You're buying all the drinks though.' I said.

'All the drinks?'

'All the drinks.'

'You're on.' I finished my tea and headed back to my desk.

Pete shouted after me, 'I'm looking forward to our brief encounter!'

Jill overheard.

'Saucy.'


I killed the afternoon by convincing an internet illiterate client to give us 30k for a social media campaign. When I was on it, I could sell ice to the Inuits like no-one bar Big Cock Miles. Digitally duping an old duffer was like flogging time-shares on the Costas to lower-middle-class social climbers: they knew everyone else was doing it and wanted a piece of the action to keep up appearances. The rub was they didn't have a fucking clue how the thing worked. Which was where we came in. A tour guide to Tron, giving our accountants hard-ons and us a carte blanche to piss about on the internet for hours while someone else footed the bill for broadband and Bellinis.

Today however I used the free time not to Facebook-stalk future ex-girlfriends but to gen up on the seemingly unsordid world of speed dating. Like a typical PR man, Pete didn't give me the whole story – we had to submit a thirty-word biog for the briefing sheets. As if I didn't have enough bullshit to write. As ever, Google was my most steadfast friend. A few searches later I came to realise that, like every secret society, this lot had their own language. A lexicon of love, it was cheesy as fuck. But I'd promised Pete. I'd promised him. This was my chance of only suffering a flesh wound in his demented corporate killing spree. I'd go along. I'd support. I'd try to enjoy. First off, I'd better learn the lingo. Didn't want to look like a dog in a cat fight. So here goes:

- **GSOH** – Meant 'Good Sense of Humour' (While I could appreciate the simplicity of a man falling off a log, and had laughed, once, at situation comedy *Friends*, it'd only be fair for my date to realise my sense of humour *was* good, but dark. Very dark. With the odd cock joke thrown in for good measure).
- **WLTM** – Meant 'Would Like To Meet' (A more toned down subversion of other acronyms I was familiar with, like MILF etc.).
- **LTR** – Meant 'Long Term Relationship (Let's have a drink first, yeah, sweetcheeks? Could also be visually represented by her post-coitally holding her knees up to her chest and counting to twenty).
- **OHAC** – Meant 'Own House And Car' (I *have* a home. My non-car owning status was my little planet-saving protest. Plus, I was mostly too drunk to drive. Yes, believe it or not, I did have a moral code of sorts. Underperforming in work/bed I could handle, killing a kid who'd chased his ball into the road and getting arse-raped in prison, I couldn't).

- **WE** – Meant 'Well Endowed' (!) (On a first date? Well, maybe this was going to be an interesting night after all…).
- **CTAA** – Meant 'Can Travel And Accommodate' (The standard issue Morgan & Schwarz GPS Flakberry could direct even the freshest off-the-boat cab driver back to number 35 after a night of meaningless sex at someone else's place. It was best we didn't go back to mine – drunk girls, stiletto heels and holes in the bathroom floor really didn't mix).
- **AC/DC** – Meant 'Bisexual' (Something that could be a plus-point in a partner, as opposed to being a school-uniform-wearing ginger metalhead. Although, thinking about it, that could rock too, as long as she didn't look like Angus Young).
- **SWF** – Meant 'Single White Female' (If the film was anything to go by also meant 'avoid like crabs').

Jesus, this bullshit was nearly as bad as PR. This biog was getting binned off. My chance to sell myself replaced by the worst words any spin-doctor could commit to copy: 'no comment'.

# Chapter 12

I checked my hair in the mirror, sprayed on cologne bought by an ex-girlfriend's mother four Christmases ago, brushed up my GSOH and hit the town.

'Really?'

'Yeah, and then the doctors said I'd never be able to chew properly again but I think I've proved them wrong.' She ate so quickly the poor food stood no chance of mastication regardless.

'Really?'

'Yeah, and like I always say, "don't bite off more than you can chew". Ha!'

A bell rang loudly, three times. I'd spent the last 3 minutes talking to an overweight hypochondriac and the 3 minutes before that being cried at by a woman taking her first steps into the dating world after catching her husband of 7 years balls-deep in her sister while on a caravanning holiday in the Lakes. The previous 3 minutes were spent speed-drinking bourbon at the bar, my sophisticated drink of choice, to pluck up the Dutch courage to appear interested in these poor souls; my 'dates'. This was the world of speed-dating, where a fog of desperation hung in the air and everything came in 3-minute intervals. This, when I really couldn't be jacked to put the effort in, was about my average anyway.

We were in a cocktail bar in the city. The kind which changed its name and decor every two years, while retaining the same atmosphere of try-hardness. A beacon of light for the social stupids who flocked like flies before realising the fluorescent light was just, well, a fluorescent light. Spend too long near it and you'd almost pray you were swatted just to bring an end to it all. We'd ventured in about six months before the next gutting. The chocolate brown sofas and vintage wallpaper were tired. The bar staff resigned. The last few clientele clinging on, waiting for the cycle to begin again.

We were in the upstairs room, out of the way. The place they stuck the salsa nights and tango clubs which supplemented income now even the finger-off-the-pulses realised the place was flatlining. My company tonight was oblivious to any of these harsh truths. They had bigger fish to fry. Matters of the heart. Twenty unlucky in love/time poor/social leper/supportive friends, split evenly between the sexes, although you had to look hard to distinguish which, even under the flattering low lighting. We'd got the last two male places. Pete had been pleased with that.

'I'm pleased with that,' he'd said.

There was a break in the proceedings for 'mingling'. I scoured the rectangular room looking for a potential, a maybe, an after-five-pinter. I'd had at least five pints. Pickings were slim, even if no one else was. Pete interrupted my neggy thought-train, which was grinding itself to a halt anyway.

'How's it going, big guy?' he said. He was being less formal than usual. He'd had a Tia Maria and diet Coke.

'Good. Good,' I lied.

'Spoke to any future Mrs McDares yet then?' He nudged me with his elbow.

'Not unless one of them dug my dad up and carried him down the aisle.'

'Bill!' He looked shocked but remembered we were meant to be having fun. 'What are you like, yanking my chain like that?' This was 'banter'.

'Just kidding, Pete. How about you? Struck gold yet?'

'I don't want to curse it, but I'm getting warm. I'm getting very, very warm.'

'Tell me more, Casanova.' I cringed at this, but it was in keeping with his expectations of laddish behaviour and I didn't want to disappoint.

'Well, I've got to say I'm pleasantly surprised. I have met a couple of what you would call p-p...' he struggled for the next word.

My heart said 'pigs', my mouth said 'peaches?'

'Peaches! A couple of peaches. One of the young ladies had a really warm character. She reminded me a lot of my Auntie Vi.'

'That's not a good thing, Pete.'

'It is. She was a very warm person. A lovely woman.' It was confirmed. Pete was beyond redemption, but at least he was having a good time.

'And then another who told me all about her battle with anti-depressants. I felt like a voyeur watching one of those Oprah Winfrey type shows. Intriguing.'

'Right, and she was a peach?' I asked.

'No, no, not her, Bill. She wasn't a peach. Another one really caught my,' he paused, 'glad eye, as they say.'

'So, what did she look like?' I pushed.

'Gosh, it's not all about the looks, Bill.' He rolled his eyes behind his contact lenses, his black frames relegated to the bedside table for the evening, 'But if you must know, she was very well turned out. Yes. Very well turned out indeed.'

'Well that's just brilliant, Pete.' I gave the barman the wink and he begrudgingly poured me another.

'She started telling me the most fascinating story about the Italian town of Pompeii. The whole place was exterminated when a volcano erupted in around...' he did his recall face, '... 80 AD, I believe.'

'Right, yeah, and...' I asked.

'Well, that's the thing. The bell rang before we could finish. I'd love to hear the end of it.' This was typical Pete, more turned on by talk of ancient civilisations than carnal pursuits. But who was I to judge? It was nice to have common interests, particularly non-substance based ones.

'There she is, talking to the chap with the 'trendy' haircut,' Pete said. He made inverted commas in the air when he said the word 'trendy'. She was facing the opposite way to us. Neither a J-Lo nor a fat ho. In a town with so many fast food joints, this was a solid foundation. She wore a flowery dress just above the knee and had a severe bob-cut. She looked classy enough, and well in control. The 'trendy' haircut milled away and she turned back into the room. Her face was inoffensive enough. She caught Pete's eye and shot him a smile.

'You're in! You are so in!' I squeezed his shoulder the way teammates standing next to each other on the halfway line watching a penalty shoot-out unfold at the goal would. He looked at me, wide-eyed.

'I'm going to ask her for a drink. To finish the story...'

'Easy, tiger,' I replied, 'you know the rules.' I didn't know the rules until an hour ago, but thanks to their constant repetition over a tinny microphone by a failed TV quiz show host type, I now very much knew them.

The rules of speed-dating (brought to you by **Brief Encounters – Modern Mating Services**) were:

1. **Respect the bell – when it's time to move on, move on –** (While this left Pete on a conversational cliffhanger, the bell proved my saviour from numerous nutters telling me about their cats, cataracts or cat o' nine tails – apparently there's *always* one into bondage).

2. **Be polite** – (This was VERY FUCKING HARD. But I did it. For Pete).

3. **Don't ask judgemental questions about age, occupation or where your date lives** – (Meaning I didn't have to explain why I looked at least 5 years older than twenty-nine (the booze), explaining what PR was (no, it is not 'like promotions' and no I am not a 'personal assistant') and it's best we don't get into the whirlwind of woe that was number 35).

4. **Don't exchange phone numbers** – (Trust me, on current form this lot weren't worth the 12p a text).

5. **Don't judge a book by its cover (Meet everyone!)** – (The rule most likely to be used against me before the night was out).

'And you're here because?'

'I'm providing moral support to a friend,' I answered.

'Of course you are,' she said. She took a slug of her drink. She was drinking cocktails like sodas. Common interests: it was a start.

'Rumbled,' I said. 'Very perceptive of you. You've let the cat out of the bag, I'm here to find my life partner.' I was trying hard to obey rule number two, albeit sarcastically.

She looked me up and down – well, to my midriff, we were sat at a sticky table – like a big cat weighing up a new piece of meat.

'Okay. I believe you, millions wouldn't.' She took another slug of her drink. She had teeth like tombstones.

'The first time, I meant. As in, I believe you're here with a friend.'

'Well, thank God for that.' It was hard to turn this sarcasm off.

'Snap,' she said.

'Sorry?'

'Snap. I'm here with a friend too. Although it's difficult to remember who initiated the coming. We're regulars at this kind of thing.'

'First-time caller, long-time listener,' I said.

It was her turn to say, 'Sorry?'

'Oh, nothing. Woah, though. To your earlier confession. I mean, you must really enjoy these kinds of things then?'

'I'm not sure "enjoy" is the right word,' she said. I was pretty fucking terrified of this woman. I tried to turn the conversation away from the two of us.

'So which is your friend, then?'

'The girl over there.' She pointed disinterestedly over to her right and rattled the ice cubes around her glass. It was the bob-cut girl.

'That's the girl my friend likes!' I showed a little *too* much enthusiasm here.

'Well, what are the chances?' she replied in a flat one-tone voice. The voice of a girl on a dirty phone-line, tired and emotionless after telling the other end of the receiver she'd been licking the world's biggest balls all night long.

'I wonder if she'll like him?' I said. Screw worrying about the eagerness. This was Pete; it'd been a while.

'Does he have a cock?'

'Sorry?'

'A cock?'

'I assume so.'

'Then, yes. Yes, she'll like him.' We were being used. I was a poacher turned gamekeeper.

The bell rang.

'I've never known anyone waste 3 minutes so badly. Let's go for a drink later to see if you can do the same again. You bring him, I'll bring her.'

'It's a date,' I replied.

'It's a double date, darling,' she replied. I was TERRIFIED of this woman. Deep breaths. This was for Pete.

We'd made it out of Brief Encounters alive, for now, into a tapas bar down the block. Pete was an only child. The one other time we'd been for tapas together, a Morgan & Schwarz social, he'd ordered albondigas and patatas bravas for one. The thought of sharing was anathema to him. 'It's part of the experience,' we'd said. 'No thank you very much,' he'd said. The bob-cut one and the terrifying one looked like they had dirty fingernails. I could see Pete was plotting an uneasy mental map of where their paws met his calamari. He put on a brave face and cracked a dad-gag.

'So, ladies, what do you fancy…? You can say me.' They picked up the sticky menus in silence.

Tapas suited me. Its one-for-all nature meant I didn't have to embarrassingly leave a still-full plate in front of me. Eating was cheating.

'Cocktail, ladies?' I offered.

The terrifying one was silent no more. 'Screwdriver.'

'That's a funny name, isn't it?' said Pete. Bob-cut smiled at him. The terrifying one gave me a 'where the fuck's my drink' look?

'Anyone else?'

The bob-cut spoke.

'Oh, thanks, um…'

'Bill.'

'Thanks, Bill. I'll have a… Cosmopolitan,' she said.

'I could tell you were cosmopolitan,' Pete threw in. She laughed. I was unsure if it was a false one. It was harder to tell than with an orgasm.

'Pete?' He looked the menu up and down.

'I will plump for one Virgin Mary, my good man.'

'That's got no booze in it,' I told him.

'Oh, really? Drat. I liked the name.' They both laughed now. They thought Pete was being ironic. He wasn't.

'Okay, what about a Singapore Sling?' he added.

I nodded and fled to the bar.

Well this wasn't quite how I saw today panning out. Who'd have thought when I avoided the mirror and swallowed some mouthwash this morning I'd end the day on a quasi-double date with Pete. Pete who'd not had a jump under this government, Pete to whom this was the social event of the millennia, Pete who was… I looked over my shoulder… making the brace of broads genuinely laugh back at the table. A misspent youth standing next to large speakers at loud gigs had left my hearing fucked so the content of Pete's comedy escaped me. He was all hand gestures and animated expressions. He was relaxed in the company of women; he just never seemed to fuck them. I took a moment to reflect on how the reverse was true for me.

The terrifying one broke my contemplation with one of those 'booze-or-I-kill-you' looks again. I ordered, waited for the slick prick of a barman to flip a bottle onto the back of his hand in an attempt to preen in front of a nubile and naive looking colleague, and then headed back like a 21st century hunter-gatherer to the laughter.


'The worst thing was, they were totally oblivious to what was going to happen. I've read things which say that they were just going about their daily business, eating and bathing, blissful in their ignorance.' The bob-cut didn't look like she knew a lot about ancient history, but as *Brief Encounters* told us, don't judge a book by its cover.

'Quite, quite incredible,' said Pete. 'I'll have to make sure I've got my wits about me the next time I'm in the tub, just in case.'

'Put your rubber duckie on red alert,' she said. Her warmth belied the severity of her hair do. They were hitting it off. She continued the history lesson. 'They say that when they saw the first sign of smoke, they were more curious than anything. '

'What is it they say?' Pete replied.

Bob-cut started, 'There's no smoke…'

'Without fire,' Pete finished. They guffawed in unison.

'Speaking of which, I'm going to go outside for a cigarette,' the scary one said. The booze had calmed her, but frantic laughter had turned to boredom.

'That,' I said, 'sounds like a very good idea.'

'Do you feel like we've gatecrashed the nerdiest first date in history?' She cackled smoke out of her mouth and nose like Pompeii plumes.

'She may seem boring, but she will fuck literally everything that moves. A variation on this happens every time we come to these things.'

'He's quite the opposite,' I said, 'but a good ride would do him the world of good.' An image entered my mind: Pete, slick-haired, wearing a smoking jacket, sat around the boardroom table drinking scotch, slapping his thigh, laughing heartily.

'Well, let's just say, he'll have his own eruption later.'

Christ.

'And what about you?' she said.

'What about me?'

'Do you fuck everything that moves?'

'That's a very personal question.'

'Yes it is.'

'Well, I'm not sure I should answer that.'

'Do you want to fuck me?' she said.

Christ.

Before I'd finished my smoke, she'd flagged down a cab and her chipped fingernails were tearing at my pubic hair.

Pete would have to make his own way home.

I awoke with the familiar of unfamiliar surroundings. It was some clattering outside the door that did it. It sounded like the usual morning sounds: wardrobe doors opening and slamming, showers gushing, the low hum of a radio host. I was alone in an unmade bed. The room was blank and bare. So was I. I was wearing one sock. It said 'Wednesday'. It was Thursday. This great escape couldn't involve months of planning and dirt-dispelling through holey pockets. I had to get the fuck out of dodge, and now. I looked down to my left to find last night's clothes in a pile. My boxer shorts were draped on the radiator. This was not a good sign. I dressed like a fumbling first-time necessity stripper in reverse. No sock in sight. This could help the next operation, which was all about stealth. I was hardly feeling my most cat-like. I turned the handle before pulling the door towards me to silence the opening. What would Pandora's door reveal? The radio got louder. The shower stopped. A corridor ran ahead of me with stairs leading off it. There was light at the end of the tunnel. I moved quietly, touching the near wall, quietly hovering over the carpet and down the stairs towards the chink.

Flashback: neat house, neater spirits. Her: aggressive, domineering, wanting to slap and be slapped. Call me… what was her name? At least once you'd think I'd be able to remember her fucking name.

There was a bureau by the front door: take-away menus, charity collection bags, free newspapers, mail. I picked up a circular. Diana Davies, that was her name. Diana Davies. I slipped out of the door to safety.

An overwhelming thought smacked me in the jaw. The name on the letter wasn't Christy.

# Chapter 13

Young Boy Scouts in more enlightened parts of the world have the pleasure of rubbing sticks together and holding maps upside down while looking lost, not just with other spotty spec-wearing runny nosed boys, but with girls. Wandering in the woods together. Losing innocence under the star-smudged sky. No such luck for me. I was stuck with Geoff, an ageing outdoors type who liked to ramble and hit young boys with sticks, often from distance. His wife chose to go by the name of 'Badger', perhaps in allusion to her greying perm. Which I can't help thinking now seems a little cruel. Bereft of the distraction of bare-legged girls in green, I started to carve out a burgeoning career for myself in the city's 81st troupe. I won orienteering competitions in record time. I erected tents efficiently and securely. My divining rod often found a source of water. At the tender age of twelve, I reached the lofty heights of Seconder. The Sixer was getting on a bit. His balls had dropped and it wouldn't be long until his Wednesday nights wouldn't be spent in the scout hut but in the park with a bottle of White Lightning and ten Regal Superkings. This was a young man's game. My eye was on the prize.

So, it seemed, were Russell Stevens'. One evening after winning a game of table tennis and reciting a passage from *The Jungle Book* I'd committed to memory, Geoff called me over to one side. He told me this was to be my last night as a scout. Allegations had been made regarding the spiking of Badger's drink. A cup of lemon squash laced with shampoo. I was out on my ear. No ifs. No buts. No chance of appeal. I knew what had happened. The little cunt had grassed me up for a crime I didn't commit. And now I was on the scoutheap.

Stevens had a clear run to the top. In the lunch queue, I'd overhear tales of him picking up crab football trophies. Of him winning capital cities of the world quizzes. Of him making Badger laugh. I sat patiently. I bided my time. I twiddled my thumbs with vengeful intent.

But there was no need to put my masterplan into action. Six weeks later the stupid fuck set fire to the scout hut. The victim of a roaring campfire and a strong wind. With just one gale, exuberant 'Kum-Ba-Yah-ing' and marshmallow-toasting turned to cries of woe and scorched canvas. Now we were both on the outside looking in.

I hadn't seen him for fifteen years until today. He was sat opposite me in the waiting room of the genito-urinary health clinic; in laymen's terms, the knob doctors. When faced with a ghost of Christmas past on the streets, I had my technique down pat:

**Step 1:** Spot ex-classmate/housemate/girlfriend's friend from distance. My excellent eyesight, even under the duress of alcohol, made this a thirty-pace affair.

**Step 2:** Drop gaze to the floor. Adopt confident stride.

**Step 3:** Reach in inside pocket for Flakberry. Hold to ear.

**Step 4:** Appear animated, pepper one-way conversation with phrases like 'two-way dialogue', 'synergy' and 'multi-platform approach'.

**Step 5:** Return gaze to 90 degrees ahead, approximately ten paces before impact.

**Step 6:** Make a 'Oh my God, it's YOU! How the hell are you? Would love to stop and chat but can't' face. Point to phone. Make the universal hand gesture for telephone with hand not currently holding a telephone.

It was difficult, nigh on impossible, to adopt the same strategy when sat immediately opposite your subject in a clinical room with the stench of venereal disease hanging in the air. I clocked Stevens and he had clocked me. After the usual cursory glance common in public situations, I'd caught him looking my way again, just to make sure. I shot him a confirmatory look with some self-satisfaction. I was wearing a high-quality three-piece hand-made Italian suit. He was wearing tracksuit bottoms underneath a gut that hung so low it was a wonder he could see his dick to stick it in anything in the first place. My smugness lasted for just a second: we were in the STI clinic. Cock rot was a great leveller.

On the bus across town, Dr Carter's referral note had hidden like a filthy secret in my inside pocket, brushing up against commuters on their way to their day jobs and their desks. I was off to show my dick to a white coat. Again. At least now I was in the right place. Yes, the problem would be sorted, the weight would be lifted. Less need to bag the boy up when on manoeuvres then. More skin on skin, less skin on bin bag.

My eyes, doing all they could to avoid Stevens, scanned the space around me. It had the look, if not the feel, of a low budget airline departure lounge. The frequent flyers dotted liberally on the rows of frayed seats wore the air of an unforced error: leaving the bar and coming in here too soon. Or leaving the bar and coming into something quite different too soon. The administration in our municipality clubbed men and women together in the same waiting area, leaving most of the blokes with faces as red as their privates.

Stage-left a brunette entered our Heartbreak Hotel of sexual liaisons gone gammy. Ripped denim clung to her long legs. She wore a cropped t-shirt splashed with the name of a band I've never heard of: The Nobodies. Cute. Her walk was pure unadulterated dirty sex. She picked up a magazine from the table and sauntered to a seat. She was close enough for me to catch her eye. 'EXCLUSIVE: Coma Baby Saved,' read a headline splashed on the front page. Like all of the best – and all of the worst – women, she looked like she didn't have a care in the world. Not one. I couldn't catch her eye but I could undress her with mine. Peeling off the rock tee, ripping off the ripped jeans, down to the good stuff, the tight pink triangle of panty which hid… a FUCKING STI. Jesus, man, did I have no shame? If bad breath was a turn-off, what the fuck was crabs?

I needed to get the fuck in to see that doctor and the fuck out of here.

My earphones played loud on the way back to the office. Anything to take my mind off the doctor's hand, the cue tip and delicate end of my… anyway, enough of that. 'Oh, Mama, can this really be the end?' I hope not, I still had six smokes left in my back pocket. I decided to make it five en route to Morgan & Schwarz from the bus stop. The nicotine would be needed for an afternoon of conference calls and social strategies. I stopped my steps short of the front entrance and hung to the side of the building to draw a drag and mentally prepare myself for the working world.

One of my boozing buddies was slumped next to a bin in the alleyway I used as my drinking dressing room. Less gold star on the door, more stench of star anise from the adjoining Chinese joints. It was difficult to make out exactly which of them; a dozing down-and-out looked like a dozing down-and-out. Probably dreaming of the finer things in life: freedom, camaraderie, a cold drink. *La dolce vita*.

The horn of a passing car honked him awake. The resigned realisation that he had once again used a trash can for a pillow was visible even from where I stood. Like a short-sighted granddad grabbing for his glasses at first light, he rubbed his eyes and reached for a flagon of what I could only assume was booze. He didn't look like a Mountain Dew kind of guy. He shook the broken bones and plastic sheeting off and disappeared around the side of the industrial bin. Ten seconds or so later a trickle of piss swam across the debris like a concrete jungle waterfall. In its own little way, it was beautiful.

What happened next wasn't. He re-emerged, rubbed his hands on his street-soiled trousers, and pushed open the bin. Feeding time at the zoo. I needed a drink as much as any of these poor fuckers. But I did it with a tailor-made suit in my Berghaus rucksack, from a bottle hidden in the bottom drawer of my well-paid desk job. Even the mouthwash I swallowed was the leading brand. I was a lipstick lush. I hung my head in shame. My eyes caught my 200 note brogues, not helping the scene.

Sated for now, he clocked me from across the road. A piece of Char Sui pork clung to his face. A sad, ravaged face. It was that one. Him. His crucified eyes clung to me. In my current get-up I felt like a Jew at Calgary. His downfall was my doing and the doing of those like me. But surely he didn't recognise me? I was Clark Kent. Back up to *The Daily Planet* for a quick change before saving the day.

My foe today wasn't the Green Goblin or Lex Luther. It was Christy. Our buddy session had started off on the wrong foot.

'Where the fuck do you get off asking me questions like that?'

'I'm sorry, I…' One of the strip lights above us flickered. It gave the scene the ambience of watching the shine of late night TV when drunk, which, I'll level with you, was where I'd much rather be right now.

'What business of yours is it who I'm sleeping with or not sleeping with?!'

As you're just about figuring out, I'd made a grave error of judgment. The error wasn't in the thinking but the saying. The blurting out. Once, after a particularly trying three hour car journey with Miles when all I'd wanted to do was snort drugs and cane smokes, I'd asked a South African client I'd just been introduced to if she'd been over here long enough 'not to be racist anymore'. Only a major smarm offensive from Mr Big Dick had saved the account, and with it, probably my job. In fairness to me, this morning I had endured a cotton bud down my Jap's eye and a stare-down from a suspicious tramp. It had just slipped out.

'I really meant nothing by it, Chris…'

'Don't call me "Chris".'

'Christy… I meant nothing by it. It's just, I know what he's like and I know he was trying to make inroads…'

'Inroads? I'm not a fucking service station.'

'I'm sorry.'

'You're a dick, Bill.'

I was a dick. What the fuck was I thinking? I'd been wound up by Trent over the past week. He'd been sending me regular emails about his new 'piece of ass' and I knew Christy was in his sights. 'All in the game', he'd said. Well, typed. He'd said I knew the girl and would never guess who she was. So I didn't guess. He wanted me to guess. I guessed Pete. He told me to guess again. I didn't. Or rather I did, out loud, to my guess, Christy, about 30 seconds ago.

'You don't seem to get that this is meant to be about work. I mean, I barely even know you and you're making really offensive presumptions about me.'

'Look, Christy, I'm sorry. I wasn't thinking before I spoke.'

'Don't even think those things.'

'I won't.'

'Last time this was about our dead fucking parents and this time it's about someone I wouldn't be caught dead fucking.'

We both laughed at this. The tea, which I'd been clinging onto as a lone ally during my dressing-down, washed down the wrong hole.

'Pppphheww.' I spluttered all over the minimal white table, flecks of brown like a lost school of fish against its unwelcoming backdrop.

'Bill, are you okay?'

I coughed up some smoker's phlegm. It mixed with the tea to make the worst kind of smoothie imaginable. I finished with a sneeze. There was the suggestion of a fart. Oh Christ. This made her laugh again.

'Smooth,' she said.

'I know.'

Her face, which just 30 seconds ago was as red as her hair, was calming now.

'I hope that wasn't constructed purely to stop me being mad with you.'

'If my body was capable of such involuntary action to save my skin, then I salute it.'

'To reiterate, you are a total dick for asking me something like that.'

'I know, I know, I know. It's just that I really…' Like you? That's what I should be saying next. Like you. '…shouldn't be saying this, but the last girl…'

'Dina?'

'Yes, Dina. Well, part of the reason she left Morgan & Schwarz and now doesn't cut her armpit hair and follows the teachings of a delusional cult leader is…'

'Trent?' she offered.

'Trent,' I confirmed.

I broke the rules of the game. I wasn't sure what the rules of the game were but I knew grassing up Trent was not in the rules of the game. At least I left the date rape drug out of it. Fuck Trent anyway.

'So fucking what, Bill? So what if Trent did her rodeo style in the think tank room while Carol jiggled for tips?'

'You're right.' It was best to concede. I could see Carol through the venetian blinds. She was wearing a beige turtleneck, stood waiting at the photocopier. I don't think she'd ever 'jiggled' in her whole life.

'You know who you remind me of?' she said.

James Dean. Kurt Cobain.

'No?'

A young Marlon Brando, before the booze, drugs and delusion set in. Lord Byron. I tried my best powers of suggestion. Where was Sister Gina when you needed her?

'My dad.'

If I'd have had tea in my gob it would have joined the little snotty brown fishes all over the table.

'Your dad?'

'Yes.'

'Erm…' I swallowed hard. She continued.

'He was always worrying about me and boys. Always asking me not to see so and so, telling so and so never to call the house again, forcing me to stay in my room and not go to the park or the cinema or ice skating.'

'Well, he was your dad.'

'He is my dad.'

'I thought you didn't like him.'

'I never said that.' I resisted the teenage urge to ask if she liked me. Her big black eyes were now playful, teasing almost, showing she did like me. Just not in the way I'd hoped. More errant parent than Errol Flynn.

'Anyway,' she said, 'enough of that for one day. Are you making an appearance at Jill's birthday thing on Friday?' Jill had reached the grand old age of forty. Not being one to stand on ceremony, or go a couple of breaths without telling you to go fuck yourself, Jill hadn't gone to the trouble of sending out special invites for the poignant occasion, rather she'd announced plans in the Morgan & Schwarz Monday morning meeting.

'Because you'll all see it on fucking Facebook or something like that, yes I am forty on Friday, and yes I do expect you all to come and get pissed with me. Maybe have some food too. I imagine you'll all chip in for me. And if you don't want to, well you can just fuck off.' Miles, leading the meeting, found it difficult to tell if Jill's menace was mirth or madness, so shuffled a few papers, coughed and moved on. It was her birthday after all.

'Oh, that?' I said to Christy. 'Well, it doesn't sound like we have a choice, does it?'

'I wouldn't want to be the one to piss Jill off on her birthday', she replied. We both raised our eyebrows in a 'what's Jill like?' kind of way.

'Anyway, thanks for the buddying, Bill. I've gotta fly.' She bounced out of her chair, red hair and bare arms blurring towards the door. She opened it, turned back and said:

'Oh, and Bill, if you ever, ever, EVER, ask me anything like that again, I'll cut your fucking balls off. Kaybye.'

There was a time on work's nights out when I'd carefully co-ordinate my wardrobe to appear sharp, scrubbed up well and, if drunk, at least smooth. The nature of the industry meant there was generally an intern or a grad – who thought PR was all cocktails and celebs – to take advantage of if Trent didn't get there first. Fast forward to this Friday and my aim would be not to dress like Christy's dad. Her fucking dad. Being compared to the runaway father of the girl you're trying to lay, now that was a new BENCHMARK. Jeez, the one flicker of light in my shitfucksoullessjobnolovemeaninglesssexdeaddadcuntynewdadsh ithousewithaholeinthefuckingbathroomthroughtotheFUCKING KITCHEN existence had been Christy.

I was off to get very drunk or very high or very both. Kaybye.

# Chapter 14

'I'll give you each an animal and I want you to come up with an idea inspired by it,' Miles said, in full PT Barnum mode. There was a consensual silence across the room.

'Carol, you're a lion.' She thought for a moment, ignoring the ridiculousness of the statement, before the small eyes behind her thick rectangular specs lit up.

'We could focus on the role females have in raising their young and running the household. We could run stories which made them feel responsibility for ensuring their pride got all their vitamins.'

'Like lionesses?'

'Like lionesses.'

'Love it,' said Miles. Carol looked relieved and then vaguely self-satisfied. The wheel of fortune spun again.

'Pete, you're a tiger.'

'How kind of you to notice, Miles.' It was a shame Pete never got close to procreation. His comedy repertoire was perfectly pitched at embarrassing offspring. Sadly, the result of the Brief Encounters after-party was a phone number one digit too short. And she had loved cock by all accounts.

Miles wasn't in the mood for him.

'Pete…'

'Okay, okay, bear with me.' His emphasis of the word 'bear' went unacknowledged.

'What about a feature on the health benefits of the product? We could call it 'How Vit-Drink can give you your stripes.' Pete leaned back in his chair.

'Good, Pete.' Miles, though orchestrating the affair, was following the rule of never dismissing an idea. It could be very damaging to confidence and Morgan & Schwarz was a finely balanced and highly combustible collection of egos.

'Next up: Bill, you're an elephant.'

'Is that because he never forgets?' said Jill, apropos of nothing. My short-term memory bore all the hallmarks of an early onset of dementia.

'No, it's because I've got a long trunk.' The room recoiled. We often made bawdy comments at inappropriate moments. I was trying to join in and be a team player. It was a stroke of luck Christy wasn't there though. That quip was verging on a dad-joke. That fire didn't need fuelling.

Chais and skinny lattes were raised and sipped and slurped as I scratched around my head for an idea. The gerbil which spun my cerebral wheel was yet to get going after last night's alcoholic misadventures. I'd been sick in my hand at my desk about 30 minutes previous and had been sure that Jill had seen me. She pierced me with a callous stare and head shake that said, 'I can't believe you're worth the same pay cheque as me.' Truth was, I was on more. Miles had left some confidential papers on the photocopier last month – very unlike him. I struggled to believe it too. I felt like shit, and a shit. Not a good time, Bill. Come on. Buck up, you fuck.

'They could brand up an elephant and walk him down the High Street handing out bottles of the stuff to kids and old folks?' My intonation implied I wasn't entirely sure.

'That'd be cruel to the poor thing,' said Jill. Jill had broken the code. She'd shot down my idea in flames. Altruistic ones perhaps, but flames all the same.

'Well, this is fucking stupid anyway,' I said. I'd broken the code. I'd called the animal game stupid. We were in the midst of a thought shower (or a brainstorm, if you dug the non-PC). The team was gathered under duress in a room known through internal comms as the 'Persuasion Station'. It was where the temperamental talents of Morgan & Schwarz would assemble to pick over public relations problems and agree our strategy of attack to engage, convince and conquer. Our own little war room with Miles as Mussolini and the shirt not black but 100 per cent Egyptian cotton. These creative fluxes were, I imagined, akin to the free-form get-togethers of the Beat Poets or the intellectually enlightened riffs shared on the Parisian Left Bank in the 1920s. Except we were mainly talentless and were 'jamming' on a campaign to create a buzz around a new range of vitamin-added carbonated soft drinks. To be honest with you, I could have done with a bucket-load of the stuff to nurse me through this morning's hangover. If nothing else, it was quite revealing; the depths of despair that could be plunged upon discovering that the object of your (subtle) affections likens you to their father. I awoke at 8.27 a.m. with a deep cut on my left knee and the vague suggestion of human faeces in the air. There'd been no time for a shower before work.

'Thanks for all your input on that one, guys,' Miles said. It was hard to tell if he was being sarcastic. 'Now onto the next problem.' He was off again.

'Could I be excused for a second?' I asked. Despite the fact we were roughly the same height and sat on identical chairs, Miles somehow managed to look down at me.

'For what reason?'

'The bathroom.'

'For Christ's sake, Bill, you don't have to ask to use the bathroom. I'm not your wet nurse.'

Cunt.

Sniggers broke out around the glass table. He'd pay for that. If anyone was going to make Bill McDare look stupid it would be Bill McDare.

The Morgan & Schwarz bathroom was more can-can than can. Spotlights illuminated rectangular mirrors which hung above freestanding wash basins. Some interior design wit obviously thought we needed to feel like megastars. While the light was harsh, it did provide a perfect ambience for cutting up lines after normal office hours. Those occasional all-nighters on last-ditch pitch documents often needed an extra zing.

Yesterday's post-work drinking had started with a few calm beers on the terrace of The Accord, a fairly nondescript establishment about three blocks east from the office. The Morgan & Schwarz crowd tended not to gather there, which made it an ideal launch point last night. I caught my reflection in the acute light. The late sun had reddened the skin around my eyes and cheeks, extenuating usually non-apparent wrinkles like white valleys in a scorched landscape. Time was wearing on me, a harsh HB pencil adding lines to my look. I splashed cold water on my face for what seemed like an age, but in reality was probably 30 seconds or less. I was dizzy and losing perspective. There was only one thing for it: I'd stop at my desk for a wee dram on the way back to the brainstorm. The temporary cure to all of life's ills. And so the wheel turns again.

'So, who is the audience? Who are we trying to convince here, people?'

Miles was in mid-flow when I returned unacknowledged to the session. I hated him when he was facilitating. From what I could gather over the next few moments thoughts were being showered towards his blank flip-chart for an upcoming beauty parade for a brand of travel insurance called 'Wanderlust'. Cute. It had befallen the poor souls gathered in the Persuasion Station to preen and plot strategies to make insurance not just sellable, but sexy.

'Put yourselves in their flip-flops, people,' Miles commanded. 'Who goes on holiday?'

Like a pub quiz machine, the questions got progressively harder.

'Families?'

'Right…'

'Couples?'

'Ahuh…'

'Singles?'

'Sure…'

'Retired people?'

'Yes…'

'Rich people?'

'Yep…'

'Gays?'

'Gays…'

This went on and on. We delved deeper; why did people travel? What did people fear? Were we all inherently racist? I still felt sick. Because of the booze, or lack of booze. Because of Christy. Because I was here. Because I wasn't on holiday, supping a cocktail in the indiscriminate summer sun.

'Don't wander lost, wanderlust!' Pete had interrupted Miles and delivered his slogan a few octaves higher than had been set by the rest of the room's conversation. It was never a good idea to interrupt Miles.

'You may have forgotten, Pete, but we're in Public Relations, not advertising. We don't hawk, we have conversations. I want ideas, not catchphrases.' The other thing it was never a good idea to do with Miles was to get him started on advertising. 'Smarmy, gutless shits,' he'd generally call them. 'Overpaid cunts,' occasionally. Ad men had a skewed vision of reality; people were nice to them, their clients splashed out over the odds for column inches and air time, meaning a day didn't pass without a good old arse-licking from a happy sales schmuck. Flowers on their birthday, front row tickets to the game, complimentary city breaks. Hell, they got treated like clients. This cosseted existence made them the least qualified people to sell products or services; they got everything for free. The PR man was a cannier operator, a subtler manoeuvrer. We didn't pay to have our message carried like those flash frauds at ad agencies, we coaxed and cajoled, built relationships, planted seeds that bloomed into oak trees. Miles had lectured us on the idiosyncrasies inherent to the different disciplines of the marketing mix on so many occasions we knew them off pat by now. Jill, sat opposite me across the table, mouthed the words as today's recitation moved apace. Christ, I needed a drink. And a grilled cheese sandwich. It was only 10.17 a.m. after all; best not to go in on an empty stomach.

'Who wants to pick the ideas out of the hat…?'

'It's a bowl.'

'…the bowl, and read them out? And who's taking notes?'

A tall, gaunt boy from the accounts department agreed to scribe, Carol – buoyed by a gin and tonic (ice and a slice) – to relay the ideas to the group. We were sat cross-legged around a sunken table at one of the city's most try-hard sushi bars. It was Jill's fortieth birthday party. Miles, in a rare moment of philanthropy, had let us charge the lot to the Morgan & Schwarz account, generally used for sashimi and sake to convince clients over the age of thirty-five we were a hip young agency who could help them relive a youth they never had and with whom they should most definitely commit obscene monthly payments. Who could resist when the nigiri was this good? Miles' impromptu alms-giving had likely been inspired by the presence in our merry ranks of one Vincent Meinhoff, a short and stolid venture capitalist with a significant stake in Morgan & Schwarz and a social life so subdued (most likely revolving around vigorous squash with an old college roommate and monthly robotic loveless sex with his wife) that his unannounced office visits – timed perfectly for pub o'clock – were becoming increasingly frequent. Miles was intent on illustrating the wiseness of his investment and had relayed a message via all@Morgan&Schwarz.com to be on our best behaviour. Whilst simultaneously putting on a free bar. Uh oh. What was it Anon. said? *Know how to be content and you will never be disgraced; practice self-restraint and you will never be in danger.* Load of tosh anyway. I was drinking steadily if not yet ambitiously in solidarity with Jill, who was irked that some Germanic banker had stolen the thunder on her big day.

'In 10 years time, Jill will be married to Antonio Banderas, living in the Hollywood Hills and supplementing her film-star-wife income as a personal trainer to a select group of stars,' Carol read from a crumpled piece of paper.

Jill snorted hopefully and the rest of the group broke up in laughter. Despite being out of the office, we were unable to leave behind its rules and rituals, using the classic unmarked ideas in a pot brainstorming technique for some sure-to-be hilarious crystal ball gazing on the future of our own crazed cat lady. It said something about the weak social bond that existed between the employees of Morgan & Schwarz that we needed play time to be propped up by the structure of a creativity generation tool. I took another slug of my beer and shot a smile of faux gratitude at Miles.

'Next,' the collective cry came up.

The accounts boy – no more than twenty-one – scribbled furiously to keep up, a nervous sweat on his brow at the prospect of presenting the birthday girl with an incomplete record of the events of her special evening. Carol cleared her throat, much like a field mouse about to give a reading at the wedding of a mouse friend. If field mice could talk and get hitched, that was. She shuffled the papers around the stylised Japanese bowl.

'In 10 years time, Jill will be in the Guinness Book of Records for keeping the most cats.' Carol held the paper up to show the group. 'It says 147 here. The most cats in a one bedroom bedsit flat.'

'Who brought the fucking cats into this!?' Jill spat sake fumes perilously close to where Meinhoff was sat. Miles laughed nervously. The German seemed to be paying more attention to popping edamame beans into a dish.

'Never bring my darlings into this. Never.' Jill got her Flakberry out to comfort-look at a screensaver of her two precious furballs. Chatter resumed in the ranks. Miles took two fingers of an overpriced under-alcoholed bottle of Japanese lager. Kira would be pleased. Christy was sat next to Meinhoff, just out of polite conversation distance from me. Sitting on the floor kind of killed all possibilities of playing footsie under the table, forgetting the fact that I had more chance of an undead Marilyn Monroe stroking my shin with her heel this evening. I needed to up my game, raise the ante. In keeping with the theme of the evening, Christy looked like some goth geisha, with her trademark smudged black eyeliner and a hair-comb keeping her red locks held tight in a bun on her head. A single strand had slipped out down her temple suggesting she wasn't all kimono and no dragon. My concentration was broken by Trent, of all people, waving a pack of smokes under my nose. I refused with a sneer.

I had to tell her soon how I felt. When I'd come down so low in her estimation what did I have left to lose?

Bar. Change up to whisky on the rocks. Bill Murray was nursing a glass on a promotional point-of-sale. What a way to make a living.

Back at the table, Carol was rustling around for another dreamed-up destiny for Jill. We'd revert to the usual rules of conversation soon and the night would shuffle inconsequentially to its end.

'In 10 years time, Jill will be playing pimp from a caravan park to a newly-out and loving it every which way but loose Miles.'

Jill shrieked. Miles shouted something incomprehensible in everything but its profanity. Christy looked into the middle-distance. Trent remained steadfast against sniggers. Carol looked sick at the thought of paid-for anal sex. I returned to the table at just the wrong time holding a half-supped scotch. Accusing eyes turned in my direction. I'd been stitched up. I was a witch at Salem. This was the Dreyfus Affair. Miles readied himself to unleash ten shades of unholy shit my way.

'Ahh-haaa-haaa-HAA,' came a low, guttural laugh from across the table. 'Ahh-HAAA-HAAA.' Victor Meinhoff was in bits. His pork sausage fingers slapped the sleek surface as he rocked back and forth like a weevil Buddha.

'Dat ist very very funny! Miles as a gay boy, ya!!' I'm not sure he even knew what a caravan was. All the nuances were wasted. Miles turned towards him, visibly hyperventilating the anger out of his nose as if to pass a breathalyser test on a country line.

'Yes, very funny, Victor, we do enjoy a laugh here. Very funny, whoever that was.' He tried to catch my eye. No chance I was looking his way. Sucker. Seeing Miles cower in front of Meinhoff the money man was sad really, a bit like watching a once-mighty punch-drunk heavyweight champ brought to his knees by a newer, bigger, better opponent, or seeing your dad letting his boss win at rounders on the company family fun day. Not my dad, obviously, we were never invited.

I sank my scotch in victory and bounced to the bogs. It was time to turn things up to eleven. I reached into my inside breast pocket. This situation called for the blue pills. Ups. For now at least. The scotch on top of the beer had me on a cable car to the top of the mountain. It was time to scream if you wanna go faster. I'd drop two now and flatten out with a treat from the inside right pocket (reds) later. Zoom.

Things seemed clearer now.

I was aware of each and every single hair on my head.

The thought of my place in this chaotic universe made my heart beat beat beat.

Mirror.

I was a rugged terrain and the lines on my face swirled like roads to nowhere. Lost highways and aimless journeys. Wild goose chases.

Focus.

Focus.

Focus. I was Bill McDare.

I was 29 years old.

Bless me Father for I have sinned. It has been 14 years since my last confession.

Sister Gina has saved me. I'm going nowhere. In oh-so-many ways. But at least I'm not going in a box. Yet. I've a new motto for my monitor: Live fast, die old.

I pushed the tap. The water rushed out and I stooped to drink it in. I splashed the water on my face over and over.

Out damned spot.

The water stopped.

Focus.


Back at the table, a juiced-up Jill was showing the neurosis – if not the nose – for being as kosher as Kafka. She had just the right balance of self-hating social awareness to be a walking Woody Allen film, rabbiting on about this and that. To be honest, I was so high right now I'd run all out of context. Not that it stopped me. I tried to overcompensate in only the way an awareness of the ensuing edges of narcotics allows.

'I think you're the most Jewish non-Jew in this whole town… ' the pills said out loud. Everyone around the table stopped mid-move. Rice wine half-poured, wasabi and soy part-mixed.

Meinhoff looked aggressively defensive in the way only a guilt-ridden generation twice removed could.

'How dare you talk about the Jews like that,' he said, his flabby jowls flapping as he spoke.

I tried to reach for my drink as security but it seemed too distant. My elbow squished in a plate of teriyaki salmon. Trent nudged the glass towards me.

'Like what?' I finally replied.

'Like they are a stereotype.' The German was reddening. 'They are a wonderful people.'

'Not all of them.'

'How dare you!'

'Surely it's your answer that's stereotyping them. No one race can be all wonderful.' These pills had turned me into a contrary Sixth-form debating captain.

He really was mad now.

'The Jews are a talented and varied people!'

'Well, why did your grandad kill six million of the poor fuckers then?'

Meinhoff was verging on tears now. He didn't scare me as much as Miles though. He looked really angry. I'd only ever seen his eyes bulge this much when he had blatantly been at the beak that night we won the Walker pitch. But his face looked much happier then.

'Bill, get the fuck out of here,' Miles was a Ken doll no more. He was G. I. Joe on anabolic steroids and I was an infidel. Shock and awe.

'NOW.'

This was a bad trip.

Back to the toilets. Time for the right breast pocket.

There was a knock on the cubicle door.

'Bill…'

I knew that voice.

'Bill… are you in there?'

Christy. I swallowed two of the red pills.

'Bill, open up.' She was knocking now.

'Just a minute…' I popped another for luck and unbolted the door.

'Bill,' she repeated my name again, 'what are you doing?'

Her eyes were big and round, her tone: disappointed school teacher.

'Well, I'm not sure I can share what goes on in a male toilet with you. Why are you in a male toilet?'

'I was worried about you.'

'You don't need to worry about me.'

'If you keep pissing off Miles like that…'

'Chris…'

'…not to mention Meinhoff…'

'Chris…'

'…they'll fire you in a second if you keep on like this…'

'Chris…' She'd been ignoring me for the past 2 minutes.

'What, Bill?'

'I…'

'Yes…'

'I…'

'Yes…'

'I really really…'

'Yes…'

'Really really…' Like you, say LIKE YOU.

'Yes…'

'Huuuu-huuuu-speeeeewwwww'

And with that I threw up all over her kimono.


'Surprise!'

While Christy was cleaning bile off her blouse, back at the table Pete had burst through a Japanese screen door carrying a birthday

121

cake with forty candles. He'd missed the meeting where Jill had barked her invite, and Trent had tricked him into thinking the party was fancy dress. Musical themed. Miles and Meinhoff looked at his army uniform in bewilderment. It wasn't a good moment to come as Captain Von Trapp.

# Chapter 15

It was the sound of the letterbox that stirred me. The mail addressed to number 35 was of the depressing post-email kind: *Dine Like a King At The Taj Mahal s All-You-Can-Eat Banquet; Dear Occupant, Did You Know You re Entitled To a 10k Loan?; For the Urgent Attention Of: Mr McDare, This Is Your 3rd Reminder, Please Pay Up Immediately.* No cheques from emigrated aunts or letters from love-lorn sweethearts stationed on the other side of the country. I had bigger fish to get fried by.

I was lying in a pool of my own urine on the sofa of the front room. My suit trousers were splayed on the floor. I gave myself the benefit of the doubt for now and put the brown stains down as mud. I could see only one shoe. My pubic hair had gathered out of the top of my boxer shorts. It was clumped together with ash, or dandruff. Could you even get pubic dandruff? Hmm. My head felt like it had hosted an illegal rave and someone had forgotten to turn the sound system off. Even the surrounding pizza boxes had turned their crusts up at me. A disapproving post-it note from either Craig or Connie was stuck to the television.

I'd pissed my boss off.

I'd pissed our main investor off.

I'd pissed Christy off.

I'd pissed my pants.

In a lifetime of lows, this was a new depth plunged.

And then, out of the corner of my eye, I saw something.

It was the ginger cat.

Hanging from a broken branch.

'Hang On In There,' the bubble written caption on the poster said.

Hang on in there.

Where had I heard that before?

Sister Gina. She'd said it to me. Over and over.

HANG ON IN THERE.

So I would.

# Chapter 16

'Can I get anyone a cuppa?'

Jill spun around her chair and shot me a look seen on faces the world over at moments of unforgettable social importance: the moon landings, the Kennedy assassination, the moment the plane hit the first tower, the day Bill McDare offered to make a round of hot beverages. Cultural flagstones one and all.

'What the fuck are you after?' she said.

'Oh, I don't know: friendship, camaraderie, a sense of togetherness, maybe one in return in an hour or so…'

'But, Bill, you never make tea. NEVER.'

'Well, there's going to be a few changes around here.'

Jill looked at me with equal parts surprise and suspicion.

'Okay, not too much milk.' I trotted to the kitchen and set about my task.

If I had to pick a location for a road to Damascus moment, I'm not sure a blim-burned, piss-drenched sofa would have been in the top three but beggars can't be choosers. Not that I was begging for change. I was quite happy to drink myself silly and be a bit, well, cunty, but when, as now, it threatened my ever being able to (a) work in this town again or (b) have sex with someone whose name I remembered, then things had to come to a head.

I thought long and hard about adding a nip of scotch to my tea.

I needed to pull myself together. What did my generation have to be fucked up about? No scurvy or black plague, no offwiththeirhead monarchs, no World War, no watching yourbuddydiefacedowninthedirt of a tropical jungle. Not even the credit crunch made a difference – we still ran at 100 mph, we just greased the gas differently. Our problem was superfluidity. Cars, communications, TV stations, shoes, socks, drinks, drugs, dicks, cunts. And my problem was: which one or how much?

Well, boo hoo.

Take Christy for example: a dead mother, a boozy absent father, a mother by proxy to a bed-wetting brother in her teens. And did she complain or kill herself with lifestyle choices? Did she fuck. I'd woken up with a start this morning, a dream, or a flashback, running through my mind. It was Christy. She was saying she needed her dad. Sometimes. Not always, but sometimes. She had tears in her big black eyes. Had this happened? Was this Friday? It was hard to know what was real after weekends on the wild side.

I sipped my scotch-free tea and mulled over the next steps. What this sea change needed was a charter to avoid deviation to the old ways. I went back to my desk. It was lunchtime now, the office plate emptying with errand runners and errant lovers off into the outside to scratch their itch until it was nose back to the bullshit time. I thought about the boys outside the building, with their premium strength booze and low rent conversation…

…they'd have to wait for a tale of valour from a balaclava-clad Gulf vet. I opened the word processor, clicked 'New Document' and started to type.

This would be my Ten Commandments. This was my Mount Sinai. I knew this Catholic education would come in useful for something.

1.  Thou should probably not piss off the boss for sport, belittle colleagues because they wear tank tops and enjoy the

countryside, or amble aimlessly towards middle management without an ambitious career goal.[1]

2. Thou shalt not be drunk on whisky, wine and mouthwash during work, the walk to work, the walk home from work, the waking hours.

3. Thou shalt not increase uptake of uppers, downers, screamers and/or laughers to compensate for aforementioned lack of alcohol or otherwise.

4. Thou should most probably take notice of Dr Linda Taylor and the intricacies of her Wellness Health Check (and not just because she was a knockout[2]), particularly giving up smoking.

5. Thou should stop littering each and every sentence with words including, but not exclusive of, shit, fuck, cuntface, bugger, arsewipe, dickwad, knob-cheese and shitfuckarse bollocksssssssssssssssssssssssssssssssssssssssssssssssssssss.

My concentration was broken by a loud, repetitive shriek reminiscent of an orgasmic seagull.

'Tea… tea… do you want a tea?'

'What?

'Tea…?'

It was Jill repaying the favour.

'Erm, yeah. Go on. Yeah. Milk no…'

'I know.'

I'm sure Moses never had to put up with this.

Right, back to the redemption.

6. Thou should visit thy mother more often than on days designated special by greetings card companies and should recognise, if not celebrate, the happiness she seems to receive from that wrinkly wanker[3] Barry.

7. Thou shalt aspire to have thy own four walls and to live in quarters that do not feature an *al fresco* bathroom experience.[4]

8. Thou shalt stop being such a cynical bastard.[5]
9. Thou should try and engage with the local community and help the downtrodden, in more ways than being a drinking partner to the socially delinquent.
10. Thou should try and find unselfish love.

I felt so worthy I wanted to throw up.

PING. The email window popped up in the bottom right of my screen.

---

From: carol.cleary@morgan&schwarz.com
To: all@morgan&schwarz.com
Subject: Give-a-garment

---

Dear all,

As many of you know, not that I like to boast, every Tuesday I help out at the SoupMobile Station in the centre of the city. I'm sure I don't have to tell people as kind as you that it's a great cause and we really do try and 'make a difference' to homeless and hungry people across our city.

Now it's been a while since I last asked you all, but I would really appreciate it if you could have a root around your wardrobes for any old clothes you may have to donate. You know, the kind you don't wear anymore but are in perfectly good nick.

Any jeans, jumpers, joggers or jodphurs (well, perhaps they won't quite be horse riding just yet!!!) you find on your de-clutter will be gratefully received and will go to a good home.

Having seen the gladrags you all wore on Friday night I'm just certain you'll all have some of last season's clothes to give to someone who needs them more.

A point to remember is all donations must be clean and useable. Would appreciate any donations in by next week, before the weather turns too cold.

Many thanks,
Carol

---

From: bill.mcdare@morgan&schwarz.com
To: carol.cleary@morgan&schwarz.com
Subject: Re: Give-a-garment

---

Carol,

Have just written a reminder on my hand. In pen. Now if I don't shower in the morning, you'll know. My very own scarlet letter. I don't suppose you could do with a hand next Tuesday? At the Soup Station or whatever it's called. There'll probably be a lot of stuff for you to carry over and I don't mind hanging around and helping out.

Or not. Wouldn't want to get in the way.

Either way, let me know.
Bill

From: carol.cleary@morgan&schwarz.com
To: bill.mcdare@morgan&schwarz.com
Subject: Re: Give-a-garment

Bill,

That's really very kind of you and I must say, really very unexpected.

I didn't really think it'd be your kind of 'scene' if that's what people are saying these days! I'm sure I'll be fine with the clothes bags – Miles has very nicely agreed to my use of the pool car to ferry the donations across the city – but we could always do with an extra pair of hands at the SoupMobile. It can get quite hectic!

Would love to have you on the team if you really mean it?!?

Many thanks,
Carol

From: bill.mcdare@morgan&schwarz.com
To: carol.cleary@morgan&schwarz.com
Subject: Re: Give-a-garment

Carol,

I do mean it.

You could say I'm having a bit of a clear out myself, and not just of my wardrobes.
Looking forward to it,
Bill

PS Oh, and Carol, would appreciate it if you kept this to yourself. Don't really want the rest of the office knowing. You know what they're like.

From: peter.white@morgan&schwarz.com
To: all@morgan&schwarz.com
Subject: Re: Give-a-garment

Hi Carol,
Sounds like a great idea!
Sure I can dig out some old clobber for your charity.
Just one thing though… you said the clothes will go to a 'good home'…
Aren't they all HOMELESS?
;)
Pete

The trouble with moments of clarity was that the lucidity of your new situation hit you straight between the eyes. And getting hit straight between the eyes hurt like a motherfucker. I was, if not yet killing my babies of hooch, hits and whores, then making the first step towards a pre-meditated smothering. In the court case of McDare v Vice, today would be used as damning evidence against me. If it ever got to that. It would. It would. It would. It would. It would. It would. It would. It would. It would. (The theory of repetition posits that even the best students needed eight repetitions to commit an idea to memory).

It would.

# Chapter 17

'So, in a nutshell that's what the SoupMobile Station is all about. Remember, folks, we're giving these guys and gals a 'hand up' not a 'hand out'. There's a big difference. Now let's go make a difference!'

I was stood in a small, damp Portakabin with five or six other 'enablers'. I hadn't taken in a word that had been said for the last twenty minutes. An attempt at rousing had been made by a youngish man by the name of Nick. Behind his beads and sparse post-pubescent beard hid a face, a demeanour, an accent of privilege. I could see it now: the youngest son of the Earl of Bucklebury. When the family entertained, as it often did, he'd always slipped away into the grounds with a handkerchief full of canapes for the gardener before returning to the grand hall and drawing rolled eyes from mother for his muddied soles. After fagging for a singularly brutal master at school he refused his own boy and ended up being bullied by the seniors for his stand. He'd spent summers volunteering for Médecins Sans Frontières in the Democratic Republic of Congo, using the impeccable French he'd learnt from his Parisian au pair to provide logistical support in field hospitals. It was here that he met his first real life black person. And now this. Serving watered down minestrone and on-the-turn bread rolls to miscreants. It made him feel warm inside. His parents, the Earl and Countess, disapproved. This was his adolescent rebellion. The SoupMobile Station his teenage tattoo. Mummy and Daddy were mortified. Why couldn't he be a banker or a barrister like the other children? Bleeding heart liberals were the worst fucking kind. I made a mental note to stop these thought patterns. Nearly three decades of cynicism through the synapses was hard to stop overnight.

'Oh, and before you skip to the beat, there is one last thing everybody. We have had a few reports of over-familiarity with our female enablers from some of the diners. I've got to stress, guys, that these are isolated incidents. Let's keep on keeping on, yeah? Now get out there and spread the love!'

Carol visibly shrunk into her Berghaus like a fleeced turtle. I couldn't help thinking Nick had chosen the wrong call to action to send us out shovelling soup to sozzled sex pests. At least I'd know the audience.

We filed out of the temporary hut, modern day Nightingales against the urban darkness and all its broken baggage. The SoupMobile Station was situated behind one of the shopping district's many department stores. By daylight, thousands upon thousands of desensitised dummies traipsed the concrete paths, driven by the desire for designer names, digital goods and deep fried doughnuts. Water features and plastic trees made them feel calm. Shops had become the new cathedrals. In 2436, East Asian tourists would be snap-happy outside the remains of an Abercrombie and Fitch, while futuristic hustlers, dressed up in plastic six-packs and prep wear, vied for their space dollars.

It was a different story at dusk. While the shoppers and store workers swarmed out to the suburbs to play with their new answer to life's problems, the underfed underbelly came out of the corners to pick on the bones of the day's trade. Half-bitten burgers, dropped purses, binned receipts ready to become part of a return scam: the cyclical nature of the shopping centre's eco-system would have pleased even the world's best botanist. But there were only ever so many bones to go around. Which was where the SoupMobile Station came in. A twice-weekly drop-in dispensary offering the feral food, first aid and a sense of family. All paid for by the commercial property fund behind the retail outlets. A raging corporate social responsibility hard-on, written off against tax. It had been Miles' idea and we'd all kicked ourselves when he had it. Why didn't we come up with that? That's why he was the boss, we'd supposed. It had opened three years ago in a blaze of back-patting publicity. Morgan & Schwarz even arranged for the social justice minister to serve the first soup for a photo opportunity. '*Make sure the tramp is black,* said the brief.

Problem was, the bottom had fallen out of the commercial property game since the recession. The fund was pulling out and the place was going to close down. No more free soup for the smackheads. Time to get there before it closed. In fuck knows how many years of working for Morgan & Schwarz, tonight was the first time I'd ever gone near the place. The first thing that hit me was the smell. It reeked of piss and pea and ham soup. Sure, I was used to hanging out with society's scrotum scratchers, but always in an altered state of consciousness. Smelling the city through a sober nose was, well, sobering.


'So this is your first time here, isn't it? I don't believe I've seen you before.' I was being addressed by a ruddy septagerian dressed in entirely in tweed.

'Yes, yes it is. You could say I was a volunteer virgin.' Fucking hell, I was turning into Pete. Carol blushed at the subverted sexual side to my response and moved things along.

'Derek, this is Bill. Bill's a colleague of mine.'

Derek's sunken eyes lit up.

'Another truth-bender are you, son? Ahaaa, ha ha...' The laugh emanated from deep inside his overhanging belly and he playfully punched me in the arm. Every sinew of my soul wanted to punch him in the face. My fists clenched. Remember the rules, Billy boy. Moses wouldn't deck a red-faced pensioner, would he? Moses was a red-faced pensioner. I took a deep breath, or as deep a breath as my laconic lungs would allow.

'Something like that, Derek. Right, let's go and save the world, shall we?'

'Bill, Bill, Bill…?' Derek was shaking me by the shoulder.

'Uhhh….'

'We run a clean ship here, Bill, you hear me? We wash up as we go and we wipe down soup splats as and when. You with me?'

'Uhhh… I'm sorry Derek. I kind of drifted off a little there.' In the short period I'd been off the hooch, this had been happening a bit. Hallucinatory holidays to the inner depths of the imagination. If the booze couldn't give me a break from reality, then it seemed my brain would.

'Their ETA is in approximately 30 minutes so we need to man our stations. You know what they say: fail to prepare, prepare to fail.'

'Right.'

Derek's air of order and pomposity clearly marked him out as an ex-military man. Never a private elbow deep in the mud and the blood of the trenches, but a paperwork man, a second signatory, a minute taker and motion-passed man. His small eyes looked at me with a sympathy usually reserved for retards.

'First things first, time to don the appropriate attire.'

'You wouldn't want to get broth on your tweed would you?' My attempt at humour was ignored.

'Certainly not. Here…' He handed me a white apron, a plastic hair net and some blue gloves. I put them on very slowly.

I forced a smile through gritted teeth.

'Start buttering the rolls, will you?'

'Got it.' I located a value pack of 100 white rolls and an industrial-sized tub of margarine.

'Do about forty to start with. That should be sufficient. The rest can be done as and when.'

'Sure.'

I lost myself for a few minutes in the reassuring monotony of the task. Cut, spread, fold, cut, spread, fold. And repeat. Disappointed faces danced through my mind: Mum, Miles, Carol, Connie, Craig, Dr Taylor, Pete, Barry, the German, my Dad, Christy.

Christy.

I needed to – to borrow a phrase from that twat Nick – 'turn those frowns upside down'. And not just through the old friend of self-deprecation. Because where did that get you in the end? Where did anything get you? How did my particular set of circumstances throw me here, to a fucking soup kitchen with a retired bastard brigadier? Satan moved in mysterious ways.

A bell rang an overly jolly chime and the hungry hordes started swarming in.

'Right, Bill,' he was barking at me now, 'remember what I said; two scoops of soup into the pot, and one roll. We're very clear on that. Just one roll. Remember.' I didn't remember he'd said this before but perhaps I'd blocked out his huff and bluster. Two scoops, one roll. I could cope with that.

Carol had directed the manky mass into an orderly queue with relative ease and an unfussy efficiency. The bums seemed to move as one whole bearded, tracksuited organism. The supplicating nature of the needy addicts was instantly evident. Whether the hit was methadone or minestrone, it didn't matter. What mattered was that it was coming and things would be better, if only for a while. There were probably about forty or fifty of them in total, mostly male, mostly white, of indistinguishable age and undeniable sadness. They passed through the SoupMobile Station quietly, with eyes averted and thank yous mumbled.

I quickly got into the menial monotony of meal-time. Two scoops, one roll, serve. Two scoops, one roll, serve. And repeat. In another life, I reckon I could well have been happy as a fast food operative. In the new, cold, sober light of day, it seemed somehow more noble than pedalling propaganda for pay. Didn't it? Of course, I'd expect to start on the bottom rung of the ladder, learning the till keys, the knack to salting the French fries, the secret to the perfect shake, the leading questions to ask to tempt the customer to super size. *My name is Bill. How can I help you today?* I'd relish the opportunity to expand my horizons by working alongside minority ethnics. Every day could be a cultural exchange. In a matter of months, I'd be eyeing up the next star on my badge. In the fast food world, first you get the supervisor role, then you get the pussy. There'd be a husky-voiced hussy on the drive-thru. A one-GCSEd goer. I'd lean on the boss to give her a rota which fitted in around childcare arrangements. Let her listen to commercial radio stations in the staff room. Our hands would touch as I dropped BBQ sauce in her brown bag. We'd both know what she really wanted.

'What have you got today? Not that horrible muck we had last week, is it? I bleeding hope not.' My mental meandering had been stopped short again, but this time by what could best be described as a fathoming homeless.

'Erm, well I wasn't here last week but I'm assuming there's some menu rotation…'

He sneered back at me. Some snot dribbled out of his nose and swam through the patchy bristles on his red face. His tongue poked out, lizard-like, to taste the treasure. Perhaps a life of food servitude wouldn't have been all that.

'What's going on over here then, chaps?' The brigadier had smelt blood and left his station to investigate and be a patronising band-aid.

'Well, this gentlemen here was wondering what the choice was tonight...' I said.

'Was he now? What we have tonight, as we do every night the SoupMobile Station is in operation, are foods that are rich in the essential vitamins and minerals these young boys and girls need. You don't need me to tell you it's tough out there on the streets,' he paused at this point and looked me in the eye, 'or maybe you do, but our emphasis is nourishing the mind, body and soul for the long, cold, lonely nights.'

'But what fucking food have you got?' the hungry one piped up.

'Manners, young man, manners cost nothing. Just like this food to you. We have a tomato soup. A food stuff rich in vitamin C, essential to ward off scurvy and the like. Not to mention some brown rolls over there for a good bit of roughage.'

'But I hate tomatoes.' He was at it again. Derek tightened up like a school teacher about to hand out a beating to his favourite repugnant punch-bug.

'It is not about what you LIKE, my dear boy, but about what your body LIKES. Do you understand?'

'What about if you liven it up with a bit of seasoning, you know, spice it up with some pepper?' I somehow felt it was my turn to step in and mediate. The NATO of the SoupMobile Station. Fucking hell, it felt a change to be the least fucked up person in the argument.

'There is no pepper, Bill. No salt, no pepper, just vitamin-enriched healthy soup,' said Derek.

'Christ, I know they're homeless, but they're not animals. I'm going for a fag break...'

'You don't get "fag breaks" here, Bill.' Derek did inverted commas in the air with his wiry fingers.

'Well, I'm not being paid, am I?'

'No…'

'So then I'm taking a cigarette break. Thanks very much and I'll see you in 10 minutes.' A collective groan came up from the remaining queue. I undid the apron, threw the gloves on the floor and stormed out of there. Derek gave me a 'You've won the battle but not the war' kind of look. Fuck you, Derek, this'll be your Bay of Pigs.

I stepped off the SoupMobile Station, reached into my pocket and realised I didn't smoke anymore.

Fuck you, Rule Number 4.

Ah, one wouldn't hurt, would it?

Baby steps, Bill, baby steps.

Outside the safe confines of the ex-burger van I felt a little like a honeymooner who'd escaped the security of a shark cage midway through a 14-day break in Sharm El Shiekh, figuring that now everyone had enjoyed the big day, getting out early was better than a lifetime of limp sex and white lies. The scene before me was an uneasy mix of feeding time at the zoo and mid-morning break at a special school. Now, where was the damaged kid with the cigarettes? Looking around you'd have to say it could have been any of them. I picked out my benefactor, got ready to drop my aitches and approached for a nicotine hit.

'Why should I?' Christ, I'd picked an existentialist.

'Out of the milk of human kindness?'

'I ain't got none of that, mate.'

'Because I've just served you some soup?'

'If it wasn't you it would have been someone else…' Although relatively minor, the decision to negotiate with this particular bum looked like the latest in a long line of bad decisions.

'Okay, it's like that, is it? Well how's about this, pal? It was my idea to set this place up over three years ago to help people like you get some hot food in their stomachs. Surely that's got to be worth a smoke?' Okay, I'd used some artistic licence. And the kitchen was technically on its way out. But nicotine was on the line here.

'You set this place up?' He emphasised his first word a little too much.

'Yes.'

'Personally?'

'It was my idea.'

'So why have I never seen you here before then?'

'I'm more of a behind the scenes kind of guy.'

'So what's this then? *Undercover Boss*?'

'How do you even know TV programmes? You're homeless.'

'Don't judge me just because I'm taking your handouts. I'm a lot smarter than you think.'

'Right…'

'You know who else set up a soup kitchen? Al Capone, that's who.' Fucking hell, I was arguing with some trivia tramp for a cigarette. Not drugs. A CIGARETTE. We picked our own battles, I suppose.

'Right, here's a fiver. Give me one NOW.' His face lit up. Well as much as it could for a man who shat in a department storey doorway.

'There…' He passed me a soggy box.

'My brand too.'

Victory.

Light.

Inhale.

What I'd have given for the hit to be harder than a Golden Virginia.

My head rushed and thoughts followed. I'd spent far too much time with this city's underclass for a man that pulled a wage that could have put the Brady Bunch through college. Sure, you could buy drugs from flash wheeler-dealers or other bored executives, but moving amongst the street people offered an anonymity appealing to someone prone to blackouts and the black dog. Too many times doing too much coke with alcoholics in alleyways. But tramps couldn't afford beak and beak wasn't brown. We'd all always known this. Our little secret.

'Right everybody, grab-a-garment will be starting in a few minutes over by the First Aid station. Be sure to get some warm clothes, guys and gals, Jack Frost is going to be out in force over the coming weeks.' Nick projected like an over-friendly politician desperate for your cross in his box. The bums sprung to life, albeit a low level one, the sound of rustling shell suits, wheezing lungs and petty squabbling bouncing back off the tarpaulin roof.

I was suddenly flung forward by an unexpected force from behind. My hands reached out to soften my fall and took the bulk of the blow. Blood gushed from my grazed palms and brought tears to my eyes, visions of playgrounds past flashing through my mind.

'Get up, man. You shouldn't have been leaning against the bloody door to the Station, should you? Ridiculous place to rest yourself.'

Derek.

Fucking Derek.

A few stopped their rush to the hobo Harrods sale and gathered around me. I pulled myself to my feet and felt a calmness come over me. I rocked onto my right foot and directed a left hook at Derek's ruddy right cheek.

All 200 pounds of the 60-plus retired military man and part-time volunteer hit the deck. I think punching a senior citizen probably outweighed the good karma I'd earned from my earlier contribution this evening. Yin and yang. Ringside let out a demented yelp. The others had now swelled the Madison Square Concrete crowd. Before I knew it I was lifted onto shoulders. I was the Rocky of the Reprobates. The Sugar Ray of the Underpaid. As they spun me around, faces flashed by. Nick – angry, Carol – stunned, the bums – toothless and happy. Then I saw him. The one from outside the office. The one with the sad, ravaged eyes. The one who looked like he'd once known life. The one who looked like he knew me.

The spinning began to make me feel sick. I got down and ran all the way home.

# Chapter 18

Ring, ring, rrrrrrrrrrrrring.

I reached through the darkness for the Flakberry. The yellow backlight showed a withheld number. Pre-revelation I'd have never answered a call like this. A random signal bounced to my cell by a satellite thousands of miles from my bed which could only lead to threats or regret. Time to face the world head on though, William. I pressed the green button. A voice sang down the line.

'The Candyman can....'

'What?'

'...cos he mixes it with love and makes the world taste good...'

'Who the fuck is this?'

'Billy boy, no need for such coarse language. Where have you been all this time? We've missed you. We've got some new stuff in. I'm calling it the Economy Seven. It'll keep you going all night for fuck all.' It was one of my old dealers. No, one of my ex-dealers.

'I've lost my sweet tooth.'

I hung up and switched the phone off. I rolled over. My bedroom was hot. And not Swedish-blonde hot. More Turkish prison hot. I'd tossed and turned and turned and tossed each and every night since I'd been on the wagon. My sleep for the past forever had been sponsored by stimulants and I'd always passed off into the land of lucid dreams drunk and dying on the inside. But asleep. Always asleep. I'd forgotten what it was to drop off as I was constantly drugged up. It felt like learning to ride a bike again. A really rusty piece of shit bike with no saddle and handlebars made of broken glass. The thoughts that pinballed through my mind when the light went out ranged from the insightful to the banal: from Christy to a contemplation on the rights and wrongs of my parents' divorce to a Madonna lyric. Fucking Madonna.

My bed felt like I'd pissed it. Now, it wasn't like I was a stranger to waking up in my own juices. The unfortunate by-product of a boozer's lifestyle was – how do I put it? – that sometimes the tap was left running when the bath was already full. The worst incidents come when in company. The man who can retain a shred of dignity after his dick showered the satin when with a sleeping ladyfriend is a more diplomatic one than I. While those days could be behind me, the alternative wasn't much better. I hoped it was an interim state of affairs. Sobriety had so far been characterised by sweating. Heavily. Suspiciously. Caught out by nature's flushing away of the things I took to fuck myself up. A walk into the office would be rewarded with fresh, damp, ominous patches like moody cumulous under the arms of a button down collar Oxford blue shirt. The anti-perspirant applied an hour previously was rendered redundant, the field test biting its thumb at the scientifically proven stamp of approval positioned by pay-rolled physicians in column inches secured by the consumer team in aspirational men's lifestyle magazines. Whether selling in a story to a hardnosed hack, dispensing of a high protein low carb lunch at an overpriced eatery, or sat in my pants mulling over which direction to take the evening's online erotic voyage, an ever-present bead of sweat sat on my temple. You'd have seen cooler paedos at a Boy Scouts' parade. This corporeal detoxification gave the outward impression I had something to hide, at the one time in my life when I actually didn't. It was worst at night. If you could have bottled the stuff up and sold it then you'd have had a distillation of dangerous fucking proportions.

I rolled over to try and find a dry patch. No dice. I was an obese man in a broken down sauna. Dressed in black. In the middle of the Serengeti. There was a light tap on the door. Someone was trying to get in.

'Bill… Bill… are you in there?'

I grunted affirmative, a tea deficit doing for my vocal chords.

It was Connie's squeaky voice. I cleared my throat. A hard phlegm lodged itself behind the teeth on my lower jaw.

'Would you like a cuppa?'

'Yes please, that would be lovely.' I fought the urge to be pedantic about the brewing process. Christ, I had changed.

'Should I make two cups?' she threw into the air.

'What…? Oh, I got you. No, no need. I'm home alone.' She squeaked a rodenty laugh.

'Thought it was best to check, hey?!'

I faked a laugh. I was awful at faking laughter. Daytime-Soap awful.

'What time did you get in last night? You must have been as quiet as a mouse. We didn't hear a thing.'

'I, erm, didn't. Go out to come back in I mean. I came home straight from work and went straight to bed.'

'Jesus, Bill. Are you feeling alright?'

'Well, yeah, I suppose…'

'Well the ravens truly have left the tower. Bill McDare tucked up early on a weeknight… stranger things have happened at sea I suppose.'

Connie poked her head around the ajar door.

'Tea and toast for one coming up!'


I must have drifted off because I awoke to a lukewarm tea and cold toast on the bedside cabinet. It was hard to work out if this was the dream or the wake. Lines blurred. I needed caffeine, at the very least. Disregarding my usual fascism against nonscalding drinks I held onto the cup and tried to take in its restorative brew. Emphasis on tried. My hand shook and spilt the tea all over the bed. Twitches and tremors were becoming increasingly commonplace. It's not like the bed was dry anyway. I was unaware of the time. It seemed less on my side, as underneath me, all around me and on top of me. Now I wasn't drinking, I had so much of it. The daily struggle had become not how to hide the hops on my breath but how to fill time interestingly enough to banish thoughts of the bottle to the back of my head. Everyday tasks were stretched to fit a diary window with no Outlook alarm to signal its end. The brushing of teeth had become a multi-layered and methodical task, ticking off ten rotations prior to moving onto the neighbouring incisor, avoiding the bitter alcoholic mouthwash like never before.

Mornings no longer meant hangovers and racing against the clock to avoid a bollocking from Miles, but wide awakenings, updates on the Flakberry's 4G and broadcast bulletins. I'd never been more over the news agenda. 24 hours, online, offline, blogs, microblogs, tweets, tumblrs, radio debates, morning briefings: give or take the odd serial killer or presidential pardon, it was a blurge of soon-to-be forgotten information. Tomorrow's chip paper didn't half fill cold turkey. I could spend forever following headlines and hashtags, which was useful, as without having the booze and blow to lean on, forever was what I had. My personal professional stock, which had previously been strained through a sock, was done no harm by my new found awareness. I'd alert clients to upcoming governmental economic announcements on which to piggyback news of jobs growth. I'd flag up the latest environmental disaster to colleagues – be it an oil slick the size of Wales off the Cape of Good Hope or a melting ice sheet in Greenland – so they could align their strategy with the corporate social responsibility cause célèbre de jour. My finger *was* the fucking pulse.

Speaking of pulses, my room looked like it had one. The half full cups, scattered shirts, crumpled clothes and greasy pizza boxes gave the ten by eight shoebox a beating heart, a warm, damp haven where civilisations of cultures were born, lived and evolved. The people of the green moss in a Cup-a-Soup left to dwell on the dresser had reached their Iron Age and recently started worshipping false gods. It was time for a tidy, a spring-clean regardless of the season. What I needed to do was first step back, move from the microcosm to the macrocosm and strategise. A Gannt chart with each and every constituent task broken down into rows and columns of collective time-killing. Being sober was fucking dull.

I was midway through allocating a traffic light system to the stinking sundries of the room when it happened. No, not (another) spiritual awakening or a eureka moment when the answer to the world's energy crisis suddenly illuminated my grey matter, but a violent, post-ominous bowel movement. I needed to unload, and now. Poo had become a protagonist of my alcohol-free life, elevated from basic human need to overriding raison d'etre. At least now I was at home, well, as at home as number 35 could ever be. Close to the reassuring porcelain. This hadn't always been the state of affairs. The worst incident had happened during a beauty parade for a new washing detergent. The potential client was a dour, Presbyterian Scot, who looked like she'd last smiled during a bout of unexpected childhood flatulence. She had a sharp black bob which the dark wrinkles under her eyes told was dyed regularly and efficiently. The air conditioning in the small rectangular boardroom was broken, or being conserved, leaving the smell of latent booze sweating out of my system to battle with the stench of bleach for scent superiority. The ammonia needn't have bothered. Miles was a third of the way through the PowerPoint slides when I'd tried to eke out a non-squeaky fart. My stomach had been performing somersaults more fitting to a circus with a poor safety record. First I had felt the release then the relief, before the realisation. Someone or something had let the safety off my trump trigger. I was damp and an unsettling aroma of inner decay unleashed itself around a room hitherto rapt by Miles' deconstruction of brand loyalty to FMCG (Fast Moving Consumer Goods for the acronym illiterate) in the Baby Boom generation. It was imperative I remained steadfast. Emotionless. Kept a straight face. What this situation called for was a good old-fashioned stiff upper lip. The sweep it under the carpet, say nothing, do nothing and be content, if only outwardly, in your ignorance approach. Hopefully, the rest of the room would fall into line, repressing the urge to speak up deep down inside them so it could well up for 30 years before exploding into a brain tumour or a cardiac arrest on a golf course in the Mendips on a pleasant autumn morning. There was ALWAYS a payback.

I searched their faces: I'd already become 'the guy who fucked off our German sugar daddy'. I didn't want to become 'the guy who shit his pants in a pitch'. Miles was far too professional to let something as small as the smell of fresh human excrement put him off when there was money to be made. The dour Scot looked aggrieved but it was becoming apparent this was perhaps her default setting. I was scared to move an inch in my seat, lest a squelch come from my direction. Unfortunately, the other Morgan & Schwarzer on the ticket that day was the one least likely to stick to social niceties: Jill. Her nose twitched like the broad from Bewitched.

'What *is* that?' Miles stopped his spiel short. The Scot looked aggrieved.

'What is that smell? It is putrid!' Nostrils flared accusatory flares. Fuck.

'Ewwwwww.'

Come on, Bill.

149

'It's… it's… it's… my new cologne!' I shouted with nervous pride. I kicked Jill under the table. She looked at me with the usual vitriol, but kept it zipped. The pitch was her lead and she wasn't about to give up a shot at the new biz bonus – 15 per cent of the fee in the first three months – that easily.

Miles broke the silence.

'Well, Bill, I think you need a new brand.' And with that, a smile broke out in the corners of the dour Scot's mouth.

On the way out I made my excuses and used the facilities. I stuffed my heavy Jockeys in the bathroom bin. Needless to say, we didn't win the beauty parade. This was a kick in the balls. I could have done with the free detergent.

Back to the now, I sped the shackles of my time-killing tidy regime and hit the pan. When I went it was akin to opening the doors of a Wetherspoons to the town drunks at 10 a.m. and seeing them burst through before laying around the edges, lifeless and stinking.

It's fair to say the relentless urge to empty your bowels was one of the more awkward withdrawal symptoms from the sauce. Thanks in no small part to the hole through to the ground floor, it was easy to hear upstairs, downstairs. A key was slipped into the lock, found its grooves and turned the door open. The draught excluder made a brushing sound as it swept over the accumulated freesheet newspapers and take-away menus.

Craig.

'Helloooooo…? Craig, Craig darling, are you in…?' And then, as an afterthought, 'Bill…?'

'Yeah… I'm upstairs.'

'Oh, hello stranger!' Connie shouted up.

But how could Connie shout up? How could she have just come in? She'd made me a cuppa less than an hour ago. Hadn't she? We'd had a conversation. Or had we? Had it really happened? Or had it all been a dream? This wasn't what drug hallucinations were like. They were full of pink elephants, two-headed leprechauns and cats with nine tails and no lives – not hot-drink-wielding housemates. Whatever was going on in this tiny little brain of mine with its blown-out, slowed down synapses, I didn't fucking like it. I strained to shit the last of the goodness out of me when a sudden wave of nausea swam from the pit of my stomach through my body and out of my mouth in the form of a vegetable soup (extra carrot). My aim was directly over the hole in the floor. The mush hurtled through the air, between the floorboards, down into the kitchen. Oh dear.

'EUUUUGH…!! BILL…!!! BILL?!'

Oh dear.

Connie appeared at the hole holding a wok equally proportioned with yet-to-be-cooked and regurgitated vegetables.

I looked down.

# Chapter 19

Oh dear.

'Here you go, my little man. Milk no sugar, just how you like it.'

My mum was fussing.

'We've got some biscuits in too if you fancy a dunk, Bill?'

'No thank you, Barry.'

'All the more for me then…' Barry leapt off the breakfast bar stool towards my mother, resplendent in a pair of tight black leather pants, '…give us the tin, ya sexpot, you.'

If I hadn't recently spewed my guts up everywhere, the behaviour of the wrinkly rocker my mum was married to would have released a vom-nado. The sight of the leather tightening around his crotch when he engaged in horseplay would have turned Cool Hand Luke's stomach. I just had nothing left to give. No goodness left inside me. Hence, the scene of post-modern domesticity you've happened upon. After sickgate I'd decided that it was best for me to lay low from number 35 for a while. Give Craig and Connie some quality time. Let the spew settle. As embarrassing as it was for a 29-year-old man to ask his mother if he could spend a few days of R & R in the guest bedroom, it was what the current situation called for. The cap in hand actions were entirely necessary for the current state of affairs. And anyway, my dead dad practically owned half of this aspirational, class-climbing, bricks and mortified toy house. Barry, frankly, could get fucked. Which, thanks to the paper-thin walls favoured by the building trade post-millennium, was something I had to pipe loud post-rock music into my ears to avoid hearing, and subsequently being sick, and then being stuck in a vicious circle worthy of a suicide attempt. But the plus sides included three hot meals a day, a 52 inch LCD screen television and quilted toilet paper. I'd told my mum I'd been feeling rundown after working myself too hard on a project to change public opinion about an incinerator planned for construction on a popular playing field. She got confused every time I spoke about work. The perfect smokescreen.

'That's nice, dear,' she'd say with a baffled look on her face. 'Now what can I fix you to eat?'

I'd googled the hell out of 'rehab diet' and decided upon a regime high in essential restorative vitamins and minerals. Heavy on the vegetables, big on oily fish and easy on the red meat. My mum had said:

'Oh, love, okay. I'll get a special shop in. We did it on the computer the other day, you know?'

'Did what, Mum?'

'Got the shop in.'

'Oh.'

'On the computer.'

'Right...'

'Shall we get it in on the computer? You can choose what you want then?'

'Okay, thanks, Mum, but I don't want you to go to any trouble.'

The thought of Barry's internet browsing history popping up on screen did nothing for my constitution.

'It's no trouble, son.'

'Problem with that bloody internet shopping though, love is the, pardon my French, the bloody Polish packers.' Head of International Relations, Barry, was at it again. 'You ask for roasting potatoes, you get a ton weight of bloody roasted peanuts. Waste of time and money, love. Don't give them the bloody jobs.'

If he threw in some Princess Di and Madeleine McCann material he could have been the *Daily Express* incarnate.

'Look, Mum, I don't want any trouble. I'll just eat whatever's going.'

'Okay, love.' She wore the accustomed look of disappointment particular to mothers.

'Well, you'll have to fend for yourself tonight, young man. Your mother and I have been invited over to our friends' on the other side of the Close, Jason and Francesca's. He's a big wheel on the town council is Jason.'

The word WIFESWAPPING flashed through my mind in big red neon letters.

'They're ever such a nice couple, love,' Mum said. 'The last time we went around Francesca cooked us a Thai green curry, didn't she, Barry? I'd said to Francesca, "I don't like spicy, but I don't mind spicy", if you get my meaning. And you know what? It wasn't spicy at all. Barry even had seconds.'

On Jason's wife probably.

Barry bore all the hallmarks of a sexual miscreant. I'd imagined he was a big name on the local swinging circuit – his poncey hair, his rock 'n' roll hips, his too-tight pants. I had every faith that he sang his solitary chart hit at the top of his voice while a 62-year-old grandmother of three gave him fellatio – the first time she'd had meat in her mouth since her husband died after a short illness – in the spare bedroom of an identikit Wimpey townhouse, my mother looking on encouragingly, not wanting to speak up against their new alternative lifestyle lest she rocked the boat.

'We can do the car boot on Sunday, as long as we're in for The Grapes on Friday night. Should be crackerjack!'

Humiliating carnal group encounters as recompense for a weekend selling bits and bobs from the back of a Seat.

This was the first time I hadn't been at least half drunk in Barry's company. It was trying.

'I wonder what she'll cook up tonight? Probably something fancy do you think, Barry?'

'I should imagine so, my beautiful wife. Righty ho, I'm off upstairs for the three sh's…'

Barry shot me a conspiratorial wink as he left the kitchen. Oh my dear fucking God. I was part of his gang. I needed to get well and get the fuck out of here.

With Mother and It off doing unthinkable things, I had the run of the house. The last time I'd had access to satellite television and a fully stocked fridge had been the summer after university when I'd lounged around on my parents' sofa for three lazy months. It had been like *The Graduate*, just with the Simon and Garfunkel, sunshine and sex with a mature lady swapped for MTV2, unseasonal rain and the 10-minute freeview. I was younger then, more stoner than day-long drinker. Lose a vice, gain a vice. Change a crutch, choose a crutch. What would my new one be? I knew what it could be. Christy. And what were my chances? Zero. I had been presented with the perfect opportunity to tell her how I feel and what did I do? Throw up on her shoes. And a little bit in her handbag. Smooth, smooth moves. Christ, I needed a drink.

Barry had quite a liquor cabinet in the garage. I should know, I'd raided it enough times. I went into the garage and looked at the bottles. Whiskies, brandies, gins, vermouths, aperitifs. I stayed and stared, rapt like a caveman looking at fire. In awe of its beauty, intoxicated by its power, aware of its danger. I went back into the house. I considered lying naked on the shag pile rug in front of the hearth in the living room but thought better of it when reckonings of who'd done the same before me added themselves up in my mind. I wandered upstairs. The last time I'd rummaged around their cupboards I'd pocketed a fistful of Citalopram. Best to avoid the bathroom cabinets this time. I turned on the cold tap and doused my face with water. Standing so close to the fire had brought me out in a sweat. I dried off, methodically evaporating the beads of water that would soon be replaced by beads of sweat, and went into the spare room. Under the bed was an ottoman full of the accumulated junk that had been hidden away since Barry had been living with my mum. I pulled it out, blew the dust off the top and opened it wide. It was a treasure trove of spoilt memories, trinkets and paper deemed significant or special enough to become personal baggage. The sum of my personal effects at my mother's house wouldn't have made for much of an estate to squabble over. Old family photographs from a 1980s beach holiday, Mum's eyes smiling worriedly, Dad's eyes giving away his sangria intake, and me, staring straight ahead at the lens. There was a singular sadness about looking at photos from your past. If only the matt-finish mouth could speak to you now and see the disappointment you'd inevitably become. This wasn't the plan, it'd say; twenty-nine, not an astronaut or spy, wears a tie to work, stopped riding skateboards. No love, no real life, it'd say, before going back to the beach or birthday party, or fun fair or family gathering. The time-worn greetings cards wouldn't have many posthumous takers either. I picked an A4-sized one up. It carried an '18' bubble, written in gold font, an exclamation mark to hammer the point home and a clearly tipsy mouse next to a magnum of champagne. I opened it up to find scribbled greetings in half a dozen different hands.

'Happy birthday bro!

Legal at last.

Looking forward to a wicked disco.

Safe!

Jinko'

I hadn't seen Jinko since I'd moved away for college a few months after receiving his kind congratulations. He'd got the first girl he stuck it in pregnant – Janine Davies: pretty face, big appetite – and fallen off the radar. Thanks to the wonders of Facebook, I now was not only up to date with his life in the preceding pre-digital revolution years – two kids now, one of each, and an assistant manager's job at a hardware store on an out-of-town development – but could be updated on his burgeoning philosophic bent ('If a tree falls in da woods and there's no-one there to hear it, does it make a sound? I thought it was bears wot shit in da woods LOL') or his appreciation for a cooked dinner ('Luv the mrs Sunday roast <3'). He poked me. I never poked him back.

'Oy oy!

Happy fucking birfday Billy boy!

Let's get mash up!

Tom'

Tom was a cab driver now. He'd picked me up from a private address at 5.30 a.m. one Saturday morning a couple of years back. I'd been snorting lines of coke the size of a midget's hard-on and had been trying to level myself out with skunk and straight up gin. I, or the large amounts of drugs I had on my person, had convinced two young girls with long legs and short dresses to leave the club, swing by another dealer's house and head back to mine to really get the party started. One of them was a perfect specimen apart from one lazy eye. I fully intended to snort drugs off their naked bodies and fuck the pair of them. I think this was evident in my demeanour. I hadn't recognised Tom for a few minutes and when I did was sure that he had clocked me but had tried to concentrate on the road and hope I'd not latch on. He had put weight on and wore a shit goatee beard. His disguise could have worked but didn't. We exchanged surprised salutations, over-egged on my part thanks to the dangerous levels of narcs in my system. He said it looked like I was doing well. I said we should lunch. He said he didn't get a lunch-break. I gave him my card. He never called.

I closed the card.

The greetings might as well have been epitaphs.

# Chapter 20

'Where the hell have you been, Bill?'

'I've been, you know… around…'

'No, Bill. No, you haven't. You haven't been at your desk for the past three days and I've texted your Blackberry every day, but nothing.'

'Yeah, it's been having problems.'

'No, Bill, I think you've been having problems.'

It was the first buddy session with Christy for over a fortnight, and the first time I'd seen her since I'd unloaded the contents of my stomach on her person. I'd lain low from work for a while, telling Miles I'd had a virus and flashing the headed paper from the wellness centre under his nose. As expected, he clocked the insignia but not the details. I'm not sure a suspected STI was sufficient excuse for a time out. Sure, I could have confided in Miles of how I'd had a booze problem and how I was trying to get back on the rails (he'd smile reassuringly) and how my work had suffered (he'd lose the smile) but how I was determined to repay Morgan & Schwarz's faith in me (half-smile), before being referred to the company shrink on full pay and benefits.

But that wasn't a game I'd wanted to play. People would talk. Rumours would fester. Jill would be the ringleader – how she'd always known I'd had a problem, how she'd often caught me reaching for my bottom drawer, how she'd tried to help. Pete and Carol would first appear surprised before shaking their heads complicitly. Trent would return to his desk, open up the Word document entitled 'Obstacles to fucking Christy' and vindictively delete my name off the shortlist.

The last man to visit the company psych was a junior executive by the name of Todd Spinks. Blonde hair, blue eyes, fresh out of college and bright as a button, Spinks had been destined to fast-track his way past clutter like me into a higher pay bracket almost from the moment he breezed into the office with his Brylcreemed hair and well-pressed Dockers. What the poor kid didn't bank on was Morgan & Schwarz's location amongst the clouds on the twelfth floor of a sleek skyscraper. Todd had suffered with sickening vertigo ever since being left to dangle 25 ft in the air in an abseiling incident as a Boy Scout, aged eleven. Morgan & Schwarz tried to fill his daytime with distractions – brainstorms, team meets, client coffees, smokin' secretaries – but he couldn't stop thinking about the windows. They were all around him, even when he shut his eyes, especially when he tried to sleep at night. Gilded glass opportunities to face his fear and fight his destiny. He was terrified of what they represented yet inexplicably drawn in by their reflective magnetism. After a month's intensive with the shrink, he'd stepped cautiously back into the fold one bright Monday morning to find his work station bedecked in balloons and foil banners welcoming him back. A tear rolled from his perfect bright blue eye. Jill put an arm around his shoulder and told him not to be down, modern medicine had done wonders and it was more than possible to live a full and rich life with HIV these days.

Todd freaked.

The rumour mill had gone into overdrive during his leave of absence. He was almost impossibly good looking, chiseled, clean cut. He smelt good and always matched his socks to his tie. Someone had seen him on a Sunday morning on the riverside leaving a brunch bar hand-in-hand with an effeminate but powerful looking Latin man. There and then Todd pulled the frame open just enough for his muscular body to fit through the gap and jumped outside, twelve floors down to the street below. During the stunned silence, a solitary balloon had followed him out and blew across the backdrop of blue sky and steel and glass.

I did not want to be Todd Spinks.

Christy's eyes called for a response.

'Look, if you must know, I've taken some time off. I'd been feeling a bit run-down recently and needed to take a rain check.'

'Well, you were sick the last time I saw you…' her eyes smiled playfully.

'Very funny, Christy.'

'Jesus, Bill, when did you get so serious?'

'I'm not.'

'Yes you are.'

'Look, I'm sorry about that, okay? Really fucking mortified.'

'It's okay, Bill.'

'It's not okay.'

'It is okay.'

'It just wasn't supposed to be like that is all.'

'What wasn't?'

'It doesn't matter.'

'Serious and mysterious. Who is this new Bill? Has Miles scooped out your soul and inserted a standard issue Morgan & Schwarz PR robot 5000 in its place?' A laugh broke out of my uptight lips.

'That's more like it. Bill might just be in there after all…' Her dark eyes weighed me up. '…Well, whatever you've been doing, you look the better for it.'

'Thanks. I think.' I took a sip of my tea. It had gone cold.

'So who's been looking after you?' She clearly wasn't finished.

'Me. I've been looking after me… and my mum I suppose.'

'Your mum?'

'Yes, I spent a few days at her house.'

'How old are you, Bill?'

'29-years-old, Christy.'

'Do not become the 30-something who lives at home with his mother. Not attractive.' We both laughed this time.

'Anyway, this is supposed to be your buddy session, not mine. How have you been while I've been recuperating in the bosom of my family?'

'I've been good, Bill, really good.' Her eyes darted to the left, betraying her answer (we regularly had body language reading classes at Morgan & Schwarz, they helped us read clients' responses to our scheming). 'Ever since I washed the carrot off my suede heels, I've been really good.'

'Ha fucking ha. Still got that GSOH then?'

'As ever.' This felt nice. Comfortable. Two old friends making up after a misunderstanding. Two old friends. Friends.

'And work?' I asked, remembering my pastoral duty of care.

'Work is… you know… work. To be honest with you, it feels like I've always been here.'

'Like in *The Shining*?'

'The what?'

'Erm, *The Shining*. The film, and the, erm, book, you know?'

'I don't know…'

'Okay. Jack Nicholson had always been in the hotel. That's the twist.'

'Well, thanks for spoiling it for me,' she said, cackled and punched me on the arm. Note to self: do not share pop culture references with the young.

'Well, just like Jack Nicholson, I feel like I've always been here. Like part of the furniture.'

'Is that because Trent tried to sit on you?' I just couldn't help myself.

'BILL!'

She snorted. It was the first time I'd heard her snort. It was a definite fault.

'You. Are. Terrible!' she shouted in staccato.

'Yeah, just kidding.'

I wasn't.

'Well the old Bill is well and truly back,' she said.

'Maybe.'

'Definitely.'

I felt my heartbeat speed up and a bead of sweat drip down my forehead.

'So, everything is good?' I asked.

'Everything is good.' Again her dark eye darted.

'And you know how to file an expenses claim?'

'I know how to file an expenses claim.'

'And you're aware of your nearest fire exit in case of an emergency?'

'I am well aware of my nearest fire exit in case of an emergency,' she repeated back, a little too enthusiastically. She was a few degrees left of slapping her thigh and singing 'hi ho'. But she wasn't 100 per cent. I could tell. Her black eyes dilated when she lied, like they did with all the good things in life. Booze, drugs, screwing and little white lies told a tale on your eyes. Maybe she was just compartmentalising for a friend in need. Yes, that was it. A friend.

'Well, we seem to have ticked all of the boxes required of the buddy session system,' I said. She made a tick in the air with the long fingers and bitten down nails.

'Thanks, buddy,' she said.

'No problem. buddy,' I said. This was another one of those moments. A chance to say something.

'So I guess I'll see you around,' she said, 'At the photocopier, the water cooler, the Christmas lunch, that kind of thing.' She was laughing at me. I think she was being sarcastic but I couldn't be sure. Sweat was now impeding my judgement. Speak up, Bill. Now, for fuck's sake.

'Well, yeah, we could meet at those places,' I said.

I swallowed.

'Or we could do other things too…'

'Like sit next to each other in Monday meets?' she said.

'Well, yeah, that too, but…'

'Yes, Bill…'

She was playing with me.

'We could do other things, like not at work things I mean…'

She was silent now and her lips had straightened and narrowed from her previous laugh into a strange kind of impassive interrogation.

'You know, I could do with a friend at the moment…'

Why did I say a friend? I was panicking.

'Sure,' she replied, 'me too.'

Her too.

Her too.

'So, where are you suggesting then…?'

Think, Bill. Think.

'Well, there's this thing I have to do next week…'

'Go on…'

'I've got to give a talk to my old school.'

'Your old school?' she asked.

'Yeah, my old school. About PR. It's a careers thing, you know.'

'Oh, really. Sure. It sounds…'

'It's just I'm a bit nervous and could do with some support.'

'You got it.' She seemed disappointed? Fuck, Bill, your old fucking school?

I threw a hook out there.

'We could go for a drink afterwards?'

'Sure, a drink.'

'Great.'

Fuck, Bill, you didn't drink. The Ten Commandments.

Fuck, Bill.

'It's a date,' I said, instantly regretting it.

'It's a date,' she said. 'A very cheap one.'

She shot me a wink and skipped out of the room. Woah. We kind of had a date. One that involved public speaking without booze. For the first time. And then going for a drink without actually having a drink. For the first time.

Maybe I would have a drink.

Fuck, Bill. Be strong. Hang on in there.

You. Had. A. Date. A ray of sunshine through the shitstorm and the sweats. Something to get out of bed for that was less than 40 % proof but twice as intoxicating.

I walked through the office with a new found spring in my step. 'Jumpin' Jack Flash' played in my head. I was in slow motion. Pete was to my left in the midst of one of his regular spring-cleans, sorting chronologically through tabloid newspapers, cleaning in between the keys of his ergonomic keyboard, sneezing at the disturbance of dust particles. Trent was to my right, minimising incriminating no-strings hook-up web windows with the agility of a sex-crazed computer-literate cat. Carol was at a filing cabinet patiently searching for an invoice to a client with initials between A and C, balanced on a box file to reach the top drawer. She smiled warmly in my direction. Jill was on the line, aggressively swirling the cord around her wedding finger, remonstrating over an incongruous headline with, I assumed, a nonchalant sub-ed, until redness highlighted the crow's feet around her eyes. She snarled warmly in my direction. I at once felt both at one and completely apart from them. Morgan & Schwarz was like space travel: a strange feeling of claustrophobia and agoraphobia all at the same time, trapped by the small ship but terrified of the great expanse outside, leaving you rooted, terrified, firmly to the spot.

# Chapter 21

My old school had held an annual careers week ever since it had opened as a front for lazy but ruthless nuns. The local diocese had obviously thought it too much of a crowded marketplace to go into the waste disposal business as cover so decided upon secondary education as a means to manipulate, torture and extol. Back in my day, careers week involved wheeling out a selection of self-satisfied nobodies. There was the disagreeable bank manager – the father of the deputy head boy (a 6 ft ginger bully who excelled at both lacrosse and the wedgie) – who dressed down a school hall's worth of 16-year-olds for failing to save a proportion of their pocket money or desultory paper-round earnings. Then there was the grey accountant who did nothing to dispel the myth that the profession was littered with boring men completing boring tasks and who invariably had mid-life emotional breakdowns and plotted out their affairs with teenage rent boys on Excel spreadsheets. And not forgetting the eccentric dentist who passed around a plaster cast of Mother Superior's cavity-filled mouth, resplendent with a pair of ruby crowns. Mother Superior did not approve of the 'show and tell' aspect of the talk and cut it short, before instructing a pair of burly brothers to escort the puzzled mouth doctor off the premises. For the remainder of the hour we were kindly given 'free time', which involved sitting upright, still and in absolute silence. Her dentures never had the same sheen after that event.

Mother Superior was the axis of ecumenical evil on which St Ignacius Roman Catholic High School span. She ruled her kingdom with silent menace, extraordinarily expressive nostrils and a legion of cruel nuns, callous monks and ambitious laypeople eager to do her bidding. This regime had little bearing on the minds of my contemporaries, who were some of the sickest, most perverted little fuckers I've ever known.

And I work in PR.

She had died last year and received a quiet funeral and an obituary in *The Times*. Apparently she'd worked with Mother Teresa in Calcutta, so it just goes to show you never can tell. The replacement headmistress – Sister Beatrix – was a moderniser, a reformer, a new, hip, youngish nun-slinger keen to pull the Catholic church kicking and screaming into the 21st century. Which is where I came in. The school was putting together a week-long itinerary of talks, trips and trade fairs that reflected the shifting industrial sands of the brave new world in which we lived. I was joined on the bill by a graphic designer, an app designer, an interior designer and an experience designer, whatever the fuck that was. It was like an even shitter Glastonbury with equally righteous headliners, less drugs and cleaner toilets. A letter had landed on Miles' desk and when he clocked the St Ignacius insignia, he assigned me to the job. Said I'd probably be better able to relate to the kids, whatever the fuck that meant. Couldn't help thinking it was a veiled kidney punch at my perceived juvenility. And yes, I realise that is a somewhat teenage reaction. I was just getting into character.

Which was apt for how I felt on the way to meet Christy. I had worse butterflies than a council estate zoo. I was on at 2 p.m., the warm-up for a comic book artist. Miles had given me the afternoon off, thanking me for putting a tick in Morgan & Schwarz's CSR box. Following on so soon from my stint serving food to the bums, I was close to becoming the company's most altruistic member of staff. Just had to try not to punch anyone this time. It wasn't so long ago that given a few hours off I'd have run straight to the nearest boozer and sunk a pint or six. Instead I was en route to meet Christy in a coffee shop near the campus. I fucking hated coffee shops. Christy was on a day's leave to deal with some 'family issues' (Jill's inverted commas, not mine), but had insisted she could still make our date. Well, not that we'd said it was a date. But it kind of was. Wasn't it?

Anyway, the sickness somersaulting around my stomach was not helped by passing the public houses I'd escaped to from school. Past The Good Companions where I'd got served my first pint, using a self-laminated fake ID claiming I was a 22-year-old Theology undergraduate (ambitious on both counts). At any one given time, there could be up to twenty Rob Burgesses in the pub at once. We'd all photocopied the same classmate's older brother's NUS card. Past The Pig and Whistle, where I'd tried to show off to Stacey Taylor by challenging a shaven headed cider drinker to a game of winner stays on. I'd put my 50p on the side of the pool table, swallowed hard and eyed the scene with a nonchalance that could only be attributed to spending all my dinner money on strong continental lager. Inwardly, I was shitting myself. Stacey seemed indifferent and more interested in the video jukebox. I was a swan. An underage drinking swan. Paddle beneath the water, Billy boy. On my first shot, I ripped right through the cloth and spilt his pint on the follow-through. I bolted out of there so fast it was the only time I'd ever made double economics on a Tuesday afternoon.

When I arrived she was sat in the window, reading an indistinguishable Penguin classic. She looked so perfect I decided to stay and watch her for a moment. It was a slightly risky manoeuvre. If she caught me stood there, staring, I'd have to do a star jump and mouth: 'surprise'. I figured it was worth it. Anyway, I could do with a minute to wipe the sweat from my forehead. I'd seen a million girls in a million coffee shops over the years (okay, pubs) and wondered who they were waiting for, where they'd been and where they were going. On the occasions I'd found their story out it'd either been a bawdy limerick or a long-running series with no discernible character development. But not this time. The girl with the alive red hair, the girl with the black blurred eyes, the girl with the warm, beautiful face was waiting for me. Bill McDare. Granted, to accompany me to a talk to some jumped-up teenagers. But still.

'Bill…'

'Christy…'

Ah, the awkwardness of the greeting. A handshake? A hug? A kiss? On the cheek? On both cheeks? Or play it cool? I'd once headbutted a date, mistakenly going for the lips when she offered the shoulder. Mild concussion had been the early death knell for a Werner Herzog classic and a sharing platter at an arthouse cinema. I'd decided against fighting over the prawn tempura and sacked the subtitles off for cold beer and clinical cocaine. Let's hope lightning didn't strike twice.

I adopted the laissez-faire approach a life at capitalism's coalface had made inevitable and just stood there. She took the lead, put her bare hairless arms around me and squeezed. For two seconds. Which might not *sound* like a long time, but caught in the moment time turned malleable, stretchable. I could have ran marathons in the time she held me. I could have completed a Rubix cube in the dark. Instead I thought about putting my hands on her arse.

I didn't.

'Ooooh.' She made a noise more at home in the shakedown to close a yoga session. 'It's good to see you.'

I'd only seen her yesterday. I hadn't returned from the Western Front. What could this mean?

'Likewise, likewise. Thanks for doing this. You know, you didn't have to, especially if you've got other things on your plate.'

I was fishing. Suggestion was my maggot.

'No, it's fine, Bill. I wanted to,' she replied.

'How's your day off so far, then?' I repitched my rod.

'Christ, Bill, I think I need something a bit stronger than a latte to start opening that box!'

'…would you like a…'

'…no it's fine I'll…'

'Let me get you a…' We both stood up. The small table rocked and her book (*Crime and Punishment*) lost its place. 'Look, Chris, sit down, take a deep breath and I'll get you a drink.' She smiled a smile that wouldn't have been out of place on a nurse's face at the end of a night shift. Her dark eyes looked tired.

'Thank you.'

'Now, there's no booze in this place so how about I get you an Americano and we both perk the fuck up?'

She laughed.

'Thank you.'

I hit the coffee bar. After my early indecision, I was playing the assertive role popular culture led me to believe womenfolk liked.

'It's my brother,' she said. I smiled. I tried my best conciliatory eyes. 'Again. He's been expelled from school this morning.'

'Oh no, Christy, what did he do?' If I had the details I could help her. I was a helper. I had tissue shoulders.

'He flipped out two days ago and called the teacher a cunt.'

'Jesus, that seems a bit harsh…' She just looked at me. '…Expelling him for that I mean. If we had the same rules at Morgan & Schwarz, we'd have to leave Carol and Pete man the fort.'

'I think it's a bit different in school, Bill.'

'Yeah, I suppose so… any advice in handling errant children in light of this afternoon's engagement?' Her face screamed 'too soon'. I'd tried to lighten the mood. I hadn't banked on getting a mouthy teenager in my hot-new-girlfriend bundle. Christy took a deep breath and exhaled, pushing her average-sized breasts towards me.

'Oh, Bill, it's not his fault. He barely gets any sleep because of the nightmares, which means I barely get any sleep, and he gets irritable and the teacher was pushing him about a piece of homework he hadn't done. I'm not trying to excuse his behaviour, you know, just trying to understand it.'

'Sure,' I said. 'I thought you'd said everything was great the other day though?' I'd known it hadn't been. Those eyes couldn't hide from me.

'Well, it was. It is. Kind of. I'm really getting into my new job and don't feel like the incompetent new girl anymore, but I'm just about holding it all together.' She took another deep breath. 'I could do with my fucking dad being around.'

Silence.

What to say?

'I could help.' She downed her coffee.

'Thanks, Bill.' Her eyes said I couldn't. 'Come on, we'll be late.'

The first thing that hit you was the smell. Just like catching the scent of a woman waiting next to you at the traffic lights could bring a forgotten girl from your deep, distant past rushing back, flooding your unprepared mind with memories of the sex and the fights, the tears and the love bites, the institutional smell of a state school with undertones of vomit and gravy had the same effect. It's not something you notice at the time but somewhere down the track it'll get you, leaving you lost for more than a moment contemplating a part of your life you'd put away into a box and thrown away the key on. Smell was an unrequested locksmith.

My first sober public speaking in god knows how long and it was to a bunch of over-gelled, uber-confident little fuckers. We were never like this. Our bravado happened behind the bike sheds.

The nuns ruled with an iron rod. Sure, rules would be broken and authority challenged in the jostle for position inevitable among 800 puberty cases. The odd complicit layteacher would be co-conspirator against the horrible habits, turning a blind eye to a Benson and Hedges or a bum feel down the secluded grass banks. But on the whole, we were nothing like Generation Meh. It all comes too easy for them. Fucking hell, I'm sounding like my dad here. The digital revolution had made scoring girls easy. These little shits were definitely getting more sex than I was as a 16-year-old spotty oik. BBM, SMS, DM me, a few pokes on Facebook and it's (a smiley emoticon here, a LOL there) game on. They didn't even have to grunt a word to their prey until unclasping their sports bra. Compare that with mustering up the manhood to call the object of your teenage affections. On the house phone. Which her chastity-protecting father answered. Or her violent virginity-keeper of an older brother. Your voice squeaking when asking for Alison, giving reassurance that this high-pitched homo couldn't break a hymen if he tried.

All that gone.

All those nerves, those half dials, those preparatory nips from the spirit cupboard. Gone.

Nice one, Zuckerberg.

At school, girls had been exotic, mysterious, unreachable. At least until Laura Stanton. Every nun under the age of forty risked becoming wank material. The only sight of bare flesh we ever got was if we were lucky enough to happen upon the sticky pages of a dirty magazine strewn across the woods at the back of the school labs. These little Justins and Brandons had it beamed into their peepers 24/7 thanks to search engines and slack parental controls. The jammy cunts. Anyway, let's see if I can ruin their futures by convincing them of the merits of this sham of a career. After all, making shit sound believable was what paid the bar bills all those years.

Bars.

I'd let these kids wind me up so much I needed a drink.

'Bill… Bill?' It was Christy.

'What…? Oh, yeah. Hi.'

'You drifted off there. Seemed like you were in a world of your own,' she said.

'Yeah, it happens.' We were stood at the side of a stage waiting for the last kids to file in.

'You set?'

'As I'll ever be.'

'Then go get 'em.' She shot me a wink.

Okay, here goes. Time to sink or swim. My introductions had been made.

'So I bet your teachers are telling you that now is the time to focus on your future. Your life after St Ignacius. They'll be telling you to focus on what you want to be. On a profession that serves society and makes you happy. On a profession that makes your parents happy. They're no doubt telling you to be doctors, lawyers, bankers—'

'You're a banker!' shouted a shrill voice from somewhere stage left. An adult voice broke over them.

'Quiet, Year 12. Quiet. Mr McDare didn't come here for you to waste his time…' Just a few sniggers hung in the hollow. 'QUIET. Or do you want to waste the rest of your lives?'

Silence.

'I thought not. Thank you.' I recognised the voice. It was my old English teacher, Mr Warhurst. Old Johnny Warhurst. A St Ignacius legend, confidante to the kids, nemesis of the nuns. Like the smell, I'd forgotten all about him. I coughed and continued.

'Well, as I was saying, everyone around you is trying to point you in a certain direction. I'm here today to tell you to ignore everyone else and listen to me. Someone who just a few years ago was someone like you. Someone who wanted to leave my mark.

Someone who wanted to control situations, control people, control destinies.' They were listening now. Rows and rows of quiet, closed-mouthed Chelsea, Jadyn and Josh's. Listening or ignoring; one of the two. Either way, they most definitely were not heckling. My eyes found Christy, sat down to my right. She smiled encouragingly. Date number one had finally picked up.

'So can anyone tell me what the initials PR stand for?'

A kid at the back of the room shouted, 'Paedo ROCK ON!' I suppose I'd asked for that. Expecting above board audience participation from a room full of testosterone-tripped teens was a bridge too far. This was going to be a long twenty minutes.

Flashback.

The last time I was stood on this very stage I was drunker than I was right now. Thirteen years ago to the month. It was National Poetry Day and for homework Mr Warhurst had made the whole year learn a complete poem of our choosing off pat. In assembly that morning five names were to be called at random to recite the verse to the rest of the kids. Mother Superior was poised to punish anyone called up who was unable to pull a sonnet from up their sleeve. After the fashion to which you've no doubt become accustomed, I forgot. I'd spent the previous evening trying to spy on our new neighbours through my bedroom curtains. They looked like randy buggers (my dad had said as much) and if I could catch a glimpse of them at it then, by proxy, I'd have had sex. An early pre-cursor there to the sound reasoning that would come to characterise later life. In the toilets before we congregated in the hall, I'd had a nip of Stephen Norman's whisky (stolen from his dad who was clearly a tee-totaller or alcoholic judging by the poor choice of brand). I'd weighed up the odds – five out of two hundred made for... oh, fuck it. The whisky had gone to my head. Assembly started.

My name was called.

Shit. Shit.

The booze helped me from my seat and up the steps. I did what I'd do in hundreds of these situations in the future and thought on my feet. I'd copied a poem from a collection of love verse into a Valentine's card I'd sent in vain to Trisha earlier in the year. I called on all my reserves of memory to mumble through a few lines. If only I'd had a smell of the old foisty book. Despite my retarded recantation, I'd done enough to avoid a beating at the hands of a repressed virgin. Result.

'Gaaaaaylord!' had come up an accusation from the floor. On reflection, perhaps we weren't all that different to the kids sat fidgeting in front of me now. It seemed reciting the Romantics was enough to invoke this frankly wide of the mark response from my poetryphobe peers. I don't know if you've ever been a teenager, but being called a 'gaylord' in front of two hundred other kids kind of sticks. After my name was called for the register: 'Gaylord!' Walking through the corridor en route to double maths, a punch in the arm and: 'Gaylord!' Ordering a French bread pizza and chips from a dinner lady: '£2.60. Gaylord.' Scrabbling around for a role model's counsel, I went for the next best option and asked my dad.

'If they bully you, hit them.' Sage words as ever from Father. I resolved that whoever next called me the name, I'd punch them there and then. The unwanted tag was already ruining my chances of convincing more girls to let me have sex with them. I'd practiced the punch in my bedroom mirror a hundred times over. Straight and true. I hadn't banked on the next person to be Brother Geoff, our broad-shouldered PE teacher. Men of the cloth shouldn't be throwing homosexual invective around, even less so when directed at defenceless boys. Well, I sure showed Brother Geoff who was defenceless. I was pulling on my mauve and gold school kit when it happened, stalling to stay in the changing rooms rather than go out in the cold and wet for cross-country. I hated cross-country. The rest of the boys were waiting

174

impatiently, flicking goosepimpled legs and christening new running shoes.

'Get a move on, gaylord, we haven't got all day,' he'd said. That was it. I'd made a promise. I punched Brother Geoff hard and direct in the family jewels. He'd gone down like a sack of mash. My gym kit clad colleagues had screamed with laughter and then cheered. This wasn't Dead Poet's Society, but if we'd have been the kind of school where kids got carried to glory on their contemporaries' shoulders, I'm certain I would have been held and hoisted. News of the David v Goliath clash spread like herpes around the school. No one troubled me again.

The rest of the talk rushed by in a blur of clichés, chuckles and eye contact with Christy. Let the little fuckers have their iPhones and tits on tap. Who was I to be bitter? They had the gadgets to get fucked. We had the economy to fuck. They had no hope of getting a job anyway.

'Bill, you were great...'

'William McDare, well I never...' I hated it when two people said hello at the same time. Where to look?

'Christy, meet Mr Warhurst. Mr Warhurst meet Christy.' The voiceover to a no-hopers version of *This Is Your Life* played out in my head.

*'I ll always remember Bill, never sat at the back of the class, never sat at the front. He took a moderate interest in Shakespeare and showed a flair, if not a passion, for creative writing. To be honest, we never thought he d amount to much. Most of the kids here, they never do.*

'Well, look at you, Mr McDare. A model for our young people. A pillar of society.' I raised an eyebrow. Christy seemed proud of Warhurst's praise. He addressed her. 'We didn't mark Bill down for great things but look at him now... a fancy Italian suit, a high falutin career, his own secretary no doubt... and a beautiful wife?'

Mr Warhurst's tone rose at the end of the sentence. Christy

looked confused before her mouth broke into a smile of realisation, as sharp as a shiny pin stalking a brilliant red balloon.

*'Bill and I were forced to be buddies by our workplace and at first I wondered what they d let me in for. He always stunk of booze and his knowledge of the office filing system was rudimentary at best. But we got on, he made me laugh and then things moved on… he threw up all over me. We got over that one. Now we re really close, we enjoy spending time together. He s like a big brother to me.*

POP.

'Oh, wife? Me? God no, we're…'

'Yes…' said Mr Warhust, as if waiting for an answer on iambic pentameter.

'We're friends,' I said. 'Just good friends.' Relief covered Christy.

'Oh, I am sorry. Awfully presumptuous of me. Whisper it, but I think I've been around these bloody nuns too long. The opposite sex can't spend time together unless anointed before the Lord,' he said, then hushed, 'and all that bollocks.' The bell rang and a hundred screaming, texting, jostling St Ignacians rushed past us into the freedom of the outdoors, off for chips, fags and fingering before physics. I looked at Christy but couldn't catch her eye.

# Chapter 22

I'm not exactly sure when I first noticed that it was her. It could have been from the moment I first saw her, my soul accepting the lot of bumping against these insignificant others in the most singular of circumstances. It could have been when Christy was detailing her morning routine, my eye wandering and catching her figure, accepting her presence like a passer-by in *The Truman Show*, my mind trying to concentrate on a checklist of pre-work activities I hoped one day to be a part of. If it was neither of these times, it was almost certainly when her eye-etched hand grabbed the microphone and she cleared her throat while the assembled oddities clapped their last. It was The Mystic.

'We need to stop thinking in terms of food miles and get switched onto food feet. We don't need to buy food grown on the other side of the world under artificial lights from huge supermarkets owned by faceless corporations. Our climate is perfect for raising our own crops. We can grow all manner of fruit and veg in this country – so why aren't we doing it? Well, you know what, we are going to do it: I propose we start a community garden. Food by the people, for the people. But it wouldn't only be the food we'd benefit from… think of the employment opportunities, the way it'd brighten up the neighbourhood, the way it'd create cohesion within our community. Climate change is happening, guys. Food prices are on the up and up and it's only going to get worse. This can give us food security and wean us off a fossil fuel-supported way of life. Growing food is a basic human instinct. If our forefathers didn't do it we wouldn't be here today. The apparent convenience of modern life has replaced need with nonchalance. It's time to take the soil back. Who's with me?'

Applause rippled around the small space. Who knew The Mystic was a crusty Churchillian? She had the room rapt. Granted, many of the twenty or so gathered in the narrow corridor upstairs in The Golden Fleece looked too stoned to protest much, but either way, she'd struck a chord with the discordant.

I'd been dragged along to a transition town meeting with Connie and Craig. I use dragged in the loosest context; I'd heard them talking about permaculture through the hole in the bathroom floor, slid downstairs and casually dropped in a passing interest in sustainability. Now, I know what you're thinking; did I fuck give a fuck about the planet and, to give you your dues, to a point you'd be bang on. But in fairness to myself, I don't drive a gas-guzzling twatmobile (granted, previously down to dangerous levels of intoxication) and I couldn't tell you the last time I flew long haul. But the real reasons why I was currently sat in a damp room with some annoying hippies were altruistic, if not environmental. Following my contribution to the recent Chinese cook-off, it was time to build some bridges with my housemates/de facto landlords. Now, I'm not suggesting I was the worst housemate in the world. I paid my rent on time and rarely, if ever, caused congestion around the cooking apparatus. Still, number 35 was hardly like the set of The Monkees so the time was right to stir some homely harmony, even if it did mean going to listen to a load of jobless wonders talk bollocks. Purely coincidentally, attendance at the meeting of the mead-drinking misfits offered the chance for a sexually non-threatening date with Christy.

'She's right you know, Bill. The post-cheap oil era is an opportunity for us. Life can be better than this alienated consumer culture we've got now. We can rebuild the heart of communities and our relationships with each other, and while I'm at it, our relationships with our bloody selves. I mean, when did you last have some proper "you time," Bill?'

'Not in front of Christy, Craig…' It took him a while, but he got the joke. Eventually.

'Very good, but I didn't mean that kind of me time. It's not a laugh, this, you know Bill. This is real. This is your children's future.'

'I don't have any children…'

'That you know of…' interrupted Christy, winking and nudging. Connie snorted.

'Ahhhh…' I made the noise they make after the collective laughter at the end of *Scooby Doo*. The kind of noise where Fred actually meant 'Yeah, that fairground operator sketch *was* funny, but let's get these credits fucking rolling so I can go and smoke a doobie and try to get to third base with Daphne.'

'Anyway, Craig, you hate other people,' I said, reverting to the original conversational course.

'No I don't!' His nostrils flared a little. He seemed upset by this accusation.

'Okay, well if we're talking about community…' I racked my brains, 'you hate our neighbours.'

'I don't hate our neighbours.'

'You say that, but you did try to poison their cat.'

'It kept shitting in our garden, Bill.'

'So…'

'There have to be rules in the new society. There always have to be rules.' Connie moved uncomfortably in her chair. Christy attacked the potential awkwardness caused by Craig's admission of feline torture by saying the word everyone who's ever been in a pub wants those who've joined them to say:

'Drinks?'

Craig's eyes lit up. Craig was an ale drinker, supping everything from Bishop's Boulderdash to Ferreter's Fancy with the pomp and ceremony of the wankiest of wine connoisseurs. The offer of a free round afforded him the opportunity to go off-piste without the risk of financial penalty, sampling the strangest of brews safe in the knowledge that if it turned out to be more Badger's Arsehole than Unicorn's Fancy, he was none the poorer. Hops expert though Craig might be, he was still a grade A fucking tightwad.

'I'll come to the bar with you if that's okay? Wouldn't mind running my eye over the pump clips…'

'Great!' said Christy, nervously enthusiastic. 'Connie?'

'Just a lime and soda for me please, mate.' Christy nodded a head-held shopping list nod and drew a tick in the air. This behaviour was very un-Christy like.

'I'll have the same actually,' I said.

'Have you two got a bottle of vodka stashed away?' said Craig, his bonhomie overflowing at the imminence of his paid-for pint.

'No. No we haven't, Craig,' I said. I pitched my tone close to that of a patronising orderly in a retard's home.

'Maybe we don't need alcohol to have a good time,' said Connie, joke-sneeringly.

'Well, I'll check out if hell has frozen over out of the window but whatever,' he replied. 'Come on you.' He grabbed Christy by the arm and dragged her the short way through the fleeces and dirty hair to the bar. We were having the kind of stilted banter you'd expect from a pair of cruising couples in the first half hour of date #1. We just didn't have the party snacks and poppers to break the ice.

'You like her, don't you?' said Connie, waiting the appropriate time for our respectives to be out of earshot. Either way, the background Levellers would have drowned out her mouse-like voice.

'How do you mean?' I said, a little too defensively.

'You know what I mean, mate. You're not the old Bill we used to know and…'

'Tolerate…?' I offered.

'No, know and…' she bit her thin bottom lip and thought for a few seconds, 'accept. And love, Bill. Although I'm not sure you did…'

'Yeah, you're right. You could say I've made some changes…
'

'You can say that again.'

'Easy…' Smug Connie was less fun.

'Come on, you know it as well as I do. We don't hear you stumble in at all hours anymore. You look better. Healthier. And the smell from your room… well even that's less…'

'Less…?'

'Like something has died in there.'

'Connie!'

'Oh god, no, not you. Just like a small mammal. A vole. Or a hare.'

'Well, that's really encouraging to hear…'

'Good…'

'…that I've given up my burgeoning taxidermist career to make everyone feel better about me…' I fake cheers-ed her. Could REALLY do with a dr…

'Look, Bill, all I'm saying is that things seem better for you. This is a good thing. Don't fight good things, mate.'

'Thanks, Con…'

'And I think she's the reason why. Isn't she?' Connie performed the kind of wink and nudge move that would have fitted right at home in the range of an overbearing pantomime dame.

'84p for a lime and soda!' Craig and Christy were back. 'You two are the definition of a cheap date.' And you, Craig, are the definition of a fucking skinflint.

As much as I hated to admit it, Connie was right, you know. I mean, should I hate the fact that I didn't have to have two drinks before I could feel slightly better than a corpse in the morning? Previously, I was *always* only ever two drinks and a slug of mouthwash away from feeling better. Should I hate the fact that I could actually differentiate between the tastes of different foodstuffs? Should I hate the fact that I had, if not a girlfriend, then a girl, who was a friend? And I *was* looking better too. With a bit of luck The Mystic would barely recognise me. While it's fair to say my face had a certain rugged charm even during the darkest days, the three D's – drink, drugs and deadlines – would take their toll on even the most well-cut of bone structures. The truth was that the cut and thrust of PR agency life was a young man's game. Being half-cut and chemically thrust didn't really help. Following the regime change, my eyes were now less like pissholes in the snow and more like shitholes in the sleet. This was a good thing. I kept tripping over. Like money was drawn to money, in the drunk's case, bruises were drawn to bruises. It was a vicious circle. I was glad I was now a square.

'I think that woman was right though, you know…' said Christy.

'What woman?' I said.

'The one with the…'

'Henna tattoos everywhere!' said Craig, clearly thinking we were engaged in the kind of word-riff game that would be played for fun in a Steiner school. He meant The Mystic. Stay calm, Bill.

'Right about what?'

'The community garden idea. It takes me back to my childhood…' said Christy. In all honesty, she hardly had to turn her mind to sepia to get back to her youth.

'Why's that, mate?' said Connie.

'We used to have a little allotment… me and my brother… and my dad. We grew all sorts on there… runner beans, onions, tomatoes that stretched so far up the pole that neither me nor Joe could reach them.' She shrieked a laugh. 'We'd get into so much trouble from my dad for bending the sticks to make them drop into our hands. There was only the three of us so Dad used to make us fill up carrier bags full of the extra and drop it round to the old ladies who lived on our road. Me and Joe would always fight over who got to knock on Mrs Higgins' door. She used to invite you in and give you a glass of cold chocolate milk and the choice of any cookie from her tin.' Christy lifted her drink, put her lips around the straw and sucked. Her black eyes were starting to smudge. 'I'll never forget her front room. She had plastic covers over her armchairs and it smelt like church in there. I remember Dad said she'd been very wealthy at one time, until—'

'Did she not let you and your brother both in?' Yes, Craig again.

'Umm…' Christy looked wrong-footed, 'yeah, I suppose she did…'

'So why did you and your brother fight, then?'

'Craig!' Connie scolded.

'Are you trying to doubt her memories, Craig?' I needed to step in. Christy looked like someone who's woken from a pleasant dream to find a smoking parrot in their bedroom – confused.

'No, of course not. Just saying, is all. There was a horrible cow just like that on our street. We always used to egg her house on Halloween. Not just on Halloween, actually. She'd go mental and chase us down the street with a broom in her hand, effing and jeffing. She had a big "Beware the Alsatian" sticker in her front window. There was no Alsatian…'

'Well, thanks for that insight into your childhood, Craig…'

'Mrs Higgins wasn't a cow, Craig,' said Christy, 'she was lovely. They were lovely times.'

She missed her dad. She missed those times. The family unit. We could be the family unit. The 2.4 children. The two-up, two-

183

down. The dog walks on a Saturday, the car wash on a Sunday. The curled up on the sofa with a half price supermarket bottle of red wine and rom-com Blu-ray. Not yet. But later. Couldn't we?

Show her.

I reached out the toe of my brown Italian leather brogues under the table towards the ankle of her Converse hi-top. I'll stroke her foot, in a reassuring, I understand, I know your soul kind of way.

Bone.

Hard.

Shit.

Her foot bolted away. She shot me a look of WTF.

'Sorry,' I whispered, 'I was trying to…' The PA system crackled. A middle-aged man with a greying-gingery beard and green cords tapped on the mic.

'One, two, one, two.' He waited for the supportive sniggers to stop. 'Thank you. Thank you. Now, this movement, which each and every one of you here tonight is now a part of, is founded on the principle of *permaculture*.' He paused awhile to let the new word sink in. 'Our society faces challenges everywhere it looks these days, everything we ever took for granted has changed. Through this movement we want to equip our community – i.e. you,' he pointed at the crowd, 'for the dual challenges of climate change and peak oil. This is about socioeconomic localisation, man! It's time we took the means of production back off the man—'

'And the spoils!' shouted a just-broken voice from the table to our left.

The beard picked back up, 'We've got to be more resilient. Look at our grandparents' generation…'

'Yeah!'

'They didn't eat in restaurants, or from packets or tins, or have new mobile phones every 18 months…'

'Yeah!' (almost collectively now).

'They lived within their means. They made their means!' It was Sixth Form polemic on strong cider.

'We need creative adaptations across the board, and that's why we've got you here tonight. We want you to get involved. Collective creativity is what this situation needs. Are you in?'

'Yeah!' (pretty much everyone bar me now).

'I'm talking energy production. Health. The education of our kids. Our economy. The food we eat. It's time to adopt… and adapt, people. We need to stop living on handouts from the oil state, man. But what we need most, above all other things, is to get our message out there, to others, to more people like you, so they can become us, and we can become one!'

Christ.

'I know someone who can help!' Christy had stood up. Twenty or so pairs of eyes, many bloodshot, turned to look her way. Her frame was slight but sure. She had her back towards me. Her red hair washed down her back and rippled across her cardigan. She took a deep breath and turned towards me.

'My friend, my very good friend Bill, right here.' Some of the eyes now turned towards me. 'He can help you get your message out to the masses.' They were listening. She had that kind of effect on people. 'He's a PR man.'

'We don't need those shits!' an elderly female voice shouted. Christy ignored the heckles.

'He's a very good PR man. And he can help you spread the message about your movement. Maybe even get some funding for your community garden.'

'We don't want that dirty corporate money!'

'Hold up, people', said the greying-gingery one, 'let's hear what's he's got to say… Will, was it…?'

'Bill,' Christy corrected.

'Bill, what do you say, Bill…?' My eyes took in the scene. Craig looked like he was either finding this whole situation extremely funny or infuriating. Connie smiled an encouraging smile that would have written, 'go on, mate,' if her mouth could have held a pen. The assorted earth lovers eyed me with the suspicion of a far-right father meeting a daughter's mixed-race boyfriend. The bearded one was waiting to see if I could make his dream a reality. He had more than a look of David Koresh about him. Did I want Waco II on my hands?

But then there was Christy. Her black eyes saw through me. They softened on my sight.

'Yes, yes I am a PR man, and yes, yes I can help you get the word out there...' This wasn't among my best presentations. The Mystic gave me a knowing look. Fuck fuck fuck.

'Manipulate the media, you mean?' a voice shouted.

'We don't manipulate them, we manage them to open a dialogue around your message...'

'What about money?' said Koresh.

'I'm sure I may know of some parties who'd be really interested to be involved in a project like this...' If only to partially wash their hands of the fact they tested make-up on bunny rabbits.

'Good, good. We should talk...'

'We should,' I said and handed him my card.

'Morgan & Schwarz?'

'That's us.'

'I'll call.'

'Please do.' The crowd tailed off into conversation and I sat back down. I'd just invited a potential cult leader into the offices. What the fuck was Miles going to say about that? Probably give him a fucking job.

Then, under the table and out of nowhere, Christy squeezed my hand.

Who cared if I'd committed to spinning yarns for a sustainability sect?

All was well with the world.

# Chapter 23

## SAD END FOR HOMELESS WAR HERO

An Iraq war hero who ended up sleeping rough has been found dead by a Hackney cab driver. David Jenkinson, 29, was discovered in the early hours of Wednesday morning in an alleyway behind the Queens Lane Shopping Centre. Locally born, Jenkinson served two tours of duty with the Royal Welsh 2nd Battalion in Basra province. His family has confirmed he was of no fixed abode at the time of death. Doctors say the cause of death is acute liver failure. Police are not treating the death as suspicious but have asked anyone with any information to come forward.

His former squadron leader Captain Agnew Faulkner said Jenkinson was a 'bold soldier' who 'put the lives of others before his own.' The ex-St Ignacius pupil was mentioned in dispatches for his bravery in rescuing colleagues when a grenade was thrown at his car by insurgents in 2007. His nephew William Turner said his uncle was 'an inspirational man' who 'struggled with his demons', but lived an 'ultimately happy existence.' Charity Heroes Heads claimed not enough was being done to help returning soldiers readjust to civilian life.

'Terrible, isn't it?'

'Jesus, Pete, you scared the hell out of me, creeping up on me like that.'

'Well, there's no need for that kind of language, Bill. A good man's died here.'

'I can see that, Pete.' I'd drifted off at my desk, daydreaming while the words and pictures of the local newspaper danced around my brain. It was a side effect of being on the wagon, or so my internet-based diagnosis told me.

'Isn't it ironic that he manages to avoid death out on the battlefield but can't keep his big old heart ticking when back home amongst those he fought tooth and nail to save?'

'It is terribly sad, Pete, but I'm not sure it's irony as such…' He wasn't listening to my pedantry.

'I was very nearly a military man, you know.' I could only assume the use of the 24-hour clock, sharp creases and homoerotic undertones appealed to Pete's character.

'The sense of adventure, of duty, of doing it for Queen and country, it gets me right here,' Pete said, pointing to his breast pocket. 'My family has been serving with distinction for generations.

'But what about you, Pete? You work in PR. It's hardly *Where Eagles Dare,* is it?

'There was my great-grandfather Algernon White, who took direction from Sir Douglas Haig at the Battle of Passchendaele…

'But what about you, Pete?

'And his son, my grandfather that is, Reginald White, spearheaded Operation Compass against the Italians in North Africa…

'But what about you, Pete?

'And his son, my father that is, Derek White, sailed on HMS *Invincible* in the Falklands. Or Las Malvinas, as the Argentinians would call it…

'But what about you, Pete?' My questioning was obviously falling on deaf ears during his army incest-a-thon.

'…PETE?'

'Sorry, what, Bill?'

'Enough about your heroic ancestors, what about your career in camo?'

'Ahhh.' He looked wistfully into the middle distance. I couldn't help thinking the filing cabinet in his line of sight may have detracted from the moment somewhat. 'I had a promising career in the TA's back in my youth. Those were the days. Manoeuvres in the rolling hills of the countryside…' His glasses started to mist up a little.

'Not quite a war-zone though, hey, Pete?'

'As near as damn it, Bill. The team spirit and the camaraderie we had was above and beyond anything I've known in this place.' If Miles heard Pete say that, he'd be better off at Abu Gharaib with a horny redneck.

'So why are you here bending truths instead of playing toy soldiers?' I asked. Pete looked the closest I've ever seen him to cursing. There was something particularly pleasing to the provocateur in me in pushing a puritan towards profanity.

'Firstly, Bill, I don't bend truths here.'

'Oh come on, we all do.'

'Well I don't. And secondly, it was to do with my eyesight… and the shin-splints…'

'Shin-splints?!'

'Yes, Bill. They can be treacherous if relied upon in a life or death situation.'

'I can imagine. So the great White military lineage comes to an end…'

'Not strictly, Bill. I make a pilgrimage every spring, as you know, to the war graves of northern France, and I retain a keen interest in the history of the great battles.' He looked like a toddler admiring a turd in a training pant.

'Algernon would be proud,' I said.

'You know what, Bill,' Pete said, 'I think he would.'

There had been no death of course. No tours of duty, no insurgents, no mentions in dispatches, no Gulf War syndrome or post-conflict traumatic stress. There had been a permanent homelessness, of sorts, and there certainly had been liver damage, debilitating if not fatal. There had been no valour. There would be no funeral. No triangular sandwiches with the crusts cut off, no awkwardness between second cousins, none of the obligatory platitudes about the pleasantness of the service. No ashes to ashes. No dust to dust. Sometimes it helped having influence with the media. Sometimes you could get them to print whatever the hell you liked.

Twenty-nine years ago on a Friday afternoon I'd sprung punching and shouting from my poor mother's slender loins, bringing resignation and stretchmarks. I was four days late. The behaviour of the following three decades make it pretty fucking likely I'd been waiting for the weekend. The Buddhists amongst your number will profess (placidly, granted) that when my bloody umbilical was being cut by my half-drunk father against the self-sepia-tinged backdrop of a paint-peeling maternity ward, someone, somewhere was being read the last rites. One in, one out. Balance was restored. Over the weekends that followed my first, a private eulogy was made each Sunday for the sins of the Saturday and Friday. The weekend was the carrot to my carthorse. The social sniff which dragged me through the grey days to the restrictive freedom of the 48 hours. But like a hungry baby, two sucks was not enough. Thursday became the new Friday. Wednesday the new Thursday. Monday the old Saturday. The weekend invaded the week much as if Monaco marched across the border into France. Decadent but ill-equipped. Before you knew it there was going to be a dead princess. When every day was a discotheque, the anticipation for the elevation from the daily grind couldn't change gear. There was nowhere to go. Alcohol was scratching an itch, not the treat at the end of a stretch of slog. For boozers, the weekend was dead. Today, I was going to revive it for my old drinking buddies. Long live the weekend.

I switched my email to out of office, made a barely audible assertion about an afternoon of briefings with key media targets, shot Christy a wink on reception and rode the twelve floors down to the sparkling lobby. I could see my two o'clock through the floor-to-ceiling one-way windows of the building. But these were no members of the fourth estate, even if some of their personal hygiene standards were on a level with some unmentionables I knew on newsdesks. My date was with my old drinking buddies. It had been a while.

The bums had been there for me when I wasn't all there. When I needed wingmen to bounce off, someone to share stories with, crack jokes at, or simply to stand there and say nothing, together in our silent suffering. They signposted an ominous parable that although I may well be down, I was not out. Yet.

To break the booze cycle, I'd had to bin the balaclava. Today, it was time to give a little back. A personal CSR project for McDare Inc.

Walking over to the bench they'd colonised with cider and roll-up cigarettes, I felt like a phoney, no longer a disguised desert rat. A reverse *Stars In Their Eyes*. 'Tonight Matthew, I'm going to be… me'. Well, to an extent. Today's task called for a little method acting too. As I got closer, the stench of the old days hit me like a heavyweight. Just like at school, it was always the smell that got you first.

It was Spider who turned to face me first. His dirty jeans and ripped tracksuit top almost sneered at the merino wool suit I'd once stuffed into a rucksack just yards away from where we stood. The rest of his merry men turned slowly towards me, drunk on daylight and indecision. It wasn't every day their crowd was approached by an outsider who wasn't carrying a truncheon.

'Spider?' I asked.

'How'd you know that?'

'Well,' I rocked on the heels of my handmade shoes, 'you've got a web tattooed around your right eye…' He clocked my smarts with the reaction of a man who had made corporeal violation his major. Which gave me time to explain.

191

'It was my uncle… who told me who you were…' I handed him the newspaper. He took it, unsure why. 'Here, look here…' I pointed to the story about the dead war hero. Spider pulled the pages up close to his face and studied the print, like a skinhead detective who'd lost his magnifying glass.

'I… I… don't get it… what does it mean…?'

'Oh, give it here, Spider.' A hand reached over and snatched the paper from his blackened hands. 'He can't fucking read, can he.' It was him. The one with the knowing eyes. He traced his grubby finger under the headline.

'Sad… end… for… home… less… war… hero. So. What has that got do with us?' he accused.

'Read on.'

Those eyes watched me cautiously.

'…found dead by a Hackney cab driver… David Jenkinson…' The rest of the dropouts clamoured for more information, like T-Birds to his Danny Zuko, just with less leather and more grease.

'You're going to have to explain a bit more than that, I'm afraid.' You really did have to spell it out for this lot.

'I think you knew him as Dave…'

'Dave?' Realisation came into those dark eyes of his. 'Dave…'

'What's he saying about Dave?' asked Spider.

'Dave is dead,' I said.

'Dead?'

'Dead.' The reader took a flagon of cider from Spider's hand and took a long swig. For a second, his eyes tinged a touch sadder than they already were, which, if you'd seen his eyes, you'd realise was the equivalent of the holocaust being more horrific, say.

'So, who's he, then?' said Spider.

'Like I said.' They really didn't pay attention. 'Dave was my uncle. Now, listen up…' The six or seven drunks lurched around me. '…my uncle left very specific instructions in his will regarding you lot. Now, don't get your hopes up too much because he hasn't left you a mansion, which is probably for the best as in all honesty I don't think any of you are house-trained. But what he did do is leave a small sum of money for me to take you out for a slap-up meal and drinks. So, who's in?'

A collective grunt shot up.

'Yeeeeehaaaa!' shouted Spider.

Good lord, the expenses account was going to take a battering today.

'I don't suppose any of you need to get the afternoon off work or go home and get spruced up, so let's do it…' I wanted to vacate the area before a Morgan & Schwarzer came outside for a crafty fag or clandestine phone call.

'Hold on,' said Spider. He limped up the alleyway and rustled around behind one of the wheelie bins. He returned a minute or so later with a bunch of on-the-turn flowers in his hand.

'Here, have one each and fix it on your top somehow. They're not lilies, like, but it's a mark of respect, innit? Dave would have liked that.' Behind his tough exterior lay a childlike beauty. Best get them all out of here before he shouted 'minge' at Carol again.

My working knowledge of the city's gastronomic palaces would have been second to none had there not been a thousand others like me stuck in the same career gutter. Encyclopedic recall of where to get the freshest Kobe beef in town, or the in-spots to catch the rollmop herring craze that was sweeping kitchens before it jumped the shark and the platinum-card carrying patsies started ingesting badgers' gall bladders because it was the *plat du jour* and as essential a weapon in the PR man's arsenal as an eye for a headline and a questionable moral compass. Now, I knew my dinner dates for today would give no credence to the whims of the taste-makers and would probably have much preferred to go large in Nando's, but the final decision on destination didn't rest with them. Instead, I knew just the place.

Écouter was currently *the* place, blazing through the

blogosphere and bidding snooty cuisine critics to kneel in devotion at the majesty of its malevolent Michelin-starred chef Franck Papin. His daring re-imaginings of French staples had the chattering classlesses clamouring for a table every morning, noon and night for the past three months. Which, believe me, for a restaurant in this town was a fucking eternity. Personally it got my vote because the maître d' turned a blind eye to blow in the bathroom, but when like Morgan & Schwarz you spent the equivalent of a West African republic's GDP in the joint, you could probably get away with curling a turd out on the *bienvenue* mat. Very occasionally, it was good to be part of the club.

Walking through the city streets with my current company was like herding cats on heroin. One minute 'Psycho' Sid was panhandling some Kodak-carrying tourists, the next Spider was following a yummy mummy in the opposite direction. The only one who retained an air of calm authority was the one with the dark eyes, the Reader. He'd seen it all before. He was the Doc to their Grumpy, Happy, Sleepy, Dopey, Sneezy and Sex Pest.

'Where we going then, Dave?'

'I'm not Dave, Spider. Dave is dead, remember?'

'But where are we going?'

'Look, trust me, you're going to love it.'

'You have to understand,' said the Reader, taking me away from the others, 'that it is very hard for these men to trust anyone or anything. That stopped a long time ago. They've been through too much.'

'And what about you...?' I paused three beats for him to fill in his name. Large black pupils weighed me up.

'Your name?' I pushed. His pupils dilated.

'Names aren't important out here.'

'But what's yours?'

'Well,' he swallowed, 'if you must know, I used to be called

Michael.' The wind picked up and blew his not quite shoulder length hair around his face. 'But that was a long time ago.'

'What happened to you?'

Fuck ceremony, I went straight for the jugular. I was buying lunch after all.

'That's a long story…' It felt like I was in a buddy session, although my subject this time was unquestionably less fuckable than Christy. More fucked though. Silence stagnated in the air. Time for some old PR 101: the reciprocation rule. Now, if my skills didn't escape me, social convention meant a smile sent Michael's way would make it difficult for him not to mirror me.

'Look, it's okay if it's a long story. I've got all afternoon…' And beam. The poor fucker couldn't resist.

'Okay… buy me a drink and I might just tell you…' He smiled a smile I'd seen some place before. The science of spin worked again. Another one bites the dust.

'… and anyway, you might want to fill me in on your story.'

'How do you mean?'

'I've seen you some place before, haven't I?'

FUCK.

He'd rumbled me. I was Dave, Dave wasn't dead, and I wasn't really Dave.

FUCK.

'Have you?'

'That was a hell of a left hook you clocked that fella with…'

The SoupMobile Station.

Of course.

'Well, he was asking for it. What can I say; some of my uncle's training must have rubbed off on me.'

Dave was dead, long live Dave.


The entrance to Écouter, like all of the most pretentious places on God's greedy earth, was guarded by a rope, a man, and a clipboard. Ordinarily, these kinds of situations were not conducive to being accompanied by homeless drug addicts. The man recognised me as I approached.

'Mr…' He wouldn't remember my name and blow my cover. They never remembered your name. I was just a walking AmEx.

'Good day to you,' I said. His phoney smile broke when he clocked my company.

'Sir, as you know, we have a strict dress…'

'And,' I checked his name badge and slipped two crisp fifties from the petty cash tin into his top pocket, 'as you know, Bradley, Morgan & Schwarz is a faithful and generous patron of this establishment. I'd hate us to have to take our custom some other place.' A lifetime of minimum-wage jobs flashed through his mind. He swallowed hard and looked up and down the street.

'Very well, sir. Your usual table?'

'Indeed. Follow me, chaps.'

Money didn't just talk, it screamed.


We'd probably have drawn less of a reaction from our fellow diners if we'd dressed in full Klan robes and spat Public Enemy lyrics through megaphones. Not that I'd have trusted my companions in anything brilliant white, the menace of the pointy hat diluted somewhat by the inevitable blim holes and booze stains. Our entrance must have been what Jesus felt like when entering Nazareth, just with open-mouthed stares replacing adulation. No palms were laid to soften our path. Out of the corner of my eye I spotted an ex-client, a ghastly Greek shipping magnate who had sat across from me at a dozen of these tables, gorging himself on the richest food in town and daring me not to laugh at his sexist jokes. His face now was reminiscent of mine when I took the toilet cubicle next to him and heard the desperate chokes of an Eastern European whore. I shot him a wink and a smile. His gaping pie hole mouthed a 'hello' back my way. He didn't have a fucking clue what to think.

Having been paid to manage perception for the past forever, it was almost as liberating for me to toy with this restaurant's reputation, a nihilistic cat with a ball of social string, as it was for my guests to have a hot meal in their bread baskets. Which was exactly the receptacle they demolished when our bemused waiter seated us at our table. The finest, freshest French bread, artisan-made, piss-artist-devoured. They wolfed it down quicker than the Eucharist amongst a bunch of brainwashed believers.

'Can I get you any drinks?' Seven pairs of eyes lit up like Christmas trees. I didn't need to peruse the menu.

'Seven of your finest bottles of champagne please, my good man. One for each of my companions.' The waiter's threaded eyebrows arched.

'Very well, sir.'

'And a sparkling mineral water for me.'

'Very well, sir.'

'As you were.' I had no idea why I addressed the waiting staff like a member of the 19th century landed gentry, but I rather liked it.

'Is all that plonk for us?' asked Spider.

'It most certainly is,' I replied. He smiled a toothless grin.

The waiter returned, this time with company, expertly balancing the ice buckets and overpriced bubbles.

'If you'd be so kind as to leave the bottles unopened, my good man. It's a rather special occasion and I fancy my companions might rather like to pop the corks themselves.' Wheezing laughter and mistimed clapping broke out around the table. It was like feeding time for a herd of heavily asthmatic seals. Cut-glass flutes magically appeared at their right hands.

'Right, after three, boys…' Their faces, blotchy red now from the laughter if not yet the booze, looked at me for further instruction. I caught on.

'Okay, I'll lead,' said Michael, and proceeded to show and tell the others how to get to the booze. As a rule, bums weren't big Bollinger drinkers. I knew he'd known another life. Seconds later, the troops were locked and loaded. What was the saying? Show me and I'll forget, tell me and I'll remember, tell me there's a drink resting on it and I'll nail a Rubix cube one-handed in 10 seconds flat.

'1… 2… 3!' Champagne shot through the air. Shell-suited arms flailed after corks. Shaggy heads lapped at spillages on the table. Coats were called for at nearby tables. Glasses were ignored and bottles raised to lips before being raised high like victors in a boxcar Grand Prix.

'TO DAVE. It's what he would have wanted,' I shouted, probably a little too loud for our surroundings.

'To Dave,' in chorus.

The diners who hadn't scarpered at the sight of Spider giving a frighteningly realistic impression of fellatio on a champagne bottle, did their best to ignore our party. The way you did a head-scarfed Romanian on the tube, blocking out the sound of her out-of-tune two-stringed banjo, looking straight ahead at the reflection of your detached robotic gaze. I couldn't blame these people. I'd done it myself a million times. They said you were only ever 6 ft away from a rat in this city, but that didn't mean you wanted them asking you for bus fare every 5 minutes.

The AmExodus had caused our waiter to try and hurry us along with our menu selection. We weren't helped by the fact we only counted two readers amongst our number.

'What about *navarin d agneu*?' I asked the group with, if I say so myself, almost passable Gallic arrogance.

'What the hell's that?' asked Sid.

'Well, it's a lamb dish…' I'd eaten my way through this menu twice already.

'Does it come with chips?' asked Sid.

'No, sir, it doesn't come with chips,' the waiter stepped in.

'What about French fries? They're French, aren't they?' said Spider. He wore the look of a dog who'd earned a treat.

'Well, sir, yes they are.'

'Look,' I said, 'we'll keep this very simple. Just bring us eight steaks, eight French fries, and eight side salads.' They needed at least some vegetable intake to fight off the scurvy.

'Very well, sir. How would sirs like them cooked?'

'As long as it's not with petrol,' said Michael, 'down a dark alley, I don't think these men really care.'

The behaviour of my charges continued unabashed over the course of the next half hour or so, but like the patient parent of a toddler with Tourettes, I grew accustomed to and unphased by their outbursts. The joy I felt seeing their blackened teeth chew through the best beef on the block was, I imagined, akin to that felt by Mother Teresa when out helping the poor and infirm of Calcutta, or Bill Gates after making a tax-deductible donation to a Kenyan orphanage. Warm inside in a way only the stimulants had managed before. I don't know if I'd learned to love myself, or the world, but either way, I wanted more. But what of these men? Of Michael? One bad decision, some misplaced aggression or another red utility bill away from me. The former me.

'When were they last in this situation?'

'In a restaurant?' asked Michael.

'Yes. You looked like you knew what you were doing there…' I said.

'Well,' he paused and forked the last bit of red meat up to his mouth, 'we used to eat out all the time, if you must know…'

'I did buy you that drink…'

'Yes, I suppose you did. Or Dave did.'

Christ, I was slipping up.

'Yes, you're right, Dave did. But I could buy you one after we're done here?'

'To be honest, it's probably the last thing I need.' He bit the meat from the fork. 'Anyway, I need to look after this lot.'

Keep at him, Bill.

'Who was "we"?'

'Sorry?'

'You said "we used to eat out"?'

'Oh.' His dark eyes narrowed. 'I meant my family. Every Saturday afternoon. We'd ride the bus to parts of town we'd never explored before, hop off at a random stop and stroll through the streets and happen upon somewhere at chance. Italian, Chinese, Indian, Lebanese, Turkish, Vietnamese, French not so much. You know how fussy kids can be. It was like going on holiday without going on a plane…'

His dark eyes started to mist over.

'We'd always share a dessert, three-ways. Just the three of…'

Michael was cut off by a god-awful bang from the other side of the restaurant.

'Quick quick, Mr Dave! You need to help!' Sid flung me around from the huddle Michael and I had formed. He was out of breath.

'What's going on?' I'd ignore the Mr Dave. Like Michael said, maybe names weren't important.

'It's Spider. He's just showed his knob to an old lady. She fainted and now the chef's got him in a headlock!'

What was the saying? You could take a tramp to water, but you couldn't force him to keep his dick in his pants. This situation called for some crisis comms of the highest order.

# Chapter 24

'Why?'

'Because some people don't eat meat all the time…'

'Why?'

'Because some people don't want to…'

'Why?'

'Because some people think it's wrong to eat animals…'

'Why?'

'Because they have faces and feelings…'

'Why?'

'Where the hell is your mother?!'

I was sat at a sticky table in a Wacky Warehouse with a 5-year-old walking, talking *Jeopardy!* game show. Now, I hadn't turned all Humbert Humbert. Don't fret. Instead I was meeting up with Deborah. And she'd brought a date. The road to redemption was beset on all sides by inequity.

And the content of the conversation wasn't revealing a new-found vegetarianism. Fuck that. I'd knocked the fags and booze on the head, there's no way chicken and chops were joining the list of banned substances. Rather, I'd chosen a vegetarian pasta dish from a menu characterised by transfats. Okay, I'd often eat at the best joints on the block, but my bugle intake barely left an appetite and last time I checked squashed grapes didn't count towards your five-a-day. So now, on occasion, I'd swerve the sow in favour of a vitamin-filled veggie feast. Fortunately I didn't always have to explain my decision to the Junior Spanish inquisition.

So Deborah. Debs. Debbie. *Deborah*. She came post-German lessons with Laura Stanton, post-coat rape by Mrs Jenkins, post-ruined trainers by the virginal shop assistant and pre- …well, pre-a suitcase full of one-nighters I couldn't remember the name of. Our love, and it had been love – or at least it had *seemed* like love at the time – had been markedly different from those other conquests. We were away from home for the first time. Anything felt possible and we knew all the answers. Why wouldn't we? We were eighteen and the apron umbilical had been snipped. Our only shackles were irregular Shakespeare seminars, inadequate student loan funds and a rudimentary working knowledge of Sanskrit sex manuals.

Deborah became the sticking plaster to the wounds inflicted (and in the case of Trisha, opened all over me) by my early fumblings into the carnal arena. She had deep green eyes and long flaxen hair a bit like, and I'm only thinking this now and don't take it the wrong way, a Labrador. Now, I'm not saying she was a dog, far from it, but in the early days the energy with which she bounced around my being was up there with the best in show. And her tongue wagged out of her mouth just as much.

Every teenage boy knew that a blonde was the prize stag, the arm candy that'd draw envious eyes from lorry drivers and lecturers wherever you walked. The hair shone like a spilt halo. A sandy sheen overrode facial disappointments that brunettes just couldn't get away with, turning 6's into 7's and sometimes 7's into 8.5's. In the case of Deborah (Debs), it was a mole on her chin. Not a big mole, but a mole all the same. If she had brown hair, bullies would have whispered 'gravy face' behind her back. Bisto granules would have been thrown. But being blonde deflected attention away. It was always like that. Shut your eyes and imagine Marilyn Monroe with mousy hair. Go on. Just a plump brass, isn't she?

If I went to the movies with a girl, I knew I was never going to be with them long enough for the feature to come out on DVD. It was different with Debs. I knew I liked her the first time I gave her the good egg at breakfast. I never could pull off two clean yolks. For a while there, Debs always got the virgin yellow.

But the sticking plaster started to fray at the edges.

At first, I felt like Charlie Bucket. A golden ticket of sex-on-tap and cheese-on-toast. But it didn't last. I've learnt that it never does. A morning in bed turns into an hour in Ikea turns into an argument over door handles in the kitchen zone turns into you calling her a cunt and children looking and parents scorning turns into you pushing the trolley away and shouting you are never, never, spending your sacred Saturday morning in this godforsaken hell hole ever again. Ever. She would taunt me about the respective value of our Clubcard vouchers. My life became paralysed by inertia; unable to make plans, dream dreams, book a weekend away in three months' time for the fear that I'd do it, I'd actually do it and walk away and she'd be left over with a budget return flight and a B & B for two. Life with Deborah was like the queues at passport control. We went over and over the same piece of ground without seeming to move any further forward.

I got out.

But today I was back in, temporarily at least. We'd last seen each other over 2 years ago in the express queue at a Tesco Metro. They say you're as likely to meet your spouse in a supermarket as anywhere else. Well, I met hers at least.

'This is Steven', she said hesitantly (the leap of faith on the 'v' over the 'ph' was mine and mine alone).

'Hi, Stephen', I said.

'Hi, I'm sorry, I didn't catch your name?' he said.

'Bill,' she said. 'This is Bill.'

'Oh,' he said, his face turning less friendly with the realisation that this was *that* Bill. 'Oh.'

My shopping basket contained only white wine and extra strength condoms. We all looked down at it and then away.

And that, as they say, was that.

Until now.

My Flakberry had beeped three days ago with a text message from an unknown number:

'This is my new no. Please update yr records. Deborah xx'

I didn't have her old number. It was evidently a group text. I was now just an anonymous member in a group, filed away alongside old school pals and former colleagues. But still in the file.

I gave it some thought and messaged her back. I mean, how bad could it be? I'd already served soup at a Meals On Wheels for salvation; saying sorry to Debs should be a walk in the park.

If that park was full of really fucking annoying children.

'So how do you know my mum, then?' he asked.

'We're just old…'

'…friends,' Debs finished. 'Just old friends.' He slurped his Coke and looked up at the ceiling.

'Is he Daddy's friend too?'

I said 'no' as Debs said 'yes' and then 'yes' as she said 'no'. We looked at each other and smiled and it was as if nothing had ever changed.

Except it had.

'Kid?' I called.

'His name is Charlie.' How apt, she'd named her first born after the third wheel in our relationship.

'Charlie…'

He kept slurping on his Coke.

'Charlie…'

How were you meant to get a kid's attention?

'There's a fiver in it for you…'

He was all ears.

'Why don't you go and play with the other kids in the ball pool over there?' Faint pre-pubescent screams of excitement and the vague stench of urine wafted over from the children's activity area at the other end of the 'pub'.

'I don't like other kids,' he replied.

'I know how you feel, kid, but I'm sure your mother's told you by now that sometimes in life you have to do things you don't want to do.' I took a crisp note out of my top pocket and pushed it along the table to him. He snaffled it up and ran off. I resisted the urge to ruffle his hair as he passed.

'Wow, you've sure got a way with the young, Bill.'

'It's nothing, really,' I said in mock humility. 'I'm like Willy Wonka, just without the chocolate factory.'

'And the Oompa-Loompas,' she said.

'And the Oompa-Loompas.'

We both smiled. It had been Debs' smile which had first attracted me to her. It was the first day of university and, full of the zest of the fresher, I'd followed the typewritten instructions left on the desk of my 1960s dorm room to attend a course registration day at 9 a.m. on a bright autumnal morning. It was to be the one and only time I'd step foot into a university building before noon in three years.

Scores of lost looking teenagers slowly trundled around the perimeter of a room lined with trestle tables manned by keeno second years wearing hoodies advertising membership of the debating society (Deb-Soc) and prepped like bad double-glazing salesmen to coax you onto a Romantic Poetry and Prose module over an Irish Literature one.

'Byron was mad, bad and dangerous to know, a bit like all of us in Rom-Soc. You should totally study it.'

And there she was, stood in the corner being loudly lectured at by a mature student – you could always tell by their beards and local accents – on the merits of Milton. She smiled her way through the patronising, somehow still looking a little bit more lost than the rest. I knew I was going to like her from that very moment. Her green eyes had then sparkled with a youthful naivety. Today they looked like chipped marbles being kicked around by crows.

'So,' she took a deep breath and exhaled, 'how have you been, Bill?' She broke into nervous laughter.

'Oh, you know me, Debs…'

'Knew you…' she said.

'Well, not much has changed… You knew me then, you know me now.'

'Oh.' She looked disappointed, and down towards her latte.

This wasn't true. I had changed. I wasn't the Bill she knew, the one who broke her heart like that.

'Well, maybe that's not strictly true. I don't drink anymore for a start.' She spat bad coffee all over the table.

'Christ, Debs!'

'I'm sorry, I'm sorry,' she snorted. A vaguely attractive Eastern European waitress came over with napkins to dab away the mistake. They watched you like hawks in these places.

'Is that such a surprise?' I asked, knowing the answer. She cleared her throat and composed herself.

'I'd have been less surprised if you'd have told me you were gay.'

'Thanks, Deb.' I took a sip of my orange juice. The acidity hit my stomach.

'Wow, Bill, just wow. What the hell brought that on?'

'Oh, I don't know, a few things really…'

'Like?'

'Oh, you know, work I suppose…'

'But you always used to drink *for* work. "It's part of the job, Debs" you'd say…'

'Well, I suppose it is, but the less time I have to spend in bars with lonely clients, the better really…'

'Right.' She looked unconvinced. 'So what are the other things?'

'What?'

'You said there were a few things…'

'Oh, right.' She still never forgot a word you said. I was forever being pulled up on pissed-up promises made without the slightest intention of fulfillment.

'Well, you could put it down to a Sister Gina, I suppose.'

She spat coffee all over the table again.

'Debs!'

'Fucking hell, Bill, have you turned God squad? Is that what this is all about?' The waitress again came to mop up, this time leaving a roll of tissue on the table for the spillages of the next revelation.

'God squad?!' I said.

'Sister Gina? A nun convinced you to quit drinking?'

'Oh, fucking hell no. God no. She's a psychic.'

'A psychic?!'

'Yeah…' I realised this sounded almost as ridiculous.

'You really have changed.' I sipped my orange juice and longed for the dull bite of alcohol. A bead of sweat became apparent on my left temple. And then my right.

'Yes, I suppose I have. That's why I wanted to see you actually…'

'To invite me to a seance?'

'No, Debs, not to invite you to a seance.'

'That's good because I'm not sure I would want to go to a seance with you. All of my dead relatives hate you.'

'Thanks for the reminder.'

The sound of hyped children battled with the songs of Simon and Garfunkel interpreted through the pan-pipe for background noise.

'I wanted to say sorry.' Her green eyes trained on mine.

'Debs, I'm sorry.'

'Well,' she swallowed hard, 'that's okay Bill. It's okay that you're sorry. It all happened so long ago that it seems like another lifetime away. It is another lifetime away.'

She was too kind. She was always too kind. My actions would have still haunted a Buddhist seven reincarnations down the line. So, where to begin? At the beginning I suppose. Well, you already know the beginning, and a fair bit of the middle. The bit I fast-forwarded was the end. So now for the slo-mo and director's commentary. It's the least you deserve this far down the line.

The pill wasn't working for Debs. Well, when I say it wasn't working, it was *working* but it wasn't 'working'. It was making her fat (it wasn't) or moody, or moody because she was fat (she wasn't) or fat (she wasn't) because she was moody. So she came off the pill, and I came, well, not into her. Well, that was the plan at least. And the plan worked for a while. It was hard for it not to really; we barely touched each other. If it had been in the early days, we'd have bankrupted ourselves with the rubber bill. Deep down, I couldn't help thinking she'd concocted the whole thing to put the final nail in the sexual side of our relationship. But I was scratching that itch with so many others, it mattered little.

She paid half the rent. She swept the floors. She made sure we had in-date milk. Okay, she didn't put out, but there were plenty of fish in the local pond for that. Until one night I stumbled into the one bedroom of our flat; drunk, high and emotional.

A night with Trent had been cut short when he left – with the coke – to go fuck the intern he'd been manipulating since the last one caught onto his bullshit. I'd nursed a beer and chaser with the bedside manner of a back-street abortionist while weighing up the options for the rest of the dark hours: go home and sleep under the roof I shared with my live-in girlfriend, or go hunting for a score under the stars from the men who lived nowhere. Choose your own adventure. I rolled the dice.

I don't have to tell you what happened.

But it'd been a bad hit. I'd gone south, inside myself, emotional; wanting to put things right. What the fuck was I doing taking drugs with strangers on the street when I had a home to go to and work in five, four hours? I was going home. To talk to Debs. Just maybe not with words. I tripped over my jeans getting into the bed. She stirred.

'Did you have a nice evening?' Evening. It was always 'evening'. It was a fucking night, not an evening. I pulled up close to her.

'Bill, what are you doing?'

'Sssh.'

'I'm tired, Bill.'

'Sssh.'

If I didn't insist, then I demanded. You know what I mean. You've been there.

'Bill, we don't have any condoms.'

'I'll pull out…'

I didn't pull out.

A month passed.

Then six weeks.

Seven.

Eight.

'Bill… I'm…'

I wasn't ready. She wasn't ready. We weren't ready.

I wasn't ready.

An appointment was booked at the Grove Banks Medical Centre. 2.15 p. m. on the 24th September. Ask for Dr Drake on reception.

I thumbed complacently through *National Geographic* magazines, lost in a photo-led feature on the world's longest waterfall range. The spray showered my subconscious. A gap of quiet hung in the air. Behind the door, silent screams soaked in the blurred colours of a collection of Rothkos placed tastefully on the walls.

After it was done we drove to her mother's house. I sat sipping tea in the front room, unsure if she knew the reason she'd prepared the spare room was so her daughter could convalesce after killing her unborn grandchild. I thought it best not to bring it up.

We said our goodbyes, me hinting at a crucial few days on the Henderson account, her mum nodding and Debs' green eyes looking more lost than ever. I got back into the car and knew exactly where I was pointing the wheel. I went where I always went, even if the places were different.

The girl was the same. A different body, different perfume, but the same.

The next morning the latch on the front door opened. Soft footsteps in the corridor. The bedroom door was eased open. One eye looked up at Debs and her mum, holding an overnight bag and the weight of yesterday. The girl was still asleep. The bedroom door was shut, and then the front.

All I could think of was the waterfalls.

'Mum?'
'What is it, Charlie?'
'Can we go now?'
'Yes, Charlie, yes we can.'

# Chapter 25

Her full lips were mouthing the shapes of words grasped from and exhaled into the air of a cafe bistro decorated in a non-ironic homage to the 'great shows and performances of the musical theatre'. I was listening intently but wasn't hearing a word she was saying. I tuned back in.

'...so he said you're meant to weigh parcels on the franking machine before you stick them in the postage bag and when he said it I was 99 per cent certain he was staring at my breasts.'

For starters, breasts were not Christy's thing. If I wanted to remain on-message for the inevitable 'favourite part of the turkey' question from bawdy Barry in the projected future life of Christy McDare, I'd have to answer I was most definitely a leg man and always had been, gazing reassuringly over the cracker-strewn table at her black eyes, tired but happy in equal measure at the inaugural Christmas celebration with our beautiful but sleep-depriving first-born. (It is worth noting that this is a medium-term projection. Barry would be killed off in a longer-term vision with his place at the table and my mother's side taken by the impotent but kind-hearted head of a sustainable fishing company. My mother loved the sea).

It was perhaps unfair on Christy to judge her breasts in the current context of the voluptuous cane-carrying centrepieces of the framed Broadway posters that lined the walls.

'Bill...'

'Sorry...'

'Are you here? Helloooo,' she waved her thin arms in front of my face as if she were trying to set off a smoke alarm. A bobble from her cardigan fell into my tea. It was too milky anyway.

'Yes, I am most definitely here, if a little tired. It was so hot in my room last night I barely slept.' And not hot how I'd like. These sweats. Still.

'That house is freeeezing,' she said, chattering the ee's. She'd had the pleasure of visiting number 35 for a fundraising evening Craig and Connie insisted on for that fucking community garden. I'd boarded up the hole with a Tesco value box before the hippy hordes arrived. I should have expected this would have sparked off a one-sided debate about the corporate rape of the local high street. I'd only wanted to save Christy from the ignominy of peeing in front of a public gallery. I was certain a bucket in the back yard would have been better than the provisions the crusties were used to.

'Yeah, yeah it is. Craig and Connie don't believe in burning fossil fuels.'

'And I see your tired, and raise you a teenage nightmare's nightmares.'

'Still bad?'

'Still bad.' Her sad eyes betrayed her breezy attitude. I shot it out there.

'How long can this go on for?' The theme from *Les Misérables* hummed low in the background.

'What? Our lunch hour?'

'No, Chris. Bringing up your brother on your own.' I'm not sure what the hell I was fishing for here. Was I implying they both move into Craig and Connie's and we set up a free love commune? I very much doubt it.

'Well, what else do you suggest, Bill?' She clung to her coffee cup.

'What about trying to find your dad?' She spat her latte all over the table. This was fast becoming a theme of my dining experiences.

'I'll take it by your reaction that you think there's as much chance of finding Lord Lucan riding Shergar?'

'What the fuck, Bill?'

I'd snookered her with a pop culture reference once again.

The waiter, an impossibly camp man in his late-40s with a neat moustache and tight pants, broke in and mopped the coffee up. His presence extenuated the silence between us.

'I'm sorry. I don't know what I was thinking.'

'It's fine.'

It wasn't.

'It's just—'

'I know exactly what it is, Bill.'

I wish she'd tell me because I didn't.

'Oh.'

'Because of the way things worked out for you, you have this ideal of the family unit up on some pedestal. Well, you know what? It just doesn't exist. Not for any of us.' She took a sharp sip of coffee.

I thought about what she'd said. Maybe she was right.

'You know what? I wish my dad wasn't missing and my mum wasn't dead and my brother didn't wake up screaming in the middle of the night but that's my lot,' she said.

'Your dad is missing?!'

'Yes, Bill, my dad is missing.'

'Christ, I just thought you weren't in touch.'

'We're not.'

Smart arse.

'Clearly, but I thought you knew where he was, roughly.'

'We don't.'

This was news to me. I'd assumed Christy's dad was at arm's length in a halfway house somewhere, not actually MIA.

I tried to pick up where she'd left off.

'Well, okay, I wish my dad wasn't dead and my mum wasn't

shacked up with a walking mid-life crisis and that I could take a dump in my house without looking down and seeing a relative stranger making a Cup-a-Soup, but we don't live in a perfect world…'

'Because if we did Morgan & Schwarz would only be open two days a week and pay a seven figure sum…'

'And Pete would actually have had sex…'

'And Jill wouldn't be so bat shit crazy…'

'And Trent wouldn't be such a sex pest…'

'And Carol would occasionally swear…'

'And Miles wouldn't be so silently terrifying…'

We fell to the table laughing. A grandmother with tattooed-on make-up and tight blonde curls peered over her teacup at us from the adjacent table.

The opening bars of 'Beauty School Dropout' kicked in.

'Christy, I'm sorry.' I swallowed. I put my hands together, lowered them onto the table and edged them towards her. Were it not for the hum of the waiter whistling show tunes, time could have been standing still.

'I'm sorry too, Bill.'

My hands were an island swimming solo in a sea of glass-covered ticket stubs and theatre flyers. I looked down at them. Her hands touched the table top. They slid slowly towards mine. We touched. The dial turned down on the background buzz. Punters passed by in a slo-mo blur.

I genuinely have no idea how long we sat there for or if we said anything at all.


'Oh, and before you get back to your desk, I've got a message for you,' Christy said.

'Fire away.'

'It's from the man from the Transition Town group,' she said.

'Tell him I'm not here.'

'He's not on the phone now.'

'Well, he'll call back another time I'm sure.'

'Bill, that was the eighth time he's called for you this week. Can you just call him back, please? He's getting more than a bit tetchy with me on the phone now.'

'Sure I will do. Just not now. I'm busy. Really busy.'

'Deadline stuff?'

'You could say that.'

Saving the planet from climate change was going to have to wait. What good was saving the world if all the people left had broken hearts?

# Chapter 26

*'We found love in a hopeless place, we found a-love in a hope-less place .*

The music played loud and fast.

'Come on, people, let's crank the resistance up half a turn. Half a turn. You can do this, people. Now we're going to sprint for one whole minute in five-four-three-two-one-sprint people!'

A collective grunt sprung up from the group. In a new addition to the Morgan & Schwarz employee benefits package, alongside the charge card, dental plan and option on a week in a gîte in the south of France, we now had our own in-house personal trainer. His name was Andrei and he was an early 20-something Armenian, built like a brick outhouse with all of the charisma. Perhaps I was being harsh. A spin class was perhaps a difficult forum for the complex facets of a personality to reveal themselves. Particularly when the poor fuck was herding out-of-shape PRs to improved cardiovascular levels. It was a million miles away from being Madonna's yoga guru, but them's the breaks, Andrei. At least you're the fuck out of Yerevan.

'Halfway there, people. You can do this.'

*'In a hope-less place, we found a-love in a hopeless place.*

'I want to see those wheels turning, people.' Andrei weaved between the static bikes, clapping and cajoling. He stopped next to Pete.

'Come on, Peter, you have an iron will. You are my main man, Peter.'

216

Following in the great tradition of all the best motivators, Andrei's attention served to galvanise Pete and push his body to previously unforeseen heights. As with everything he set his mind to, Pete had taken the spin class very seriously indeed. He was dressed more than appropriately for the gym, the only slight problem being that the gym he'd dressed for seemed to be located in 1980s Miami: Lycra shorts, headband, sweat bands and a luminous yellow vest lest the bike take off and he be faced with traffic at dusk.

In his slipstream rode Jill, resplendent in a lilac velour tracksuit. A *Hello Kitty* towel draped from her handlebars. Sweat congealed in her curls as she tried to keep pace with the beat. She took a long, needy swig from her water bottle.

'*In a hope-less place*

'Pssst…'

'*less place,*

'Pssst… Jill,' I hissed.

She looked over her left shoulder to me, coating Pete in salt water as she turned.

'What?'

She had her war face on.

'Can I have a drop of your water please?' Like an anarchic Boy Scout, I was ill-prepared.

'No.'

'Oh come on, I'm dying here.'

'I wouldn't piss on you if you were.'

She turned the bottle upside down and poured the remaining liquid over her head. It was reassuring to know that even as I tried to change, Jill steadfastly remained a grade A sociopath.

My previous perspiratory pursuits were the by-product of illicit drugs and explicit sex. On the wagon, a bead was permanently etched on my temple. On the bike, it purged from my being like a wet sock being wrung dry.

Andrei brushed between me and Christy. Yes, she was there. Yes, she looked fucking great in Lycra. He looked at my red face and took obvious inspiration.

'Remember, there are only two rules, people. Rule number one is—' He smiled wryly to himself. 'You must sweat more than me.' Considering the Armenian's apparent lack of awareness of antiperspirant, compliance with this regulation was going to take Tour De France levels of effort.

Andrei held up the fingers of his left hand like Churchill. A frayed leather shag band sat on his wrist, his face sterner now.

'And rule number two, people—' His eyes stared fiercely ahead like he was recalling some wartime atrocity from his broken Eastern European home. 'You must remember to…' He stalked through the bikes like a boot camp instructor.

'…you must remember to… SMILE, people!' He broke into laughter. Christy, previously a blur to my left, turned to me, her legs slowing now, and took Andrei's advice in my direction.

Melt.

I needed to concentrate on the imaginary road.

Compose.

This was not the situation for a full-on hard-on.


It took quite extraordinary powers of imagination to transport to the cliff-cutting roads of the Cote D'Azur when flanked in all directions by a pungent collection of my colleagues.

Pete steadfastly turned the pedals over and over, grunting and grinding his way onwards to Andrei's acceptance. The outriders of our deviant diamond formation were Trent and Carol. Trent was sulking. I'd revved him up this morning with rumours of a new peroxide-blonde Bosnian PT by the name of Llana, with hot abs and a pressing need for a visa. He'd hogged the changing room mirror pre-session, spending a good half hour plucking his chest hair and applying body bronzer.

When we entered the gym and his hungry eyes set upon a 16 stone Armenian, his face was like a scene from *The Crying Game*. The effort he put in over the ensuing half hour was in direct proportion to his disappointment. He burnt far more calories shooting me a 'fuck you' look. If his bike hadn't been static he'd have toppled over.

Carol, on the other hand, was as diligent as ever. Her application had been honed over the years through a series of athletic endeavours for countless charitable causes. She had her own JustGiving domain and had mastered the pathos required for an email to almost apologetically push colleagues into a tax deductible donation. We joked around budget time that stopping Carol running half-marathons was as pertinent a fiscal policy for the chancellor to consider as lowering the higher rate tax band or raising the stamp duty threshold. She cycled onwards, resplendent today in a '10k for Cassie' tee; not the quickest, not the slowest, ever-moving onwards, oblivious to the sped-up R & B that played loud in the foreground.

Miles wore the metaphorical yellow jersey, dressed head-to-toe in white Ralph Lauren, blonde hair swept back and just so, looking to all the world as if he was on holiday in Mustique. Which he often was. He sat on the bike at the peak of the formation, driving his men forward from the front like an Ivy League captain parachuted in to lead a ragtag platoon deep into the jungle of Iwo Jima.

*'In a hope-less place.*

'Okay, people, time for just one more 5 minute sprint…' said Andrei.

'You've got to be fucking kidding,' screeched Jill, a furball of cusses, curls and sweat.

'Oh come on, Jillian,' pleaded Andrei, his wry smile planted across his chiselled chin, 'I am joking. Maybe we sprint some more next time. Just me and you. I joke, Jillian, I joke!' Jill had her back to me but I could feel the heat from her scowl through the back of her head.

'Okay, people, take it down to eighty, ease up now, people. And then down to sixty...' Rihanna now jarred with the pedal revolutions, like hard house at a tea dance.

'Slow it up, people, you're nearly home...'

As we warmed down, my mind wandered on how to warm up the existences of the people around me, the people who, like it or lump it, I spent the majority of my waking hours with.

Jill, Pete, Trent, Carol, Miles.

And Christy.

And those not here; Craig, Connie, Mum, even Barry.

And Christy.

To misappropriate Spinal Tap's Nigel Tufnel, it was time to turn it up to eleven.

'Great job, people. Great job. I will see you all next week.'

# Chapter 27

'We can't eat an elephant whole,' was one of Miles' most well-worn edicts. Perhaps for the first time in my professional life I was about to follow the Big Dog's advice.

As with most things at Morgan & Schwarz, it came back to one man. If we could find a pot at the end of the rainbow for Pete the perennial virgin, surely salvation could be grasped for all of us damned souls. Despite what old wives would have you believe, the route to happiness for the modern man wasn't through the stomach. Pete was still rather traditional. We'd gone for lunch.

Being particular with his pennies, he jumped at the mere suggestion of a free lunch, albeit suspiciously.

'You know what they say don't you, Bill?' he said as we walked the two blocks to the restaurant, squeezing our way through the rest of the suits.

'They say lots of things, Pete.'

'Yes, I know that, Bill,' he chuckled, 'but I meant what they say in relation to our current little escapade.'

'No, what do they say, Pete?' I humoured him.

'They say there's no such thing as a free lunch.' He winked and nudged me in the best bawdy fashion, pushing me into a pinstriper who broke his stride to tut in my direction.

'Look, Pete, can't a man take his fellow man for some Dim Sum, friend to friend?' Because like it or not, that's what Pete had become. Sure, in my fantasies I envisaged myself rolling around town with Keith Richards and Baudelaire, dressed as dandies, stinking of sex and dripping in drugs, gadding about on the guest list and living life as one long, continuous hangover-free party.

But I didn't.

The reality was if I had a friend at all it was Pete, and he told me not to scrimp on tyres because it was a false economy, or to always check the rate with at least three Bureau de Changes before committing to a currency exchange, and I told him to shut up or I didn't listen and we stood there or sat there drinking beer, and not even that now.

I'd picked this spot specifically for lunch for its waitresses. It was a Dim Sum place that had flirted with the lower reaches of the hot list around three years ago (or twelve seasons if you counted like that, which on the culinary scene in this town they very much did). It was now very firmly not hot. Still, though, despite the best efforts of the chef, the broads who brought the dumplings were, the ones in the know knew, the wrong side of smoking, the right side of willing and with a grey area over their legality. Pete was not in the know.

And before you get all high and mighty with me, I do know what you're thinking. Pete was better than these girls, Pete deserved to meet someone nice, someone to share interests with and settle down with. Believe me, if I knew those kind of girls, Pete's would have been the first hand I'd offer to them.

'Oh, hi, this is Pete. He loves hill walking too, I can't believe I've not introduced you guys before.' But I didn't know those kind of girls. You had to stick to what you knew. If I'd got out of my comfort zone on this kind of gamble, all hell could have broken loose and that was the exact opposite to what we were trying to achieve here.

So what were we trying to achieve here? Well, ultimately for Pete to get his rocks off, so to speak. Sure, love was the end goal but love could wait. Pete needed to get on the scoreboard first. Otherwise the minute he did meet someone who shared his passion for comparison websites and car boot sales, he'd shoot his load within seconds of black lace (or, if we're being more realistic, white cotton). This was purely an itch-scratching exercise. Fortunately the girls waiting the tables had very long nails.

We'd take a table for two by the service hatch in order to optimise our options with the hired help. The waitresses were a smörgåsbord of the second world. A little rough around the edges but that only served to make them more fuckable.

'What would make you happy, Pete?' I took the lead.

'You mean besides this free lunch,' he half-joked.

'Yep, that's already in the bag. What would make you truly, deeply, happy...?'

He paused for a moment, lifted the teapot and poured us both a green tea. Bad Chinese covers of current pop hits played in the background. The corners of Pete's mouth dropped from their smile.

'Oh, I don't know, Bill, that's quite a question isn't it? A bit like what's the meaning of life?'

'42,' I replied. Pete stared blankly before laughing again.

'*Hitchhiker*, very good.'

I even made sci-fi jokes for Pete. We must be friends.

'As I say, Bill, it's quite a question.'

'But isn't it the only question worth answering?' I cupped my green tea and took a sip. Lines furrowed on Pete's brow.

'Shall I get you started?' I offered. 'What about a tidy lawn, compliance with the Countryside Code, low interest—'

'High interest rates,' he broke in. 'I've got a fixed rate mortgage and it's better for the savings.' We both laughed this time. He took a deep breath and blew out against the backdrop of a Cantonese *X Factor* re-imagining.

'The usual things I suppose, Bill. The arms embracing you when you awake, the kiss on the cheek before the commute, the packed lunch, the warm welcome home, the dinner on the table, the love of a good woman. Even the odd weekend away in a country house hotel on a Groupon deal...'

'Peter White, you old romantic, you!'

He looked victorious.

'I bet you never knew I had it in me, did you?'

'I always suspected you had it in you, just not that you'd ever had it in anyone else...'

'Bill!' If he hadn't already drunk his green tea, it'd have been a hat-trick of regurgitated hot drinks.

'Well excuse the tawdriness, Pete, but you've got to start somewhere.' He smiled in resignation now. Mandarin interpretations of the sounds of the Sixties played on.

'Sadly I think you're right, old boy.' And with that, she appeared. Short, black hair, knockout hazel eyes, full red lips with just the slightest suggestion of downy hair above them. She had Latin features; that was the thing with this town, the girls never matched the cuisine.

'You guys ready to order?' she asked, her accent barely out of the swamp.

'May I?' I motioned to Pete. As more of a meat and veg man, he was accustomed to me ordering for him.

'Okay, we'll go for Char Sui Bao, some Cheung Fun, a portion of Har Gow, the same of Gow Gee, some sparkling mineral water and your phone number for my friend here.' Pete looked on in horror. I expected a kick under the table but he froze to his seat. Yolanda – or that's whose name badge she was wearing today – chewed her gum a full rotation, turned to Pete and weighed him up.

'Sure,' she said. She wrote down some digits on the paper placemat in front of Pete, blew a bubble until it popped, and sashayed away. Her sway suggested she'd have Pete for breakfast, lunch and dinner.

'Bill, what the hell are you doing?'

'Roll with it, Pete.'

'I appreciate it but I just don't need your help.'

'Oh Peter, I think we both know you do.' My eyes seemed to bore through to his soul.

I took a sip of my green tea and leaned back in my chair. He nodded in acceptance. I felt like a Chinese sage. Well, this was a new high.

Pete.

Tick.

# Chapter 28

There is something in the Code of Conduct of the APPR (Association of Practitioners of Public Relations) which states that, 'it is the duty of the practitioner to both respect the confidentiality of information relating to a client's business that they become party to through the course of the working relationship and to work with the client's best intentions to the fore at all times'.

Now this something – clause 3aii to be precise – isn't quite the Hippocratic Oath but it's as good as we've got in the PR world. In many instances, it maybe wouldn't be remiss to refer to my peers as opportunistic toads, but credit where credit is due; once we were on the payroll, the clients could get away with everything from environmental neglect to sexual misdemeanours and we'd have their backs. In another life our collective loyalty and ability to keep the beans in the can would have made us excellent lower level mafia hoods.

That's not to say there weren't kickbacks, benefits in kind. There were. And I was about to put my equivalent of the mink coat for my moll to very good use. The platform had presented itself by the most modern of methods; the errant email.

From: frank.hatcher@hatcher&son.com
To: bill.mcdare@morgan&schwarz.com
Subject: Your Faithful Servant

Master,

I have been a very bad boy. Very bad. Master would be very cross with me. I wore the leather pants to the board meeting like you requested. The metal clamps hurt my balls. Hurt my balls real good.

But I couldn't help myself Master. I know you ordered me not to touch myself but I couldn't help it. I tried to resist Master. But I couldn't resist.

When the board had left the meeting I shut the boardroom door, sat back in my chair, took off my trousers and touched myself through the leather.

I made a mess Master.

I know I did wrong Master.

I await my punishment.

Your faithful servant,

Frank.

Frank Hatcher of Hatcher & Son's was a family man. He ran a successful family hardware business that now, thanks to his no-nonsense pricing policy and honest hardworking persona lovingly crafted by Morgan & Schwarz, had a store in six out of ten retail parks across the country.

Frank Hatcher loved his wife, June Hatcher, his childhood sweetheart and company secretary, and he loved Billy Hatcher, his unfortunately freckled son and heir.

Frank Hatcher was a family man.

Frank Hatcher was also clearly a technophobe.

Like Frank, we've all sent an email meant for Harry to

Hannah. Unlike Frank, none of us have mis-sent an email revealing ourselves as sexual slaves to a dominatrix master. (Apart from you, you know who you are).

But who was I to judge a man's private predilections? What did they say about people in glass houses?

I picked up my rock and hurled it right through Frank's window.

---

From: bill.mcdare@morgan&schwarz.com
To: frank.hatcher@hatcher&son.com
Subject: Re: Your Faithful Servant

---

Frank,

I think this was sent to me in error.

Best,

Bill

It didn't take long for Hatcher & Son's IT department to call our people and claim some of their key email accounts had been hacked. Probably by some spotty student in a Shanghai bedsit. Ordered by a cheap Chinese competitor, no doubt, intent on ruining reputation and grabbing market share. Of course, the account team nodded when our geeks passed on the info.

We'll disregard all emails.

'Oh, good god!'

A thin, piercing shriek broke across the floor plate. The noise, something akin to the kind you'd expect to be emitted upon stepping on a raccoon's paw, had come from Carol's corner.

I crossed the office, my brogues hitting the parquet floor timed to each heartbeat. Christy passed me, post in hand.

'What is it, Carol?'

She looked like she'd seen her first cock; a face of joy and confusion. She pushed an open envelope across the desk. I picked it up and read.

'Pay SoupMobile Station the sum of 100 thousand pounds only. Signed F. Hatcher.' Carol looked at me for some form of verification. 'Well, well, well…' was all I offered.

'I don't know what to say,' she said, kind of contradicting herself.

'Well I did have a quiet word with Mr Hatcher. I explained how important the SoupMobile Kitchen was to him when we lunched recently, and it would have been remiss of me not to mention the parlous state of the finances.'

'You did?'

'I did.'

'Oh, Bill.' Carol sprung up from her booster chair and put her short, cardiganed arms around me. She sniffled. I pushed her away.

'Wait, what's this?' A Post-it note fell out of the envelope. Carol read it. 'It says there is one proviso. That Derek must be released from his duties. That is all. "I wish you a bright future. Yours, Frank Hatcher."'

'Well, well, well…' I said.

Carol just stared at me. Cock number two.


Carol.

Tick.

# Chapter 29

Many men have gone before us with names other than the ones their parents plucked from the air at birth. How different would the lives of Richard Starkey, Reg Dwight and Farrokh Bulsara have been had they not played them out as Ringo, Elton and Freddie?

The crux of the matter is that these showmen were destined for greatness; their made-up monikers simply added a sprinkle of stardust.

In the PR industry we were concerned daily with the illusion of image. The rub was, however hard he tried, my not-so-illustrious colleague was destined to be a mid-ranking executive whether he signed off as Kevin or Trent.

Trent needed me to help him and, in turn, help others. A coming out, if you will. His public acceptance of the Kevin brand could be a lifebuoy to all the other little boys and girls in the suburbs thinking of changing from Colin to Chas or Larry to Lake. Because every one of us was a brand. A personal brand. What, you? Yes, you. Well, that's the line we sold clients anyhow. Everything you did, thought or shat said something about Brand You, and while you couldn't control whether you were a brand or not, you could grease the Morgan & Schwarz palm to help you manage it.

I was about to take Trent on as a personal client. No one said this redemption stuff was going to be easy.

The orgasm of agency life was victory in a beauty parade. And, like the strength of a relationship, they were faster and more frequent dependent on how hot you were. At the present time,

Morgan & Schwarz was not hot. We hadn't come for a good couple of months now. Every shop went through it. Sometimes you were so smoking you were spunking new clients all over the walls, other times things were dry as a bone.

We needed some lube. And quick.

Our sights were set on a waste management company. Someone control my boner. As with shagging, you couldn't always catch the belle of the ball. But like the chub left in the club corner, the clients always had some redeeming features. Whilst the fat girl might cook, clean and gobble gratefully, the waste management company – the biggest in six territories worldwide – would pay, well and regularly.

Morgan & Schwarz had put together a crack team for the assignment, such was the importance of the financial bounty promised by our potential lay.

It started with the brief, sent to a selection of starlets sexy enough to be invited to the backstage area. On this occasion our skirt was short enough due to some previous with the second biggest player in the sector. They liked this; the chance to flirt with a rival's ex and hopefully get us wasted or desperate enough for some juicy pillow talk.

Once you'd made the first cut, a pitch required the same amount of perspiration and inspiration needed to turn a pig into a prom queen. Campaign idea after campaign idea crumpled up and thrown against the wall, long drawn drags on cigarettes through window gaps twelve floors up, name-calling, nail-biting, in-fighting, blue-skying, settling for what we've got an hour before deadline. And Domino's Pizza. Always Domino's Pizza.

The art of the pitch, as with the Pygmalion sketch, was to find some inner beauty in the client. Sure, they were a waste management company, but maybe they had a GSOH, were kind to children and animals, or carried out good deeds in the developing world.

'I've got it,' said Trent, looking up across the boardroom huddle from amongst the piles of research papers and cafetières. We looked up, as if gazing upon Moses giving the Sermon on the Mount. Yes, it was only Trent and not a bearded seer but the clock read 22.57 and the brainstorm clouds had just cleared.

'Well, come on, don't leave us fucking hanging,' said Miles. Police sirens whirred outside the window.

'What do we do for our clients?' asked Trent. Yawns were stifled. Was this rhetoric?

Carol stepped in, 'Solve problems?'

'Exactly,' said Trent. 'And what's the world's biggest problem?'

'Whether Trent is getting any pussy Friday night?' Unhelpful, yes, but sarcasm was all I had left at this hour.

'Ha-de-fucking-ha, Bill. No, while important, it's not that.'

'What is it then?' asked Jill.

'Climate change.'

He rocked back and forth on his chair with a smile of self-satisfaction.

'Go on…' said Miles.

'Well, my uncle Terry used to work on the bins…'

'Where is this going?' I nudged. When in the sand-selling zone, Trent was unflappable. You could see how his chat charmed the chicks. That and the barbiturates.

'…and they'd work in all conditions; rain, wind, snow, sleet. And do you know how they'd keep warm on those days? They'd burn the rubbish, the trash. Trash… can…'

'Trash can?' asked Jill.

'Trash can save the world,' said Trent. He leant back on his chair, post-coital without the cigarette.

'That's how we manage the waste. By burning it, producing energy and in turn, solving the world's energy crisis at the same time.'

'People, we've got our angle,' said Miles, his tone ambivalent. He hated it when other people had the big idea.

232

And just like that, the waste management pig had it: fuckability.

We worked like Trojans around the idea now, producing Prezis, infographics, slogans, strategies and online media campaigns with shareability to put puff in the plastic doll.

The day of the pitch came, with its air of inevitability and eau de parfum, freshly pressed pants and picture book hair. We were on last. This was cited as an omen.

'First or last, they're the best slots,' Miles would say, although on these days pretty much anything was seen as a message from the gods. The F5 key was pushed in and out and in again over rival PRs' social media feeds, the tea leaves of 140 characters acknowledged and analysed.

'Zara Weissman from Randalls has just tweeted about a black cat,' someone would shout across the office, while the rest of us tried to remember if that was lucky or unlucky. In the end, none of that mattered. Not with what I had planned.

We arrived pitch side at a nondescript glass office building a good hour's drive from the city and were ushered into a plush waiting area not unlike the one at the Wellness Centre.

'Did you read the register?' Miles asked Jill.

'Well, I, erm, signed us all in,' she replied. Trent and I both knew what was coming.

'And?'

'And what?' said Jill. Her trouser-suit clashed with the butterscotch wallpaper.

'What's pitch rule number one?' said Miles.

'Don't get your—'

'It's not the time for jokes, Bill.'

He turned back to Jill.

'What's. Rule. Number. One?'

She looked at him blankly, chewing gum.

'Always, always, check the name of the agencies who've signed in first. Particularly if you're on last. It's one of the benefits. ALWAYS.'

Jill's eyes, as they often did, said 'fuck you'. Her mouth said 'sorry'. Miles had been parking up when we'd announced ourselves at reception. Ever since he'd been made to quit smoking by Kira, he got antsy in these situations. He'd linger by the 'designated dying' area as he now reluctantly called them, inhaling what he could off a post room kid on his break.

When you've got the biggest dick, if your balls are on the line you've got the most to lose. That probably explained his tetchiness.

The oak double doors opened and the sound of pleasantries being exchanged echoed down to us.

'Who's this crowd?' asked Trent.

'Well, we'd have fucking known if rule number one had been followed, wouldn't we?' snarled Miles. Jill kept schtum. A bullshit of rival PRs, as was the collective noun, strode towards us. Of course they did, the hard part of their day was over. They could look forward to an evening of Rioja Joven and fucking their girlfriends. Ah, the post-pitch highs.

'Giles.'

'Miles,' said the natural leader of each quartet, all false and surprised, as if they'd bumped into each other on an August morning at the Acropolis.

'How are you?'

'Oh, you know…'

'How did it go?'

'Oh, you know…'

Giles was the CEO of Wiseman Worsley, a rival agency. Wiseman Worsley was the Pepsi to our Coca-Cola, the Shelbyville to our Springfield. Everyone needed an opponent to mock and vilify. It gave us a focus for insecurities to manifest as anger. Even Carol called them 'Wiseman Worsely', before tittering and feeling sinful.

They had a HQ in a loft development, all bean bags and yucca plants. They did exactly the same things we did for not quite the same clients. They had the same conversations with the same journalists. They used slightly different hashtags. We could have slipped into a day in their lives and only noticed the difference thanks to our email signatures. But we hated them. That was the game.

'So, feeling good about this one?' asked Miles.

'I've always got a good feeling,' said Giles. One of his flunkies snorted. (Question: were we flunkies?).

'Anyhow, stay lucky.'

And in a puff of smoke, they were gone.

'Cunt,' said Miles.

'Worse than Hitler,' I said.

'Yeah,' Trent and Jill chorused.

(Answer: we were flunkies).


The oak double doors opened for the second time and a short woman with a severe fringe beckoned us in. The catwalk – for that's what we called Pitch Zero – was dominated by a long boardroom table (oak), around which sat the severe fringe and two accompanying nondescript suits; in pitch parlance, 'the money'. There was nothing to say about them. I'd pitched to a thousand of these dull fucks and the only time there was something to say about them was when you'd created it. They were blank canvases for your campaigns. The walls hung with certificates celebrating success in industry awards. A snatch of modernity was added through an LCD screen hung at the head of the table.

Miles did the intros. Smile/smile/shake/shake.

'Does it have Bluetooth?' I asked, motioning towards the TV.

Silence.

I guess not.

I left the iPad in the bag and synced up the iBook. Trent owned the big idea so it fell to him and Miles to be our swimwear models. Jill's role was to nod, flash her teeth and elaborate through supportive comments. I'd been reduced to slide monkey.

Driving the PowerPoint (or Prezi, if you were really pushing the boat out) might seem like purely an administrative task. And maybe it was. But it was one that came with great power. Essentially, you had your finger on the throttle. Intuition was important. If your swimwear was waffling, a shift up the deck could move them on to safer ground. If they were really struggling, pinging to a video could give them a breather and blind the money with smoke and mirrors. And with great power came great responsibility. It's just that today I was choosing to ignore the second part of Peter Parker's mantra.

I fidgeted. A wool suit was not a good idea. The pressure cooker of pitches heightened the emotions. The adrenal gland went into overdrive. Add to that the skinful I'd generally had the night before – and the stabiliser in the Morgan & Schwarz men's room – and my default beauty parade smell was pure brewery. Today it was just sweat, the omnipotent bead.

Trent, on the other hand, was more fire than sweat. He was looking credible in his sector knowledge; making eye contact, a well-timed industry joke ('now don't rubbish our creative!'). Hell, he was likeable. Like a politician in a televised debate, he was referring to each of his audience by name (in this case, Imelda, Stuart and Paul). Thanks to the trusty reciprocation rule, they came back with 'Trent this,' 'Trent that', 'Three bags full, Trent.'

It was time for the next slide.

There were many reasons why I loved Christy. Often her position as Morgan & Schwarz's receptionist wasn't a priority, top trumped as it was by her warmth, her deep dark eyes, and the way her arse wiggled when she walked. But what her pay grade did afford was the keys to the kingdom, at least metaphorically speaking. Full, unlimited access all areas to a Y drive of employees' personal records. With that password I could find out Carol's next of kin (her mother Beryl, a resident at Belle Vue Retirement Village), or Pete's blood type (O positive). Or a scan of Kevin Fisher's passport.

Click.

The room fell silent.

Trent was expecting to look back at a slide detailing the target media for our campaign. Instead he found Banquo's ghost.

At first, I think the money thought the fading passport page was part of our presentation. Some clever, creative representation of the Everyman we needed to convince of the curative powers possessed by waste. But it slowly dawned upon the three that the slide they saw before them wasn't the work of our graphics team, but an eight-year-old 45 mm by 35 mm likeness of the man who was stood before them shucking his big idea. The hair a little less expensively cut, the hangover from teenage acne evident around the mouth, the nose a little wonkier, but the same green eyes. The same Trent.

Or the same Kevin Fisher.

Three pairs of eyes moved back and forth, royal box at centre court style, while Kevin's face remained steadfast sepia. Trent's, a little tighter, drained whiter and in inverse proportion to the red hue washing over Miles. And like that, he bolted around the oak table and shot through the double doors. Miles mouthed an apology and followed him.

Shocked silence.

'So, ladies and gentlemen… remember, trash can,' said Jill.

Now, you may think I failed in my responsibility to Morgan & Schwarz but that, dear friend, would be short-termism. Sure, okay, we'd bombed the beauty parade, but there would be others. There would only be one Kevin Fisher. And it was time for him to come back to life.

Trent.
Tick.

Post-pitch euphoria usually began with the simple pleasure of a piss. After an hour of selling strategies through see-through smiles while caning the caffeine, draining the lizard was the only release on my mind. But this was no conventional cruise up the catwalk.

Miles had the same idea.

I walked into the men's room to find his Prince of Wales-checked back to me. He was pissing in the middle urinal of three. I sidled up next to him.

'So… I thought that went well,' I said.

What happened next needs no embellishment.

Miles peered up from the porcelain and realised who his

bathroom buddy was. The soothing splash of pee hitting pan was overawed by a deep guttural tsunami of rage from the pit of Miles' stomach. He lurched towards me and, grabbing me by the lapels, smashed me against the cubicle door. Perhaps I should have used these instead.

'What in God's fucking name?'

'Wait, Miles, WAIT.'

His huge cock – turns out it actually was – flung back and forth like an angry metronome as he slammed me repeatedly against the closed door. Specks of urine splashed on my Italian brogues. I wondered if I could put the cleaning bill through expenses.

'Miles, put me down and I'll explain,' I pleaded. He dropped me onto my heels. I could empathise with what Jesus had to go through. This saving souls shit was hard fucking work.

'You were driving the deck, Bill; you must have known the content of the slides.'

I agreed.

'Every last one of them, Miles.'

His nostrils flared.

'Then I can't think of anything in the world you could possibly say to me which is going to save your arse right now.'

'What do we do, Miles? I mean what do we *really* do. And don't spin me those lines about "solving problems" or "adding value" or "helping organisations reach their potential" because you know what, Miles? It's bullshit. Bull Shit. Buuuuuuullshit. What do we do, Miles? We sell an image. We perpetuate a lie.' The lavender of the washroom freshener stuck in the back of my throat. I hocked and spat on the floor. Miles didn't move.

'We're not offering the answer to a happy home life; we're selling washing powder. The oil company isn't a big friend of the community; it couldn't give a flying fuck about them. That suspect sheikh who we really shouldn't have set up to meet with government ministers. This is not a noble way to earn a living,

Miles. We shouldn't be walking around with our heads held fucking high. Although it's probably the coke that does that.' His eyebrows arched.

'Don't fucking look at me like that. On more than one occasion I stole a bump from your desk drawer. A 12-year-old could pick that lock. Nothing felt finer than racking up big fat lines and snorting them off your desk through crisp fifties. The drugs and booze – oh, there was a lot of booze – took the edge off the reality of what we were doing. What we are doing. I was either too fucking high or drunk or both to care. But now I do care. And so should you, if you were any kind of man at all. That's why I did that to Trent. To Kevin. He needs to face up to the reality of who he is. We all do. You'll thank me for it.' I took a breath.

'Are we not men, Miles?'

I looked up. Miles had tears in his eyes, or at least I thought he did.

'Oh, and Miles, put your cock away, will you?'

I left him there; half naked, silently sobbing.

It would probably be the last time I ever saw him.

Miles.

I may have to find new employment.

That deserves a tick.

Out in the corridor, a short, sharp tapping noise bounced off the polished wooden floor. It was similar to one heard in the office. One that drove me slowly insane. Jill was tapping her heels. Louder now as I got closer. A death stare from ten paces. Unlikely yogi Jill. Crazy cat lady Jill. Louder. Cyanide sarcasm Jill. Naughty at forty Jill. Louder. In desperate need of a stiff one Jill. LOUDER.

'You little stinking fucking toer...' I grabbed her by her shoulders and planted a wet juicy smacker on her thin lips. It was that or punch her out and the waste management people seemed like they had an active HR department.

'Bill…'

'Jill…' Her death stare had gone, her eyes different now, adolescent even. It was 1986 and she was behind the bike sheds. I wore a denim jacket and stale cigarette smoke. The bell rang for double biology. This was a Jill I had not seen.

'I'm taking the afternoon off. Don't wait up.'

The tapping had stopped.


Jill.

Tick.


I'd be back to Morgan & Schwarz for Christy. It was time to sort out my domestics.

# Chapter 30

The pool car was parked erratically in section D1 of the car park. As the only model who'd not had a drink to take the edge off this morning, I'd been designated driver. The others had been too on edge to ask why. Even sobriety couldn't fix my reversing. Damn shakes. Jill, Miles and Kevin were going to have to ride on a one-way ticket. Anyhow, I had a feeling they'd be a while.

The interior of the car was the usual manifestation of the eccentricities of my colleagues, on wheels: a stick of nicotine gum (Miles), suspect white stains on the rear upholstery (Kevin), and a compact disc entitled *Spirit Voyage* (Jill). Pete had clearly returned the Sting CD to his home hi-fi system to soundtrack a Sunday afternoon DIY session.

I pressed play. A solitary flute whistled through the stale air of the hatchback. Chimes then. The ghost of a teenage whale called for its mother. I eased up the gears calmly. This felt good. The whale called louder. I buzzed the window down. Children ran by the window. Trees bloomed. Bells now. I stopped at an amber light. There was no spaceman. No Janie Jones. No dancing in the street. But fuck, man, this was cool. I turned it louder. I had no idea why Jill was always so stressed the fuck out if she listened to this stuff. If someone had given me this instead of *The Queen is Dead* when I was a kid my life might have been a lot easier. Actually, who am I kidding? I'd have punched them in the eye.

My existing emotional state was probably a touch more receptive.

Pete had a date, Carol had a benefactor, Trent was Kevin, Miles was cry-wanking, Jill was a woman again. My yin and yang were perfectly aligned. If the strung-out wastrel who woke up in the psychic's bed could see me now, he'd cross the road in a flash. I was abiding to my Ten Commandments, or at least my own interpretation of them. Sister Gina would be proud.

The soul was sapped out of the sky as the wheels turned into the cul-de-sac, a waking nightmare of new builds and neo-cons. My mum was in the front garden tending to a hanging basket. Her hair was tied up. The sounds from the stereo roused her attention. The teenage whale had found his mother.

'Bill, what are you doing here?' I stepped out of the car.

'I came to see you.'

'About what?'

'About nothing…'

'Oh…'

'…and everything.'

'Whatever do you mean, Bill?'

She looked old, the sunlight resting in the cracks around her eyes.

'Come on inside,' I said, 'and stop looking so worried.'

'Okay, love.' She took off her gardening glasses and placed them neatly on the step. The front door was open. *Sounds of the Sixties* could not be heard blasting from the back room. Barry was not at home.

'He's at the post office, love. Taking some packages for his friends off of eBay. He spends an awful lot of time talking to them on that computer.' I bet he does. I smiled at her. She smiled back. Good old reciprocation.

'Let's sit in the posh room shall we, Mum?'

'Okay, love.' I pushed the glass door open. 'I'll just get the kettle on… Oh, and take your shoes off will you, love?' she called from the kitchen.

243

I kicked my brogues off. The shag pile tickled my toe through a hole in my socks. A minute or three passed. Deep breaths.

'Here you go, love, it's hot,' she said, handing me a cup of tea.

'Thanks, Mum.'

'You look very smart today, love.'

'Thanks, Mum. We pitched for a big new client.'

'Did you win?'

'We'll win in the end.'

'That's good, love.' She took a sip of her still-steaming tea. Worry lines clustered on her forehead like the contours of an Ordnance Survey. There were more than I'd ever noticed before, although I rarely got this close to her. The last time I'd asked her for a chat had been… had been God knows when. We didn't 'chat' in our family. We just existed next to each other, the constant coming together eroding edges onto the smooth pebbles we once must have been.


I took a deep breath.

'Do you remember you and Dad always used to tell me to be true to myself?'

They never had told me that. We barely spoke. And certainly not in a rules-to-live-your-life-by way. It just seemed like an appropriate opening to what I was about to tell her. Verification that we were getting up close and personal because that was her parenting mantra come to fruition. Warts and all because that's how she wanted it.

'Well, that's how it's going to be from here on in. I'm going to be true to myself,' I looked her in the eye, 'and to you.'

She nodded silently. The lines grew deeper.

'Whatever it is, love, you can tell me,' she said. 'What is it, Bill… are you…' she smiled reassuringly, '…gay?'

I spat the cuppa out all over the shag pile. This was becoming a fucking trademark.

'Bill?'

'Mum.'

'It's okay, love, it's…'

'I did not sit you down to tell you I'm gay. Jesus.' My trouser legs were damp with tea.

'It's okay, love. Barry has a nephew…'

'I AM NOT GAY, MOTHER,' I stood up and shouted, flinging the teacup across the carpet. A neighbour appeared in the window. They gathered this was not a good time.

'Okay, Bill, okay. Sit down will you?' I reached down to pick up the cup and saucer.

'Leave it, love, I'll clean it up later.'

I counted to ten, or at least two before she started again.

'So if you're not gay then, love, what is it…? Drugs?'

'Mum!' I screeched.

I was fourteen again.

'Well, it's either that or the other these days, isn't it?'

'Mum!'

'Well, it's always in Barry's paper.'

'Mum, okay, well, it is drugs. Or was drugs.' Her face paled. 'WAS. It was a lot of things but it's not anymore, it's just me, Bill, trying my fucking hardest to be a functioning member of society, doing good, thinking of others and trying to make up for all the bad things I've done over the years. Drink. Drugs. Women. Drugs. Drink. Bad things. Bad people. Bad places. But not now, mum. Not now. Now it's just me. Bill. Trying to be that little boy you told to be true to himself.'

And with that, I collapsed in her arms, tears running down my cheeks.

I was exhausted.

I don't know how long I lay there for but when I came around a cup of hot tea sat next to the remote control on the faux marble coffee table in front of me. The air smelt of carpet shampoo. Hoovering could be heard from upstairs. *Herman s Hermits* hummed in from the conservatory. These new houses had paper-thin walls.

This was their home. Mum and Barry's. And you know what, I was happy for them. Or if I wasn't quite happy for them, I wasn't quite so mad. I'd drink my tea and leave them to it.

Mum.
Tick.
Barry.
Tick.

# Chapter 31

They say a man's home is his castle. It was a shame that mine looked like it had been ransacked. It was hard to feel the security and privacy alluded to by the proverb when the kitchen had fleas and the shitter came with a viewing gallery.

I pushed the door of number 35.

The house smelt of incense. My mind jumped to a memory from a few months and a million years ago. Bad music played through the floorboards. Bad clothes draped up the mouldy carpet of the staircase. Craig and Connie were the only couple in the world for who *The Levellers* was sex music.

Today, the kitchen table displayed half-empty cans, rolling tobacco and a copy of the I Ching; proudly, ornamentally. I ripped a page from the back of the book, took a pen from my top pocket and wrote:

Dear Connie and Craig,

Sometimes a man just needs a roof. An umbrella from the elements, a guardian from the night, a cover from the cold. You gave me that when I needed it the most and for that gesture I will be eternally grateful. Man can survive under a roof forever. Correction: some men can survive under a roof forever. Some men need more than a roof. The cold kept out for only so long until internalised. Until a chill wind blows right through on the cosiest of nights. Winds lead to warm fronts. It's time for my weather to change. You have helped me more than you could ever know but now I need to help myself. I have left a month's rent in the cutlery drawer. Use my scant possessions as you see fit. I don't need them where I am going.

Yours
Bill

PS If you ever want to rent the room out again, you seriously need to sort out the bathroom floor. Not everyone is as desperate as I was.

Craig and Connie.
Tick.

# Chapter 32

The room had been booked for a week now. I'd spent lapses in between prepping for the waste management pitch searching online for somewhere special. The criteria wasn't an Egon Ronay award or a TripAdvisor top-rating. There were many factors to take into consideration. Everything had to be just right. The time had come.

I told Christy I had something important to tell her. There was no need for a PR spin on that statement. It was 110 per cent God's honest. I'd pitched it as a 'buddy session on tour' so as not to scare her off. It wasn't strictly by-the-book Morgan & Schwarz HR policy to hold these pastoral sessions in a hotel bar on the outskirts of the city, but then I never could quite cut it as the company man. The location had been methodically chosen specifically for the night that lay ahead. No one could know us. We needed to go incognito, blend in just as any other couple would. Our relationship had developed since those nervous getting-to-know-you meetings, awkward silences broken up with Health and Safety protocol, time management tips and unexpected soul bearing. After spending more and more of our time together outside of the office, I knew what Christy needed even if she didn't. She needed this even if she didn't want it.

The hotel was a good 20 miles northwest of the office along the dual carriageway which fed traffic in and out of the city, ideally located for two-bit salesmen and out-of-town conference goers to hit the bar and the hay before a day in the smoke. In my drinking days a trip this far out would have meant expensing taxi cabs there and back but my new found steadfastness put the pool car at my service.

It was getting darker. The lights of the cars flew by, white passing my windscreen, red ahead. I tried not to let the symbolism of following the red lights faze me. I was doing the right thing. I flicked through the radio dial to take my mind off what lay ahead. I'd run over this moment in my head times once, times twice, times infinity. I knew what to do. I had visualised the result.

This would happen.

The fly in the ointment could be the side effects of sobriety. The ever-present bead of sweat on my temple and nervous gut rot were not desirable traits in a man. Yeah, sure, me and Christy had got closer but I don't think we were at the 'poo in each other's company' stage just yet. When a girl had smelt the traces of your rotten insides lingering around the porcelain, it was hard to get the magic back. No one told you the wagon would be so hard.

'Arrive at destination on the left.'

We were here.

Well, I was here.

But you're here too, right?

I couldn't do this alone. Even James Dean would have struggled to make a big entrance in a roadside, 3-star, chain-hotel. I pulled down the sun visor to check the mirror. A sushi take-out menu (potentially anyone's) fell out. My eyes weren't as tired as I'd expected. Hell, I'd venture to even say that once I wiped the sweat away, I looked good. The truth was a peerless effervescent.

This was it.

I left the car and walked across the car park, past the hire cars and motor homes, through the sliding doors of the hotel. There was no welcome from a bell boy. No one offered to carry my luggage from the car. Just how I wanted it.

I was running deliberately late; around 20 minutes. Enough

but not too much. As much as I hated the awkwardness of being the one watched walking in (I never knew what to do with my hands), I wanted to see her from afar, watch her for a while unnoticed; see her look around the bar, see others look at her, area sales managers eyeing her up, imagining her back in their queen-size bed, looking, trying to catch her eye, failing, and looking again. She was sat on a table for two in the corner. It was symptomatic of a hotel bar: soulless and licensed. Her red hair shone at the side of her pale face. She reached down under the table into her bag and brought her phone out, checking the time, checking if I'd called. She turned her phone over and checked herself in the reflective back.

'Table for one, sir?' Turns out they did have staff, nondescript Eastern European staff. God bless the Common Market.

'No, I'm fine. I'm just going to join a…' and I pointed in Christy's direction, not quite knowing how to end the sentence.

Her dark eyes looked up and saw me. They smiled 'at last'. I started to walk over, awkward all over… what to do with my hands, what to do with my hands. Ah. She stood up. Put them around her. Squeeze. But not too hard.

'Hey,' I said, putting her down.

'Hey,' she said, 'what time do you call this?'

'Umm…' I reached for my phone.

'Not literally, Bill.'

'Oh, yeah,' I laughed, 'of course.'

'Shall we sit?'

'I already was.'

'Of course.'

We sat. Come on, Bill. You can do this.

'Another drink?' I offered, noticing her empty highball.

'Sure, it's table service. I'll catch their eye.'

'Cool.'

Non-threatening guitar music played in the background.

'So, how was your day?' I asked.

'My day? My day was the usual answer the phone – tell white lies – smile and repeat. I've got it down to a fine art now. But forget that, how was your day? The pitch?'

The pitch.

With all that had been happening today, I'd completely forgotten about the pitch.

'The pitch was…'

'Good?' she filled in.

'Well…'

'Bad?' this time.

'No… It was one of the best things I've ever done in my life.' If I'd said this sentence before today it would have dripped with sarcasm. Not now.

'But I thought it was Trent's thing?'

'It was.'

'Okay. Okay. Well, wow, Bill. That's great.' Her eyes opened wide. 'I'd raise a glass to that if I had a full one.'

And on cue a waitress appeared. Christy ordered a gin and tonic. I'd fucking love a gin and tonic.

'Diet Coke, please.'

'Celebrating then?' Christy poked.

'Celebrating,' I said, blowing an imaginary party horn. I felt the bead of sweat come back.

'Cheers.' She raised an imaginary glass to mine.

'Cheers.'

She leaned her jagged shoulders in towards me.

'So, Bill, pitch aside,' she was whispering now, 'how have you really been? I've barely seen you recently. The only words I can remember you uttering to me were to get the key code to the staff file—'

'Thanks for that by the way.'

'It was nothing.'

The drinks arrived. She took a long, thirsty sip.

'I've been, you know,' I lifted the Diet Coke and imagined it was something else, 'busy.'

'So. I. Have. Heard.' She emphasised every word. Morgan & Schwarz's gain was am-dram's loss.

'What do you mean?' I said a little too eagerly. I'd done my utmost to be discreet.

'Well,' she sipped again, 'Carol told me you'd helped her secure funding for the soup kitchen. That's wonderful, Bill. Just wonderful.'

Relief.

She didn't know.

'I figured it was a down payment for when the bottom falls out of the PR game.'

'Bill, stop it. It was a wonderful thing to do.'

'Well, lots of wonderful things have been happening recently.' I sipped and whispered under my breath, 'Are about to happen.' My words were muffled by the background music. The sound system played a song used in the accompanying TV ad to a campaign we'd run promoting safe sex to teenagers. The singer was a 17-year-old with hot pants and a short temper. Her name escaped me.

'How about you?' I asked. 'How's life?'

She moved back in her chair. Smoky make-up did a good job of covering up the bags under her eyes.

'You know…'

'No, no I don't.'

'Well, work I covered.'

'And…'

'And what?'

'And what about everything else?'

'And it's still really fucking hard to be there for Joe. I feel like a single mother who got pregnant aged nine.' Her dark eyes welled a little.

I was going to help her.

Over the next two drinks I cheered her up. I played the clown. We joked about Pete ('He definitely irons his tea towels,' we agreed), pay rises ('If Miles wasn't so pally with Meinhoff, I'd swear he was Jewish' – me), and community politics ('Opting in is the new opting out' – her).

All the while the elephant in the room tap-danced on the bar.

'Bill, why are we here?'

'Why are we where, Chris? Here, precisely now? Or here; the earth, the world, the universe?'

'Bill…'

'Well, you know what? I think I'm just beginning to find out.' And with that, I put my drink down, reached into my pocket and put the room key on the table.

'Bill…'

I put my hand on hers. My eyes tried to communicate a thousand things about this moment, the past and our future. I'd seen her eyes so many times before. I'd never seen them look at me like this.

'Okay.'

She picked her glass up and sunk the last sip. She was not drunk. I was not taking advantage.

'Come on…'

I settled the bill while she lingered by the door. We headed to the lobby. We moved silently towards the lift. I pushed the button. As the doors opened we caught a glimpse of ourselves in the mirror. We looked ready. We were on the precipice of something she needed.

All I wanted to do from the moment her red hair smacked me square in the face across the office floor was make her happy. I hoped this would achieve that. We stood closer as the lift moved through the floors, the rise and fall of her breath the only sound. We needed no words.

The doors opened and we walked the corridor to room 545. Our steps synchronised now. We reached the door and I slipped the key into the slot. A green light flashed. I pushed the door open and looked back at Christy. This was for her. And me. Here goes.

The light was already on. The room was everything you'd expect from a budget hotel: an inoffensive colour scheme, a 10-year-old TV; clean enough, tidy enough. Just right. Christy sat on the bed. I walked to the mini-bar.

'Drink?'

'Sure.'

I opened a single serving of gin and a small can of tonic. I took a glass out of plastic and mixed. She'd need this drink.

I'd had a hundred girls in a hundred hotel rooms before this moment but this, this would be different.

Christy kicked her heels off and lay sitting up on the bed. She sipped her drink.

It was time.

The bathroom door opened.

Christy screamed.

'Hi, Michael.'

'Hi, Bill.'

It was the one with the sad, smiling eyes. He looked smarter now. His hair had been cut away from his face. He'd shaved and moisturised. He wore one of my old Italian suits. But the eyes were the same.

Christy's eyes.

'Dad?'

'Hi, darling. I've missed you.'

They broke down in each other's arms. The tears turned to laughter and back to tears again.

I'd leave them to it. I left the room unnoticed, got into the lift and pressed for the ground floor.

The light wakes me up. I'm in the passenger side of the pool car, the seat tipped back and a suit jacket over my legs. The digital clock says it's 06. 03. I turn the radio on. The vehicles surrounding me shine in the early morning sun; hire cars mainly, red-faced men behind their wheels with conference hangovers and two-day stubble.

'…And finally, a French sheepdog will today attempt to break his own world record for riding a scooter over a distance of 40 metres in under 40 seconds. 4-year-old Ralph, from Bismarck, North Dakota, was unavailable for comment but his owner Roseanne Highvine said she was confident her pooch would remain the fastest thing on four wheels.'

'Well, ain't that something?'

I turned the radio off.

The engine revved. I followed the maze of the car park around clockwise, exited onto the motorway and drove away from the city.

# Acknowledgements

Lyrics from 'Stuck Inside of Mobile with the Memphis Blues Again' by Bob Dylan used with kind permission from Columbia.

Lyrics from 'We Found Love' by Rihanna Feat. Calvin Harris used with kind permission from Def Jam.

Although every effort has been made to secure permissions prior to printing this has not always been possible. The publisher apologises for any errors or omissions but if contacted will rectify these at the earliest opportunity.

**Further acknowledgements**
Thanks, in no particular order to Susie, Richard and all at Parthian// Jack Hudson// Lynne Barrett-Lee// Kirsten McTernan// Marc Thomas// my blood relations// Jess and Fishy (RIP)// Ninian Park// University of Liverpool's flexible arts timetabling// Kruger Magazine// Clwb Ifor Bach// Merlin// Working Word// Malky Mackay// rock and roll.